THE FATAL COUPLE
AN ABSOLUTELY GRIPPING PSYCHOLOGICAL THRILLER

A SERGEANT EVELYN "MAC" MCGREGOR THRILLER
BOOK 2

JULIE BERGMAN

Copyright © 2022 by **Julie Bergman**

The Fatal Couple: An Absolutely Gripping Psychological Thriller

Copyright © 2022 by Julie Bergman, The Fatal Couple: An Absolutely Gripping Psychological Thriller. All rights reserved. No part of this publication may be reproduced, distributed, or transmitted in any form or by any means, including photocopying, recording, or other electronic or mechanical methods, without the prior written permission of the publisher, except in the case of brief quotations embodied in critical reviews and specific other noncommercial uses permitted by copyright law.

This book is a work of fiction. Any reference to historical events, real people, or real places is used fictitiously.

Neither the author nor the publisher assumes any responsibility or liability whatsoever on behalf of the consumer or reader of this material. Any perceived slight of any individual or organization is purely unintentional.

Neither the author nor the publisher can be held responsible for using the information provided within this book. Please always consult a trained professional before making any decision regarding the treatment of yourself or others.

ISBN: 979-8-9860820-3-5

Library of Congress Control Number: 2022916468

A special thank you to my wonderful husband who has shown me unwavering support and dedication and took on a demanding job so I could quit mine and follow my dreams. My wonderful children, friends, and family have shown me fantastic support and jumped in with some wicked proofreading and editing skills. Without my fantastic editor and mentor, my stories would be a mess. Thank you to all my brothers and sisters in the military who have served and are currently serving our county.

"The belief in a supernatural source of evil is not necessary. Men alone are quite capable of every wickedness." - Joseph Conrad

JOIN JULIE BERGMAN'S NEWSLETTER

Thank you for supporting a Woman's Disabled Veteran-Owned business by purchasing this book.

Receive a Free Short Story:
Join Julie Bergman's newsletter and get your free short story, updates about future books and get to know the author only at juliebergman-author.com.

PROLOGUE

BRANDON WAS RUNNING LATE. He took one of the corners too fast and felt his tires slide on the wet pavement. His boss was expecting him at the club twenty minutes ago, and he was supposed to be the DJ that night. It was one of many jobs he did to make ends meet and send money home to his mom. He didn't mind this one so much; it allowed him to get out and enjoy a little nightlife and watch all the sexy women dancing from up on his platform. This job certainly had a better view than his construction job, where he worked with a bunch of stinky, sweaty men.

He wasn't a pervert or anything, he just really enjoyed beautiful women, and sometimes the universe smiled on him, and he would go home with one. He looked like the typical beach bum with shaggy black hair, tanned mocha skin, and a muscled body that he had earned through his day job. He got lots of compliments about his looks, but he figured it was just because he was a little different. His dad was a black man who had disappeared when Brandon was young, and his mom was a beautiful Latina. The combination gave him an exotic look with high cheekbones and large eyes. The good thing about his day job was it helped build a nice physique. If all went well, he could afford to go back to school by the end of the year and stop working all these dead-end jobs.

His beat-up Jeep slid to a stop in front of the club, and he made a run for the back door, pulling a dark-blue shirt on as he went. Right as he walked in, one of his buddies spotted him. His overly skinny body was leaned up against the door; Brandon thought his friend looked perpetually stoned with his messy brown hair constantly dropping into his eyes. He reminded him of Shaggy from *Scooby-Doo*. "Hey dude, you better get up there. The boss is hunting you."

Brandon appeared on stage seconds later, just as the lights went down. He kicked on the smoke machine next to his equipment and looked to his left, signaling his buddy to hit the strobe lights. A kaleidoscope of different colors flashed around the large dance floor in front of him. The music started thumping, and the crowd began to dance.

He took a deep breath, looking over to his left, where his boss stood shaking his head. Brandon smiled and gave him a thumbs-up, hoping he would still have a job tomorrow.

A sea of bodies danced in front of him. He could barely make out what people looked like in the dark smokiness, but he could see basic silhouettes to let him know which ones had nice bodies. As his shift wore on, he glanced at his watch, relieved to see it was almost time to call it a night.

The crowd had thinned a bit, allowing him to see a woman dancing alone. She was in a tight emerald-green dress, swaying her hips. Her red hair draped down her back and touched the top of her perfectly round ass.

He couldn't stop staring. This woman was mesmerizing and, more importantly, alone. She pulled her long hair to the front, dancing with her bare back to him. The dress dipped low with tiny spaghetti straps holding it in place. He let his eyes wander down her back. He enjoyed how her short skirt hugged the bottom of her ass; he might get a show if she moved wrong. He wondered what kind of panties she was wearing, or if she was wearing any at all.

He was so distracted that he almost missed the song change. He started "Cherry Pie" by Warrant. He loved the old classics.

She turned around to face him, and his breath caught in his throat. She was the most beautiful woman he had ever seen. She looked up at him, and her full red lips lifted into a seductive smile.

He couldn't believe his luck. He gave her a goofy smile as she swayed her hips. She ran her hands up and down her body, teasing him. He tried to focus on not getting a hard-on, but it wasn't easy.

Another man came up and started dancing with her. Brandon felt jealous as he watched him press his body against hers and sway to the music. Finally, the song ended, and he switched to another song, waiting to see what she would do. The man she was dancing with walked away. *That guy's an idiot,* Brandon thought. At that moment, he would do just about anything to press himself against her. *Just one dance won't hurt,* he told himself.

She curled one finger toward him, beckoning him to join her on the dance floor, and he couldn't resist. He could always get another job, but a woman like her wouldn't come around again.

He jumped down without hesitation. She met him halfway and slid her body into his arms. He looked down at her porcelain skin, losing himself in her pretty green eyes. She pressed up against him and laid her head on his shoulder, then without warning she laced her hands around the back of his head and pulled him down, kissing him deeply, passionately, almost animalistically. She pulled away, and he didn't know what to say.

"Hi," she whispered in his ear.

"Hi yourself," he replied breathlessly. "My name's Brandon."

"Nice to meet you, Brandon. Would you like to go back to my motel room for some fun?" she purred.

"Seriously?" He swayed back and forth with his arm around her waist, stunned at the invitation.

"Seriously, Brandon. I'm just lonely and would like a little company, and you're exactly what I've been looking for." She knew that the best way to hook the bait was to stroke the ego. All men had one, and they would do anything she wanted. She had yet to be turned down and loved the powerful feeling associated with it.

On the other side of the club, her husband watched. He grinned broadly as the lyrics "my girlfriend is a dick magnet" came over the speaker. He loved that Theory of a Deadman song and thought it should be changed to "my wife is a dick magnet."

He was becoming aroused as the other man pawed at his wife. The contrast between the guy's dark skin and his wife's lily-white body made the show even better. He kept letting his hand slide down over his wife's perfect ass. The man knew it was a little sick to be turned on by that, but hey, he was one sick puppy. He enjoyed watching her get turned on by other men. Every time she walked into a room, especially dressed like that, all the men and plenty of the women just stopped and stared. Who could blame them? He liked to watch it, too.

"I just need to shut the place down," Brandon said apologetically. "Can I meet you at your place?"

"Sure honey, I'll be ready and waiting," she said, pressing her body against his. She slid the address and room number into the front pocket of his jeans. "See you soon, lover."

Brandon watched her leave the dance floor and began running around, shutting things down. It was almost time to close anyway, and he didn't want this one to slip through his fingers. He caught sight of his buddy. "Hey man, would you mind closing up shop tonight?"

A shit-eating grin crossed his buddy's face. "Why?"

"You know why. Now help me out. No one should have to pass up a piece of ass like that. Now, please," Brandon pleaded.

"Sure man, I got you."

"Thanks, dude; I owe you one, big time." Brandon grabbed his wallet and keys and headed for the door.

"Damn straight you do," his buddy called after him. "I want details."

Brandon arrived at the motel a little breathless. It was a slightly older place, weathered by the hot sun and heavy rainstorms in this part of the state. The room was on the bottom floor with an outside entrance toward the back. Brandon knocked lightly, and when the door opened, he couldn't believe his eyes.

"What do you think?" she asked, leading him into the room by his shirt.

"Wow," was all he could say.

"You like it?" She said with a grin. She stepped back so he could appreciate her. Her hair, which was a wig, sat in a high ponytail. She'd changed into her favorite outfit: a tight black bodysuit that pushed her breasts out into full view with a tight-fitting corset wrapped around her waist, elbow-high gloves laced up her arms, a choke collar around her neck with fishnet stockings climbing up her strong legs, and a pair of knee-high stiletto boots. "I hope you don't mind it a little rough." She grinned.

"You can do anything you want to me," Brandon said, pulling his shirt over his head.

Her smile stayed in place as she glanced at the closet where her husband sat watching. She knew he was already playing with himself and getting off on her dominance. She liked putting on a show for him and found it especially exciting when he watched her with other men.

She strutted across the room, spun Brandon around, and pushed him on his back. The bed had been conveniently moved to the center of the room. He grinned like a big doofus. She was going to enjoy every minute of this. She looked down at her prey, thinking about how men always underestimated her and how few understood her true power and what she was capable of.

She climbed on top of his bare chest, sliding her hands up his arms and pushing them above his head. He didn't resist anything she did to him. He was just happy to be with a goddess like her. *He's in for one hell of a surprise,* she thought. Her hand wrapped around one of his wrists. She clasped a handcuff around the left one in one swift move and quickly flipped to the right. Before he realized what had happened, he was handcuffed to the bed.

Hell, I can do kink, Brandon thought. *This might be fun.* She kissed his neck and ran her red fingernails down his chest. He was getting more excited by the minute. He lifted his hips, trying to get his hard erection closer to her, but she was too far forward on his chest.

"What do you think, lover?" she said loudly. At first Brandon thought she was talking to him, and he thought she was unbelievably amazing—until a lanky man walked out of the closet.

"What the hell?" Brandon blurted, staring at the naked man standing next to the bed.

"Oh, don't worry, sugar," she purred. "I just like an audience when I play."

Brandon didn't know what to think. The other guy seemed chilled out, but Brandon had never performed in front of anyone before, and he wasn't sure if he could—but then she started stroking him and he lost all ability to think.

The other man took a seat next to the bed and watched. Brandon glanced at the other man; he was stroking himself. Brandon closed his eyes, hoping that the other guy watching wouldn't bother him if he focused on her touch. Even if he wasn't cuffed to the bed, he wasn't sure he would walk away.

He took a deep breath as she moved down and started licking him and playing with him. Eventually, he felt her move off him. He was hoping it was finally time. He was about to explode, but he didn't want to open his eyes and see the creepy guy watching them.

He had read about cuckold situations but had never been involved in one. He wondered if that was what this was. It seemed like she was taking longer than she should. He slowly opened his eyes to see her standing over him with a whip. It wasn't a normal whip; it had a long, thick handle with multiple leather straps coming from it.

He tightened his abs in anticipation, thinking it would hurt, but it didn't even sting when she struck him. At first she ran it up and down his chest and genitals, but she slowly became more aggressive, hitting him harder. It only stung a little. "Do you like that?" she asked as she circled to the other side of the bed.

Actually, he kind of did. He wasn't sure if he liked watching her with the whip or how it felt on his skin, but there was undoubtedly something arousing about it. The whole situation was a massive turn-on except for the creepy guy in the corner, but he could tolerate anything as long as she kept touching him. He felt like he was about to explode. "Please," he whispered.

"Please what?" she hissed.

"Please let me have you," he breathed.

"Not yet. You've been a very naughty boy." She grinned. The harmless whip disappeared in one swift move, and then she was holding a bullwhip.

"Wait a minute," Brandon said, feeling a little alarmed.

"Are you scared?" she asked, tilting her head to the side.

"Um, I don't like pain. Can we go back to the other thing?"

"No, Brandon, you may not." With that, she flicked her wrist, and the whip rose in the air and struck his stomach, leaving a long red welt.

She grinned at her husband, and he walked over and placed a gag over Brandon's mouth to keep him quiet. This was the best part. She struck him again and again until his entire body had welts across it. He cried out, but it was muffled by the rag placed over his mouth. She was getting more and more excited as Brandon whimpered under his gag. Her husband walked from one side of the bed to the other, pacing like a lion waiting for his next meal.

Just as quickly as she had started whipping him and abusing his body, she stopped. The two of them stood side by side, staring at him. Brandon had tears streaming down the sides of his face. He normally never cried, but these two were scaring the crap out of him. He looked around the room for a way out but saw nothing.

She walked over to him and he flinched, which seemed to please her. Every time he moved or struggled, the cuffs would bite into his wrists. This was getting out of hand, or at least Brandon thought so. She brushed his hair back and caressed his cheek like she was consoling a child. She let her fingers run down his body to his penis, which was lying there lifeless and scared, just like he felt.

She began playing with him again, and he couldn't help himself—his body responded to her touch. She climbed on top of him and slid him inside of her. She was tremendously excited and entirely too sexy. Brandon thought it would be a hell of a story if he survived.

He began to enjoy himself again, looking at the beautiful woman moving up and down his body. He had lost track of the man and even closed his eyes after a few minutes. He hoped she would take off the cuffs so he could touch her stunning body.

Just as that thought entered his mind, he lost the ability to breathe.

She was always amazed at how excited she felt watching her husband kill while she got off. The strangest things would happen to a man's body when he was strangled. Sometimes he would ultimately lose his erection as the life drained out of him, but in this case, Brandon remained rock hard.

It was mesmerizing to watch his eyes bulge from his head. He turned different shades of purple, red, and blue. She couldn't take her eyes off Brandon as he began to kick and sputter. It was just like she imagined riding a wild bull would feel. Slowly Brandon began to lose consciousness. His body became limp sooner than she would have liked. Her husband continued to pull the strange rope tighter until he was sure the young man had passed.

She climbed off the dead man, grabbed her husband's hair, and pulled him onto the bed next to their fresh kill. It was the wildest sex they'd ever had. Typically their love life was intense, to put it mildly, but nothing compared to this. They couldn't get enough of each other. It was an extreme high.

CHAPTER ONE

MAC'S ARM was draped over Hudson's large frame as he snored softly. She had been awake for hours, thinking about her new assignment. She was supposed to leave on Monday. Part of her was excited to go, but the other part was hesitant.

It seemed like a lifetime ago, but it had only been six months since she had tracked down and killed her mentor. He was a chief master sergeant in the Air Force and had been her friend and advisor for years. Everything changed when he went to Afghanistan, suffered a head injury when a female operative planted a bomb, and he decided he needed to seek vengeance on her. In reality, he had been back in Washington killing innocent women who looked like the woman who had planted the bomb.

Mac had ended up in his sights, and he'd tried to destroy her and Hudson. She had trusted him and believed in him, and his betrayal left her feeling off-balance. The best thing about the experience was lying right next to her. He was strong, supportive, and seemed to understand how she felt.

He stirred next to her, slowly opening his eyes to look down. She snuggled up next to him. "I'm going to miss you," he said in a sleepy voice.

"I'll miss you too," she said quietly.

"Can I come visit you while you're there?"

"Without question." She smiled back, enjoying the warmth of his body in the cold house. Hudson always wanted to keep the house cold; his large body produced a ton of heat. By contrast, Mac was a small woman standing just under five foot four and was always cold. They made quite the pair.

"So, what do you want to do today?" She smiled seductively.

"I'm sure I can think of a few things." He ran his hand down her naked back and softly patted her butt. He couldn't get over how lucky he was. She was stunning, with soft curves that he simply couldn't get enough of. Her beauty was only half of it; she had a warm heart, and she cared deeply.

Hudson's phone started ringing.

"Leave it," Mac said, softly guiding his large arms back around her body.

He smiled and let her lead him back, not thinking twice about the fact that he was on call as a First Sergeant and was supposed to always answer the phone in the event of an emergency.

He pulled her up on his chest and gave her a deep, slow kiss. She could feel herself becoming aroused. She thought, *Life just doesn't get much better than this*—until his phone started ringing again.

Hudson growled softly. "Nothing like ruining a perfect morning," he grumbled, sitting up on the edge of the bed. He answered the phone with an impatient tone. "Sergeant Hudson."

Mac grabbed her phone, realizing she had six missed calls and three text messages. She had left her phone on silent without realizing it. She was about to return the call from her boss when Hudson placed his hand over her phone and raised his finger, indicating she should wait.

"Yes, she's here," he said into the phone, and handed it over to Mac.

"Sergeant McGregor," she said with hesitation. No one had called Hudson to find her before.

"Mac, sorry to bother you guys on a Sunday," her boss's voice came across the line. Captain Stanton had been her supervisor for the past few years. They worked in the Area Defense Counsel's office together. She'd recently been reassigned to a task force to identify violent offenders in the military. However, she was pleased when Captain Stanton had negotiated for her to still fall under him as a defense investigator. He was assigned a new defense paralegal to help with the daily cases and assist her with the more serious ones. It was uncharted territory. As far as Mac knew, this was the first position of its kind in the JAG Corps.

"No worries, boss. What can I do for you?" she said.

"Kibble keeps calling me. He's working on that concurrent jurisdiction case we talked about," Stanton explained.

"Yeah, I'm familiar. They told me I would be assigned to that one shortly after I had…" She trailed off.

They'd had this conversation many times, but he had been the first person Mac had ever killed. She hadn't even intended to kill him—she just wanted to stop him. It weighed heavily on her that she had taken someone's life, even if it had been the only way for her to survive. She was still having a hard time rationalizing it.

Ali had been the last woman he'd abducted before Mac hunted him down and saved her. Stanton knew how hard it was for Mac to make peace with it or take credit for her heroism.

"Yeah, shortly after that." She stayed silent for a moment. "So, what's Kibble worked up about?"

"They just found another body, and the young man was one of his clients. According to Kibble, he was a good kid with lots of potential. He saw Kibble about a simple underage drinking charge where they were offering him an Article 15, non-judicial punishment. It was just what the kid needed to scare him straight and get him back on track with his career. It should have been a bump in the road. Kibble had a fondness for this one. He said there was something about him that he liked."

"How many bodies are there now?" Mac asked.

"There are three with the same markings, and two others in question."

"In question—why?"

"The victimology is all over the map. The two in question were too decomposed to determine if they had the same wound pattern. All the victims have been pulled out of different bodies of water. Not one the same. The two bodies were found in the Puget Sound along the coast, one of the bodies was pulled from Bonney Lake, and another was found in the Snohomish River. This is a multi-jurisdictional case, so we have to tread lightly. The military now has a stake in it because one of our own had similar injuries, but we also have the Tacoma, Seattle, and Port police involved. To top it all off, they're considering pulling in the FBI because of the potential serial-killer angle. What are your thoughts, Mac?"

Hudson was lying on the bed listening to her side of the conversation, which wasn't much at the moment. He ran his fingers down her back, and she swatted his hand away playfully, but also let him know this was serious and not the time to play.

"Well"—she absently chewed on her fingernail—"I certainly have more questions than answers right now. Can you send me everything you have?"

"Sure. When will you be leaving?"

"First thing in the morning. I just need to submit my TDY orders through DTS. I'm always behind on the paperwork side of things. Would you mind ensuring my temporary duty orders get signed through the Defense Travel System folks? I have my work computer with me and can follow up. I should be able to connect through VPN once I get there."

"Sure, no problem. Is there anything else I can do?" Stanton asked.

"Not that I can think of," she said, already running the case through her mind. "Actually, I'm not familiar with JBLM. I have been down to Seattle a few times just to visit, but haven't spent any real time there. What intel do you have for me?"

"Unfortunately, I haven't been either. I know Kibble has been to Joint Base Lewis-McChord on several occasions to represent clients, but I don't think he's been stationed there. I know that all four services are on the base, and it's primarily led by the Army with a significant Air Force presence. It sounds like the local law enforcement is putting together a task force, so you should have some folks who know the area well at your disposal. You'll have to get with Kibble for the details."

"I'm on it," she said, portraying confidence she didn't entirely feel.

"Sounds interesting." Hudson smiled as she hung up. "How about you tell me everything over breakfast so we can put together a game plan? I'm starving," he said with a grin.

"You're always hungry, and I desperately need some coffee. What sounds good?" Mac asked.

"Let me go see what we have." He swung his long legs off the side of the bed, standing up with a stretch.

She whistled loudly. "Go put some clothes on or we're never getting breakfast."

He shook his ass at her and grinned. "Invitation accepted."

"After food and some liquid life." She pointed toward her tiny kitchen.

"I guess I can wait until after breakfast and your much-needed coffee," he huffed.

He truly was a fantastic cook. She hated always asking him to take on that responsibility, but she certainly wasn't good at it. His mother had taken the time to teach him some fine culinary arts skills. Her mother had taught her survival skills and hand-to-hand combat.

Mac watched as Hudson went into the kitchen. He had to be the sexiest man she had ever met. His long, lean body had no flaws as far as she was concerned. Even his scars made him look sexy. She smiled as she slipped out of bed and into a worn pair of sweatpants and one of Hudson's old t-shirts.

She sighed as she walked into the kitchen. "Watermelon Crawl" by Tracy Byrd was playing on his phone as he cooked in her tiny old kitchen with cracked countertops. It terrified her how much she had grown to love this man.

CHAPTER
TWO

MAC LEFT for Joint Base Lewis-McChord with the taste of Hudson still on her lips. They had gotten up early that morning to make love before she left. She was on an open set of orders and wasn't sure how long she would be gone; they could close the case in a week, or be down there for months. At least he was only about five hours away and could come to visit.

She liked routine and preferred to be more familiar with her surroundings, which didn't bode well as a military member. As she drove, she found herself distracted from the pending case by the ever-changing landscape between Spokane and the Seattle/Tacoma area. Spokane was green with lots of hills and mountains, then she passed into what looked like a desert environment. A few hours later she was in the lush, thick forest of Mount Rainier National Park. That was her favorite part. She thought she could get lost in the woods for hours, though she'd heard it was also a great place to get rid of a body.

That didn't seem to be this guy's style. He preferred to submerge the bodies. She wondered if it was simply to destroy evidence or if it was part of his fantasy. Maybe he had a link to water or had suffered something tragic that had to do with water. She wasn't sure.

Her trusty little SUV got her to Tacoma without any issues and only one stop for gas and food. She knew the base was led by the Army and was unsure what to expect. It only took her about five hours, which was what she had anticipated. Her legs were tired; she hated sitting all day.

Finally, she arrived at the entrance to JBLM. Before she could even get to the gate guard, she wound around the visitors' center and finally looped in to the main gate. This one was a bit more sophisticated-looking than the one at Fairchild: it had lanes with an electronic indicator telling her which one was open. A young guard member checked her identification and gave her directions to lodging.

She entered to find a beautiful tree-lined entrance with towering pines and lush forest throughout the base. It struck her as quite welcoming. The base was large and spread out, with white stucco buildings sprinkled amongst brick ones. They had expanded with some upgrades, but had left some of the older buildings intact. At Fairchild, many of the airmen didn't own cars because they could walk to most of the places they would need to go, but this place looked like it required a mode of transportation.

The Rainier Inn & Complex was nicer than most billeting. The Holiday Inn line of hotels had landed a contract on the base to run their lodging. She walked into a very tall building with *Candlewood Suites* at the top. A young lady with dark hair sat playing on her phone at the front desk. Mac walked up to the counter and cleared her throat to get the woman's attention.

She finally looked up from the game with wide eyes that made her look surprised. "Good evening, what can I do for you?" the woman said with a friendly smile. The woman's nametag said she was Alice.

"Hi Alice, there's supposed to be a reservation for me. I'm Technical Sergeant Evelyn McGregor."

Alice typed lightly on the keyboard in front of her, and a confused look came across her face. "Um, will you be staying with us for a while?"

"I'm not sure. Is there a problem?"

"No problem, they just booked you in the officers' quarters here in the Candlewood Suites. They're quite nice with a full kitchen, microwave, and a full-size refrigerator. You should be very comfortable," she explained with a perplexed look on her face.

"Nice, thanks."

Alice gave her directions and the key card to her new room. When she arrived, she thought there must be a mistake. The room was huge and, accurate to Alice's description, had a full kitchen with a bedroom that was separate from a living-room area. It looked like a small apartment.

She sat down on the bed and called Captain Kibble to tell him she had arrived.

"Hi Mac, I'm so glad you got in," his booming voice came across the line. "How soon can you get settled and get to the Area Defense Counsel's office?"

"Thanks for the nice room," she said. "Give me a few minutes to get settled, sir, and I'll be right over."

She walked in thirty minutes later. The waiting area where the ADC clients would sign in and wait to be seen was inviting, with nice leather couches and a few straight-back chairs along one wall. A television played a local news channel in the background. On the other side of the room, a small shelf held a buzzer and a clipboard with client intake sheets.

A few seconds later, the door to the right of the sign-in counter made a strange electronic sound and then clicked open. Mac walked over, pressed the buzzer, and noticed a small camera in the upper-right corner shift slightly to look at her. She waved at the camera and turned so they could see the name on her uniform.

She pushed open the door to find a young man with blond hair and deep dimples that sank into his slightly round face when he smiled. It made him look much younger than he probably was. "You must be Mac," he said, grabbing her hand and shaking it.

The man standing in front of her was not what she'd expected. He seemed a little too young to be Captain Kibble, but she had met a couple of attorneys over the years that still looked like they were in high school. He wore tan khaki pants and a blue Air Force golf shirt, but had no nametag. "Hi," Mac responded. "Are you Captain Kibble?"

"Oh no, I'm Senior Airman Carter. I'm the paralegal here. I was just heading out for a volunteer event. We get more cooperation from leadership and our clients open up more if we're visible on base."

"Yeah, I took a similar approach when I was in your shoes," she said warmly.

"I hear you've moved on from the daily grind and are now hot shit for solving that case at Fairchild. I'd really like to hear about how all that went down." He smiled broadly, like a kid meeting a celebrity.

"I was just doing my job. Nothing hot shit about it, my friend," she said, but Carter didn't look convinced. "We can talk later," she offered. "Can you point me in the direction of Captain Kibble?"

"Sure." He turned without another word and pointed her in the direction of an office down the hall.

CHAPTER
THREE

CAPTAIN KIBBLE perfectly matched his voice. He looked just like a big grizzly bear in man form. He sat behind a huge old desk that had probably been built inside the small office, never to be moved again. It was a huge solid piece of furniture in the traditional dark-brownish-red shade that the JAG Corp favored.

He held up his finger, indicating that Mac should wait while he finished his call, and then pointed to the seat on the other side of his desk.

Mac sat down and looked around. This was clearly the visiting attorney's office. There were generic pictures of the Seattle/Tacoma area on the walls and one of the front gates of the base right behind Kibble's head. Otherwise, there was nothing personal about the place, just a desk, chair, and some notepads.

"Well, if it isn't the infamous Mac. It's a true pleasure to finally meet you in person. Stanton tells me good things about you," Kibble said, smiling broadly, showing off dazzling, almost too-white teeth.

"All lies."

"I doubt that," he retorted, coming around the desk with his hand outstretched.

She shook it and smiled. He wasn't a particularly tall man, but made up for it in girth and attitude. He looked like a man who ate helicopters for breakfast and spent off-time in those strongman competitions.

She liked him immediately and could see why he was such a successful defense attorney. In the courtroom, the facts and circumstances of the case were only half the equation. If the members—the civilian equivalent of a jury—liked the defense attorney, they had a much better chance at an acquittal. If they liked the accused, it was a pretty sure bet.

Mac had spent hours watching the members' reactions and reporting back to her boss. The information was beneficial to winning a case and how to approach the court. She found it fascinating how the human factor could change the outcome of any court, even if the government had their guy dead to rights.

"So, Mac, what do you think so far, and what do you know?" Kibble's booming voice broke into her thoughts.

"I'm afraid I don't know very much. I had hoped you could give me an overview so we could start looking at strategy." She paused and looked down. "I'm really sorry about your client. That's always tough when you lose one of yours…" She let her words trail off.

"It's a sad situation when anyone is murdered, but it really pisses me off that this asshole took one of our brothers. I'll certainly feel better when we catch this slimy bastard," he said with gritted teeth and clenched fists.

"I couldn't agree more," Mac said. "Now, lay it out for me. What do we know, and who are we working with?"

"As you know, we have three victims that the coroner is fairly certain were the work of the same man. All three were found in different bodies of water, and each had unique ligature marks across their throat, but that's about where the similarities stop. Two other bodies in question have been dead for much longer. They were weighed down with cinder blocks tied to their chests and feet. Both have damage to the throat, but the marine life in Puget Sound removed most of the flesh. If they hadn't been weighed down, they may have been swept out into the ocean and never found, but instead, both bodies were found near land outside Olympia and Everett. This guy seems to be all over the map, and we aren't even sure if all of these deaths are related."

"Interesting," Mac murmured as she took notes. "Is it possible to visit where the bodies were found?"

"Sure, but most of them were submerged, and they don't seem to be related. The local police and now the FBI has gotten involved. The only reason why they're allowing us access is because of Airman First Class Collymore."

"Okay, so let's start there. Tell me everything you know about his case so far."

CHAPTER
FOUR

IN HER WILDEST dreams she'd never thought being a killer and marriage could go hand in hand, but here she was, blissfully intertwined in a relationship with a man just as vicious and talented at inflicting harm. They had spent ten wonderful days sitting on a beautiful beach in Hawaii—hunting, torturing, and killing. The trip was fantastic. The passion was intense, and the murders acted as a kinky aphrodisiac. The euphoric sex was like a drug right after a fresh kill.

They had been back for almost a month, and she still missed the sand, so she dragged her new husband out to Sunnyside Beach to relax and bronze her skin in a tiny black bikini. She never cared for the rainy, cold weather they endured in Tacoma, but she enjoyed the summers.

As a natural redhead, she couldn't stay out too long or she would burn to a crisp. Her wonderful husband lay next to her. He could tan to a deep golden brown without ever seeing any red, which made her jealous. She wanted to look especially good tonight, which didn't include a burn on her perfectly toned, sculpted body.

They had plans to go out that evening and tear up the town. They hadn't gotten into any mischief since their return. She could feel the anticipation building at the thought of their next naughty adventure. She was getting excited just thinking about it. If it could only be like this forever, they would never have to be normal again. Now that would truly be amazing.

They went back to their house on the water, which cost a small fortune. She had received a large sum of money from her parents' wrongful-death lawsuit, which allowed her to live a bit more lavishly than anyone could afford at this point in their career. Her husband seemed to like it as well. It afforded them privacy and the ability to play undetected. It was an amazing place with a dock that ran out into the water.

The home sat at the edge of the water, four stories tall. Each level was not very big but served a purpose. The bottom level had three exquisite bedrooms, one of which had a glass wall that showed a view of the water. The second level had a sectional couch, television, and sitting area for people to relax. The next level up was the kitchen, an office, and another living room area, and finally the top level was a master bedroom with large windows offering an amazing view. It was simply stunning, with a luxurious bathroom that looked like something out of a spa.

They often opened all the windows to hear nature and the water lapping up against the dock. She had loved being at Bellows Air Force Station while in Hawaii. It was similar, but the waves were larger, and she enjoyed listening to them crash against the rocks as they slept each night.

"Hey gorgeous," her husband said, coming up behind her. His strong arms encircled her waist, and he rested his head on her shoulder. "Are you going to be ready soon?"

"Almost, love. Just give me a few more minutes," she said, smiling back at him. "Do you have our supplies and bags packed for tonight?"

"Absolutely. Did you want the black outfit for tonight, or would you prefer something else?"

"No, the black one will do," she said while expertly applying her makeup.

He couldn't believe how lucky he had been to find someone who finally understood him. She was the first and only person he had encountered who connected with him on every level. She had fully accepted his twisted past and wanted to join him in all the naughty pleasures life had to offer. His excitement was starting to grow.

He whistled softly as she walked out of the bathroom. "Wow, you look breathtaking."

"Thanks, hopefully it'll do the trick." She smiled wickedly.

"I can't imagine it wouldn't," he said, coming over to her and kissing her neck.

"Now, don't start the fun until it's time." She reached down and swatted him on the ass.

He took her hand and helped her out to their car. It was a small, white, unmemorable compact Ford—just the way they liked it. He looked over at his beautiful bride. Her body was stunning with her long legs and thin waist. She was without question a perfect ten.

They parked at the small motel that sat on the outskirts of downtown Seattle. It seemed silly to have two places to stay, but it was essential that no one could trace their steps. They had to be careful at home on the water and only occasionally brought victims back to play, but down here they could be completely anonymous, which was perfect for their evening out.

They left their tools and playthings in the room and locked up a few valuables in the motel safe, just in case. It wasn't the most secure-looking hotel—not that anyone would be dumb enough to mess with them or survive it if they were—but it was better to be safe.

They walked arm and arm through the streets of downtown Seattle, stopping at a little street café for dinner. They could see the beach from the front of the restaurant. It was truly breathtaking, and there were so many yummy people walking about. She almost couldn't get enough. She looked at each person who passed by, wondering who would be chosen for tonight's activities.

Her husband smiled at her. "What are you thinking about?"

"You already know. I'm just wondering which one will present themselves to us." Her eyes gleamed with excitement.

"Be patient. It'll be dark soon, and then we'll hunt."

CHAPTER
FIVE

THE FOLLOWING DAY, Mac and Kibble were standing on the bank of the Snohomish River where A1C Collymore's body was found. It was a beautiful place under different circumstances. The body had been discovered by some hikers just past Spencer Island Park. She could hear the I-5 freeway buzzing and wondered if the killer had taken the I-5 to dump the body here or if he had left the body upriver and taken a little trip.

It was a reasonably well-populated area in some sections. Still, there were other places along the river where someone could dump a body undetected, and no one would ever see them, especially under cover of night.

"The local police have been up and down the river looking for clues, but haven't found any," Kibble said. "There's so much area to cover, and it's rained several times since the body has been discovered, let alone since it was dumped. So, it's unlikely we'll figure out where he was dumped, and if we do, there won't be any evidence left."

"Are we certain he was dumped and not killed here somewhere along the river?" Mac asked.

"It's possible, but there's evidence that he strangled and revived Collymore, and it appears that he may have sexually abused him before killing him, and that takes privacy."

"Sexually abused how?" Mac asked.

"There was evidence of bruising along his thighs, genitals, and an anal fissure present on the body. There were ligature marks along the wrists and ankles, indicating he was bound. It's still inconclusive, but some of the marks could have been caused by a whip or something that could leave long welts on the skin."

"Poor guy," Mac said with a disgusted look. "How could a human being do that to another person?"

"No idea, but we aren't going to find the answers here. After lunch, let's head back to the office and look over what we have."

The man stood on the other side of the river, watching. None of the other investigators were getting anywhere close. He had heard about Mac and was pleased they'd sent a budding celebrity to hunt him and his beautiful wife. He had read all about the case at Fairchild and how she had saved the day. He wondered if she would be a worthy adversary. He was getting bored with this. He needed a little excitement.

He and his wife had fallen into a pattern, and he was ready to shake things up. The need to up the stakes was like a drug; he always needed more. The victims would whimper and cry and carry on about why he should spare their lives and what they had to live for, but none of it was exciting anymore. He needed to bring it to the next level. He needed to feel the rush he'd felt when he had killed his first. Admittedly, he and his wife hadn't meant to kill a military member, but the guy was at the wrong place at the wrong time.

As a junior in high school, he had read every serial killer book out there. He loved reading about all the greats: Son of Sam, Ted Bundy, Jeffrey Dahmer, and so many more delicious creatures. He'd learned from them and found them fascinating. He didn't find most of them impressive, actually. They made stupid mistakes or just weren't very intelligent. He was baffled at how so many of them were able to kill for so long. He knew DNA and forensic science had come a long way since some of the greatest predators had been active.

He found the Green River Killer extremely interesting. Though he was much more intelligent than Gary Ridgway, he'd still given him the idea to submerge his victims to erase the evidence. He had to admit he liked putting them in water and watching them drift away, or immersing them so he could return later for a visit.

They were meticulous about not leaving any DNA behind and went to great lengths to clean up after, especially since his wife liked to get so up close and personal. His mom had always told him that cleanliness was next to godliness.

There was a great deal to be learned from others' mistakes, and he had read and researched every bit of information he could find, from past serial killers to forensic science.

Mac and Kibble headed back to their car with none of their questions answered.

CHAPTER
SIX

MAC AND KIBBLE stopped for lunch at a little café on the way back to base. The place was painted a bright yellow with a little porch out back that overlooked a small river. *It's a lovely place to eat*, Mac thought.

"So, how many times have you been to JBLM and the Seattle area?" Mac asked while waiting for their food.

"I've only had three cases here over the years," Kibble replied. "I'm currently stationed in Alaska, but you already knew that."

"Yeah, I did. How do you like it there? I'm not sure I would survive. I have enough trouble with the winters in Spokane. Is it really six months of dark and then six months of light?"

"Something like that. It's not solid dark or solid light the entire time, but close, and it can be hard to deal with. My wife can't wait until our assignment is over. We've already done a year and a half, so I should get another assignment soon."

"I can't say I blame her. I wouldn't be a big fan, either. Do you guys have any kids?"

"Yeah." A warm smile came across his face. "We have three kids and one on the way."

She found it interesting how expressive his face was, especially for an attorney. It would be interesting to see him in court; could he mask it, somehow? Showing emotion while defending the case could be helpful, provided compassion was expressed for the accused, but if the accused disgusted the attorney, it would make things more difficult.

Their killer disgusted her.

If the case ever came to light and they caught the guy, she wondered what kind of defense would be put forward. They wouldn't be on the case since they had actively investigated. She thought a sanity plea would be one of the better bets.

"So, tell me a little bit more about Collymore. What was he like?" she asked.

"He was a good kid. You know those clients you instantly like. He was just a young guy trying to figure out life. He had been caught underage drinking right before his twenty-first birthday. I mean, come on. He'd figured he was close enough, but his leadership disagreed. He was drinking with some of his buddies, but he hadn't hurt anyone. He wasn't drinking and driving or causing trouble, but they were in the dorms and were getting loud, wrestling, and fooling around. Someone called the cops, and they all got arrested. Nothing serious, just kid stuff. It could have happened to anyone."

"Yeah, I can remember some wild times when I was a young airman just starting in the military. It didn't seem to be such a big deal back then if people did a little underage drinking. Most people figured that if you were old enough to serve and defend your country, you should be old enough to have a beer. I guess I was lucky and just never got caught. Of course, I came in when I was a little older and certainly wiser." She smiled, thinking back to a simpler time.

"Agreed. The bottom line is, he didn't deserve what he got. No one does. Now it's just a matter of figuring out how this young man ended up in this psycho's crosshairs," Kibble said.

"What do we know about Collymore?" Mac asked.

"Not much, really. He worked in the communication squadron; he had only been in the military for about two years. He was well-liked by his coworkers and his leadership, but that's about all I know. I haven't talked to anyone about the night in question yet."

"It only happened last Saturday. Do we know of any witnesses?" Mac continued.

"Maybe. It sounds like he was out with some friends at a place called Kremwerk about thirty minutes outside of the base. The local cops have already questioned the other guys, and they said they hadn't seen anything, but they may have just been scared to talk to the police. At least, that's what I'm hoping."

"Okay, so we need to interview the guys he was out with and hit Kremwerk to question the staff." She was jotting down a list in a notebook she had pulled from one of her many uniform pockets. "Is there anyone else we should talk to? Is he dating anyone?"

"Not that I know of, but as I said, the two guys he was with weren't really forthcoming. Anything is possible at this point. I would suggest we start from the beginning and go from there. As far as I'm concerned, we need a fresh set of eyes and a different approach."

"I agree, but I have a request for you. Let me interview the young airman without you, and on their turf," she said, expecting protest.

"That's an excellent idea. If an officer shows up, they might clam up, and people tell me I can be intimidating." He grinned widely. "But I would like to go over the questions before your interview."

"No problem, I could see that," she offered with a smile, referring to his intimidation factor. "Now, what do we know about the guy who's doing this, assuming it is a guy. I try to keep an open mind because you just never know. People always amaze me."

"We shouldn't discount anybody because we don't know anything about this guy or lady. The FBI thinks there's a serial killer out here with a new hunting ground. The killer hasn't left anything behind that's been discovered yet, and keep in mind you and I aren't the only ones looking. Which reminds me, we have a task force meeting this afternoon with all the parties. I intended to go in my blues. Did you bring that uniform with you?"

"Of course. What time?" Mac hated her blues. She wasn't sure what kind of sadist had designed the women's uniform, but they were guaranteed to bunch and pull in all the wrong places. It most certainly wasn't a woman.

"In about two hours. They set up shop at the Tacoma Convention Center. It'll be a good fact-finding mission. The rest of the victims are civilians, and we haven't been afforded the right to all the information yet," Kibble grumbled.

CHAPTER SEVEN

GENNAVIE SAT on her balcony after work, wasting away the evening. The news was on in the background, broadcasting all kinds of horrible things, including the dead bodies discovered. She wasn't worried; there was no way to link them to anything. They had been cautious, unlike the first time.

She remembered how it all started. It seemed like yesterday, but it had already been almost eleven years since the first incident. She thought about how scared she had been. *I'm completely screwed!* she had thought. How could she have been so wrong?

Her days in Florida had been blessed, and life was good until things weren't. Back then, she couldn't believe she was facing a mess for simply whipping a man. Okay, so if she was honest with herself, she had gone a bit too far. Her uncle, a well-known defense attorney, told her she could be facing second-degree attempted murder charges, and that was only if Joe survived. It all seemed a little over the top. After all, he was a willing participant. He knew the risks and knew that he should have used his safe word if he had wanted her to stop. It was part of the game they played.

They had been dating for three years. Joe knew she preferred to be in control in the bedroom. They had been experimenting with increasing levels of BDSM over the past year. He seemed to enjoy it as much as she did, but this time they—or, more to the point, *she*—had gone a little too far.

Joe was into it as much as she was, and had even gone as far as calling her Mistress Gennavie. It made her feel empowered, unstoppable, and in control. It was one of the most significant highs she had ever experienced. Having the power to make Joe submit and bring him to ecstasy by dominating him was like a drug to her. She began to crave it, asking Joe to submit every time they were together in the bedroom.

She replayed that night in her mind. She had answered the door as Mistress Gennavie in her standard dominatrix outfit. She wore a laced-up red leather corset with a sheer lace choker around her throat and a short, black leather skirt. Her long, muscular legs were covered in sheer black nylon and knee-high boots with spiky four-inch heels. She liked towering over her sub. She already stood taller than most women at five foot eight, but with the boots on, she was nearly six feet tall. A pair of black, elbow-high gloves topped off the outfit.

Joe showed up at her door looking sheepish and wanting. He looked her up and down like she was a delicious meal to be devoured. He reached to touch her and she slapped his hand, leaving a little red mark.

"I did not give you permission to touch," she seethed. But she knew it was all part of the game. They thrived off of taking the stakes higher each time they played.

She took him by the collar and led him to her guest room. Joe was a tall, lanky man with well-defined muscles like a marathon runner. She liked his sleek body and enjoyed the things she could make him do.

Her playroom was in the back of the house. The makeshift dungeon had dark walls and nothing but a leather bench, a couple of chairs, oversized hooks on the wall, and a large assortment of sex toys and outfits in the closet. She had opted for wood floors in this room to keep things from getting messy. It was always hard to get lubricants and the occasional blood splatter out of the carpet. With the window facing the backyard, it was the perfect place to unleash her inner dominatrix; no one could see.

She lightly shoved him in the center of his back. "Now take off that silly monkey suit you're wearing and dress for your mistress!"

"Yes, ma'am," he said with a shy smile, and began to slowly remove his business suit. Joe was a young attorney at her uncle's law firm. He knew he was playing with fire by sleeping with his boss's niece, but he couldn't help himself. She was entirely irresistible with her beautiful body and long red hair that cascaded down her back.

She stood back and watched as he took off his jacket, pants, and shirt, neatly folding them and putting them over the chair in the corner of the room.

Joe stood in front of her in his tighty-whities, waiting for her command. He could never deny her anything she wanted.

She threw him a leather harness that strapped over his chest so she could tie him to the wall if she wished to. "Now, put on your leg cuffs," she directed. He did as she asked. "Now the hands," she said.

A shiver ran up his spine as he waited for his punishment. She walked over and shoved him against the wall. "Now stay still and be a good boy," she sneered, and cuffed him in place.

Things were going along as they usually would. She hit him lightly with a riding crop, leaving small marks on his chest and arms until he started begging. "I need more," he challenged.

"Challenge accepted," she said with a wicked grin.

"Please," he whimpered.

She gripped her favorite bullwhip that was strapped to her left hip and struck him with it over and over. At first she was doing her best not to break the skin, but her excitement grew as she saw the whip marks turn to bloody streaks across his chest and legs.

"More," he whispered.

Her focus was solely on Joe. Her vision blurred as she folded the whip and wrapped it around Joe's throat. She began to choke him, pushing all her weight against his neck, feeling the wetness between her legs increase as his eyes began to bulge. His face was turning a grayish purple, but she couldn't seem to stop herself. She was simply fascinated by the way his face had contorted into something inhuman.

Finally, the sound of her front door opening made her loosen her grip. She released, watching Joe gasp for breath and eventually return to a normal color. The entire experience had been exhilarating and terrifying. She hadn't intended to kill Joe, and she thought she didn't want to, but why hadn't she stopped? She looked at Joe, worried that she had really hurt him. He still hung there with his eyes closed and head dangling like a rag doll.

She slapped Joe across his face to wake him up, but he gave no response. A red mark materialized on his face. He wheezed softly. Grabbing her robe, she covered herself and ran to the living room to see the only person who had access to her house.

Uncle Frank looked up as she walked in. "I was wondering where you were." He smiled and then looked down at her boots peeking from below her robe. "Um, sorry, was I interrupting something?" He looked down nervously.

"Not anymore, but I may have a problem. Joe is hurt," was all she said as she spun on her stiletto boots and headed back to the bedroom.

He followed her cautiously.

She crossed the room and quickly wrapped a sheet around Joe's waist. "I didn't mean to," was all she could say.

CHAPTER
EIGHT

UNCLE FRANK LOOKED at the ligature and bloody whip marks and sighed. Where had he gone wrong? He had raised her. How was she capable of this? He had been appointed as her guardian after her parents had died in a car accident when she was thirteen. It had left her scared and made her feel like everything in her life that was stable could change in the blink of an eye. So she lived life to the fullest, taking unnecessary chances and always living on the edge. He knew she was into some crazy shit, but he had never actually witnessed any of it.

This is going to seriously screw up my life, she thought as she helped Uncle Frank drag Joe's body to the car. She knew she was self-centered, considering the state of Joe's body, but she couldn't help it. She had always been a bit selfish, self-centered, and willing to do just about anything to take care of herself. She would never have made it without Uncle Frank's help, but he worked all the time, ultimately leaving her on her own.

Uncle Frank broke her train of thought. "So, what's your plan?"

"What do you mean?" She looked at him, perplexed.

"Do you think we can just take this man to the hospital after what you did to him, and no one will ask questions?" He looked down at her like she was still a little girl. She hated when he made her feel like she was stupid.

"Well, no, but Joe would never press charges. I'm sure of it," she said, trying to sound convincing, but she wasn't sure of her convictions.

Uncle Frank stood to his full five feet, eleven inches and squared his overly broad shoulders. He ran his fingers through his gray hair. When he stood in front of her like that, she always felt small. She hated feeling small. "You know I love you, right?"

"Yes," she whispered.

"So, I need you to listen and listen well. If they convict you of attempted murder, you face possible life in prison. I can't handle you going to prison, and I'm sure you don't want to be there, either," he said, softening his voice.

She stood there thinking for a moment and then looked over at Joe. He still wasn't moving. She really could be in some big trouble here.

"Let's get him to the hospital and then figure out what we'll do," Uncle Frank said. He could see the fear in her eyes. Every time he looked at her, he pictured that sweet little girl, especially now that she had changed out of her outfit and stood there in shorts and flip-flops. Her long red hair was pulled back in a tight ponytail. Nope, he wasn't about to let her go to prison.

Uncle Frank got behind the wheel of Joe's silver Lincoln Continental. It was a nice luxury car with plush leather seats. They had put Joe in the passenger seat and strapped him in. Uncle Frank checked his pulse and was relieved to find the young man still had one. *I need a vacation*, Frank thought.

Of course, this wasn't the worst thing he'd done. As a defense attorney for high-profile criminals, he found himself walking a fine line where the law was concerned. It used to be a very defined line for him, but it had become blurred over the years.

Gennavie climbed into Frank's dark-blue Lexus and followed him to the emergency room. Her heart was pounding as they drove. What if they were pulled over, or someone witnessed them loading Joe's body into the car? She tried to calm her nerves, reminding herself that it was late and no one would be watching. It didn't help; she simply wouldn't survive in a box. Prison wasn't for a girl like her.

They pulled up in front of the hospital with the bright *Emergency Room* sign glaring down at them. Frank parked the car in the drop-off zone right in front of the emergency room doors. Thankfully, no one was standing nearby. He turned off the engine and laid the keys in Joe's lap. They had put clothes on him prior to delivering him here. The least they could do was leave the man with his dignity, and hopefully he would heal from his injuries.

Frank wiped down Joe's Lincoln, taking the time to inspect Joe's body to ensure Gennavie hadn't left any hair or follicles behind. She swore she hadn't gotten that close, and thankfully she had been wearing elbow-high gloves as part of her outfit. That would reduce the possibility of her DNA or fingerprints being left behind.

Now it was time for Uncle Frank to take care of business. As she pulled away, he slid a burner phone out of the breast pocket of his suit jacket. He called the emergency room number. A gravelly voice answered the phone. Frank calmly explained that there was a man in the passenger seat of a silver Lincoln parked right outside their door, and the man needed immediate medical attention. As soon as he was sure the man on the other end of the line understood, he hung up the phone.

"I'll check in on Joe later, but first we need to get you taken care of," he grumbled.

She stared at him with her huge eyes. He couldn't look at her. He was going to miss her so much. She was all he had left, and now she had to go away. He felt her piercing green eyes staring at him, wanting him to make it all better, but it would never be the same again.

Finally, she worked up the courage to ask, "What do you have planned?"

"You're not going to like it," he said, not making eye contact, "but it's better than prison."

CHAPTER
NINE

MAC AND KIBBLE arrived at the convention center building dressed smartly in their blues. She wondered if Captain Kibble had to have his specially made. Her technical instructor in basic was so large that he had to have all of his uniforms custom-made because they didn't come in his size, but unlike Kibble, that guy had an ego the size of Texas. Mac thought there was a special place in hell for people like him.

It was a huge glass building with five floors. They climbed into the elevator and headed for the fourth floor, where all the meeting rooms were located. When they arrived, a young officer directed people to a room called the Mississippian.

It was set up like a classroom with dark-blue tablecloths over long tables with uncomfortable-looking blue chairs lined behind each table. The carpet was a hideous-looking blue, yellow, and white combo that did not add to the ambiance, but Mac figured that wasn't what they were after. It was functional. She was actually impressed that someone could get it on such short notice, especially with this much space.

A case file for the teams that represented the investigative agencies sat at each table. It appeared that each agency had sent a team of two or three. She saw many people in plain clothes and suspected they were the local detectives from the various police departments in the area.

Several of them turned to look at Kibble and Mac. Kibble looked straight ahead while Mac tried to smile at some of them. They didn't smile back. *So that's how it's going to be,* Mac thought.

A pencil-thin woman stood at the front of the room. Her blond hair was pulled back in a tight ponytail that made her pointed nose and sharp features look even more severe. She was wearing a no-nonsense blue pants suit and sensible heels. She was flanked by two men that made Captain Kibble look small. They were at least the size of Hudson, but didn't have his kind eyes or soft smile. They still reminded her of how much she missed him.

Kibble and Mac took their seats close to the back. Kibble had said they weren't welcome and were only invited as a courtesy to someone higher up on the Air Force food chain. Mac understood and promised to try and keep her mouth shut. It was the one thing that could really get her in trouble. *I should probably install a filter,* she thought, smiling at herself.

The bird-looking woman tapped three times on the microphone to get everyone's attention. "Thank you all for coming out today. I'm Assistant Special Agent in Charge Bardot with the FBI." She paused, looking down her sharp nose at everyone sitting at the tables. "I'll be leading this task force, and all information will be filtered through me. You are not to take any action pursuing the perpetrator without checking with me first. Is that clear?"

Mac wondered if she actually wanted an answer. No wonder the locals always hated when the FBI took over a case. She looked around the room and saw some of the others nodding their heads, agreeing to her demands. Mac found the whole situation fascinating. The local police seemed absolutely resigned to the situation and already looked defeated. The two FBI agents flanking their boss just stared straight ahead like they were afraid to make eye contact.

It was interesting how their worlds weren't really all that different. It reminded Mac of the times she'd been in a commander's call with an Air Force general barking order, and everyone else just had to sit there and take whatever abuse was being thrown at them. Maybe she could get one or more local police to work with them and keep them informed. Clearly they weren't going to get any information from the lady on stage.

ASAC Bardot nodded toward someone off to the left of the stage, and a slide presentation came up. It was very organized and quite impressive. She wondered what poor sap had spent hours putting it together. Bardot cleared her throat again. "We have three probable victims that present with similar unique ligature marks. Two other victims were submerged in water, similar to the other victims, but they were weighed down. These two have damage to the throat area, but the bodies were too decomposed to show the pattern or marks on the flesh. We only have damage to the bone to work with."

The slideshow advanced, showing a picture of a skeleton with little pockmarks and visible bits of flesh hanging from it. It almost looked like it had been barbequed for too long, and the flesh had seared to the bones.

"The first two bodies were found in approximately the same state. The coroner estimates that the first body has been in the water for over a year. As you can see, it's completely decomposed, and the marine life has scattered some of the remains. We were only able to recover parts of the first two victims. There's evidence that these first two victims had been weighed down. The divers found cinder blocks and bits of rope near some of the remains."

Bardot paused to let the information sink in. "This first victim's name is Roni Thomas. She's an Asian female; her driver's license information says she was a hundred and ten pounds and only five foot two, age twenty. She's from California and was in Seattle attending Seattle University for her undergraduate in biochemistry. Her roommate reported her missing last year after failing to return from a night out on the town. We were able to positively identify her through her dental records."

The next slide came up on the screen. "The second body, which you can see is almost completely decomposed, has been in the water for approximately eleven months," Bardot read from the report. "The victim's name is Theodore Harris, a white male; his driver's license lists him at six foot two and two hundred and ten pounds, age forty-six. He worked as a law clerk in downtown Seattle. He was reported missing by his girlfriend a year ago after he didn't return from work."

"Now, for the more recent victims." Bardot looked up for a moment. "Fair warning, the rest of these images are quite gruesome, and each body is in a slightly different level of decomp. Several factors contribute to this. For instance, one of these three bodies was in saltwater, and the other two were in freshwater. The temperature and bacteria levels in the water can also accelerate or slow down the process."

Mac had to give her credit; she was extremely thorough and professional. She could just imagine how tough a woman would have to be in the predominantly male career field of the FBI. She knew from her own experience how hard it could be as a woman in the military, and she wasn't nearly as high up on the food chain as Bardot appeared to be. She wondered if Bardot ever allowed herself to show emotion or if she was always stone-faced.

"The third victim is Emily Sandburg, one hundred and forty-three pounds, five feet, five inches tall, and thirty-one years old. She's a white female born and raised in the Seattle area. According to her mother, she was working as a photographer and was an aspiring journalist who reported her missing eight months ago. The level of decomp on this body is consistent with the timeframe in which she would have gone missing," Bardot explained.

"The first three bodies were found in the Puget Sound. The next two bodies were found in freshwater. This next victim is Tamara Addison, a small black female, thirty-six years old, ninety-eight pounds, and five foot even. She was reported missing by her husband three months ago. She was a nurse working at a local hospital and didn't come home from the night shift," Bardot said, looking defeated. "She was found in Bonnie Lake not far from the city." Her small remains were up on the screen for everyone to see. Mac thought it was awful that they had to dissect people's lives this way, but also necessary.

"The final victim that we know of is Airman First Class Ryan Collymore." She paused to look at Mac and Kibble, acknowledging their existence for the first time. "This victim was five foot nine and weighed a hundred and sixty pounds. He was twenty-one years old and a white male of Italian descent, and he was found in Snohomish River. He was on active duty in the United States Air Force and had served his country for a little over two years." The young man's bloated body was almost unrecognizable on the slide. Mac had seen pictures of him while he was still alive at the ADC office, and the slide looked almost alien rather than human.

Bardot paused again, looking at Kibble and Mac like this death caused her pain. Mac knew that every victim was equally important, but this one seemed different for Bardot. Mac wondered if the woman had served previously. Many military members went on to serve in one of the three-letter agencies. They ran things like the military, which made it an easy transition. Mac had considered it herself a few times.

"To summarize, we have five potential victims ranging in age, ethnicity, background, and occupation. Normally in these cases, the victims have distinct similarities. Still, in this particular case the only thing tying the victims together is the distinct ligature marks found on the last three bodies and the fact that they were all in watery graves."

A slide appeared on the screen with close pictures of skin at various angles. The skin looked weird and distorted on the slides, but Mac could still see what Bardot was talking about. On some of the better pictures, there was about a one-inch mark of grayish-colored skin that ran in a straight line. It had a zigzag pattern with ridges along the edges. Mac was pretty sure she had never seen anything like it.

"Do we have any witnesses so far, or anything to link the victims?" one Seattle police detective asked. He was a short, dark-haired, heavy-set man who looked like he was quickly approaching retirement.

"Not so far," Bardot responded. "We're still interviewing family and friends to see if there are any connections between the victims, but we've come up empty so far. Currently, there seem to be no witnesses. We can account for their whereabouts until just before their disappearance.

"At this point, we need to divide and conquer. I need each of the local police agencies to canvass the areas where victims were last seen. Pull any video surveillance, interview witnesses, and tap into your local informants to see if you can dredge up any information. My people will be going through their digital lives to find out if there are any connections that we have yet to see."

She paused and looked directly at Kibble and Mac. "I need the two of you to report back with any information you can find about Collymore. You have much better access than we do, and so far, we have little to go on in his case. Everyone reports back to me. You'll find everything you need and my team's contact information in your folders." Bardot gave a curt nod and walked off the stage.

CHAPTER
TEN

SHE SAT at work trying to focus on her tasks, but she couldn't seem to keep her mind from wondering. She often thought about how she had ended up in the military and how things had turned out the way they had. Though she did not go by Mistress or Gennavie in this environment. Her uncle's words ran through her head for the thousandth time: "You're either going to jail or going into the military for making a grown man squeal." She acknowledged that she had done much worse to Joe than make him squeal. That would have been acceptable even if invited, but she had lost control.

Uncle Frank had let her know that Joe had been fortunate to survive and was still suffering from vocal dysfunction due to the damage she had done to his throat, even to this day. He told her Joe would have died if she had continued. Since that night, she had studied and honed her skills. She couldn't entirely give up her need to dominate, but she learned that she needed to never lose control again. Joe never pressed charges and kept asking when she was coming back.

Uncle Frank told her that Joe not testifying or pressing charges was only half the battle. There was still a police report and evidence that could easily lead back to her. Frank had caught wind that the prosecuting attorney was out for blood because it was a fellow attorney that had been assaulted, even if Joe didn't want to press charges. That had all blown over now, but there was still no going back.

Uncle Frank had once defended a high-level colonel in the Air Force and saved his career. After a few phone calls, Gennavie found herself in basic training at Lackland Air Force Base in San Antonio, Texas. She had a new name and even a new look. He had even created her a new past to get through the background checks and obtain her security clearance. At first she was pissed, but she found she liked it once she arrived, or at least she liked the regime.

They started every morning with a good workout and then a good meal. She loved being physically active and thrived as a new airman. The feeling of belonging to something bigger than herself was rewarding, and she even liked some of the other airmen she had trained with. She had made expert marksman, which according to her TI was extremely rare. The military had all walks of life from every part of the country imaginable. She had never experienced such cultural diversity.

Eight and a half weeks later, she graduated. Uncle Frank showed up and hid at the back of the crowd, but she knew he was there. He didn't want to blow her cover, but she knew he still cared for her. The day after graduation, they got up early. They headed out to Fort Sam Houston, Texas, which was only a twenty-minute ride from Lackland, where she would attend tech school to become an aerospace medical services airman.

It really wasn't a bad gig. Gennavie was more intelligent than most people and had no problem passing the classes. It was a short course that took just over three months. She had the option to go home after she was done before reporting to her first base, but her home of record didn't really exist, so she went on to her first base.

Her former life didn't matter now. She had found a new life and new people to play with. She had several clients that she spent time with outside of her sometimes trying work that she had to do during the day, but there were upsides to it as well. She found it simply fascinating that so many men and women in powerful positions liked to be controlled in some form or fashion.

She found herself in a vast city that abutted other towns and cities.

The nightlife was amazing. She could spend her days at JBLM in Tacoma as an admired airman who was a rising star, and her nights as a dominatrix. The best part was that no one really knew who she was. She'd loved playing dress-up as a child, and now she was living a life that allowed her to reinvent herself regularly. It was great fun.

CHAPTER
ELEVEN

BY THE TIME Mac and Kibble arrived back at base, they were exhausted. They had a game plan for the next day, but they were going to rest for the night. "Do you need anything before I take off?" Mac asked.

"No, I think we're good until tomorrow. I haven't had time to connect with my wife and kids much over the last few days," he said, grinning. "The little ones like the video chat features."

"Sounds like fun. I'm going to hit the gym and blow off some steam. My backside hurts from sitting in those awful chairs today," she said as she was walking away. "See you tomorrow."

Mac was shocked to find there were several gyms on base. She decided on the McChord fitness center simply because it looked like the closest one. The gym was adequate for her workout. It had all of the basic amenities, but she was disappointed there wasn't a punching bag to take her frustration out on, and there didn't seem to be any sparring mats.

She absolutely hated running, and was looking forward to avoiding it over the next year. Instead, she decided to lift some weights and get some cardio in on one of the elliptical machines. She was happy with getting a ninety-three on her recent annual fitness test.

She plugged in her headphones and started to work her shoulders.

She could see her shoulder muscles straining against the weight in her tank top. She liked the way her traps were shaped. They were pronounced and well-defined but not unfeminine. She was facing one of the big mirrors and could see a woman behind her, watching. She figured it was only because she was new to the gym, and then she realized it was Alice from the front desk of the Holiday Inn billeting.

Mac made eye contact and smiled warmly. She didn't intend it as an invitation, but Alice walked over.

"Hi," she said, looking down at her feet.

"Hi," Mac responded. "How are you doing?"

"I'm good. Um, I'm sorry to intrude on your workout, but I wondered if I could buy you a drink or dinner or whatever when you're done. I think I may have some information for you," Alice said in a whisper.

"I'm all ears. Can we meet up somewhere at eighteen-thirty hours?" Mac realized that Alice was probably a straight civilian and corrected herself. "I meant six-thirty."

"I know military time," she said, sounding slightly offended. "I've been on base and around the military for a while."

"Okay, good to know. Where would you like to meet?"

"How about Black Bear Diner? They have delicious food, and it usually isn't crowded. If you want, I can meet you in front of billeting and we can go together?"

"Yeah, sounds great. I'll see you then." Mac was interested but slightly annoyed, because she had to rush through her workout. She raced from one station to the next, trying to get in the bare minimum. It was a promise she'd made to herself a long time ago: never skip a workout. Even if you find yourself at the gym really early or really late and only get half in, don't skip.

She could remember many times when she hadn't wanted to go anywhere, let alone to the gym, but once she was there she always felt better, except for the times she had to run. The thought of running made her groan internally, and she wondered if she was doing it wrong. Most people made it look so easy, but for Mac, it was pure torture.

By the time she was done, showered, and ready to meet Alice for dinner, she felt one hundred percent better. She was proud of herself for not throwing in the towel and just going to dinner. She was famished, and it was definitely time to eat. She hoped they had something other than greasy burgers at this place.

Her diet wasn't the cleanest, but she tried to stay with the eighty-twenty rule. Eighty percent of her food was healthy and clean, and twenty percent was questionable at best. With that and eating six meals a day, Mac could keep the weight off, but she really struggled when traveling. She reminded herself to stop by the store tomorrow to buy groceries for her room. That always helped.

The thought of food had her distracted, but this case kept creeping into her thoughts. She wondered if all the murder victims were connected, or if Bardot was trying to make connections where there weren't any.

CHAPTER
TWELVE

VINCENT LOOKED at his beautiful wife. "What ya thinking about?"

"Just thinking about the past and how we got here," she replied casually.

He went to take a shower, thinking about where he had come from. His past was a bit more complicated, but she knew the story. They had long since shared all their sordid stories. Since homicide wasn't acceptable in polite society and he didn't want to spend the rest of his life in prison, he had to find an alternate means of quieting his demons.

At a young age, he'd felt disconnected from the rest of society. It was odd that he seemed to be the person everyone wanted to be like. He couldn't connect with anyone, but boy could he put on one hell of a show. He had learned to mimic the actions of others and had become quite good at it.

People told him he was charismatic and charming. Thanks to his mother's side of the family, he'd inherited a high IQ which made school and college easy for him. His need to kill had consumed him from a young age. He strived to be and feel normal, but his dark desires wouldn't rest unless he took another victim. He had honed his skills over the years, but after his last kill, the authorities started to take notice.

At the time, to evade capture he had decided to join the Air Force, hoping that the great US government would find it convenient to pay him to kill. He had always wanted to fly and dreamed of taking out people from the cockpit, high in the air. He felt like a great and powerful eagle swooping down to pick off all the defenseless mice who scurried about in his dreams. He preferred a more hands-on approach when he killed, but he thought that would be fun.

Unfortunately, things hadn't worked out the way he had planned. He hadn't passed the depth perception part of the physical, and they said he was color blind and couldn't be a pilot. Though, not all was lost. He had managed to change gears and join the 22nd Special Tactics Squadron at Joint Base Lewis-McChord. He had yet to see any real action and had been through more training than he cared to think about, but at least he could hone his combat skills and, more importantly, his evasion tactics.

He fondly remembered his first kill in Seattle. It hadn't been the first time he had killed a person, but it was the first time in his new hunting ground. He had been out drinking beer with his buddies from the military. He was constantly scanning the room.

"Whatcha looking for?" one of the men had asked. Auston was always inquisitive, so Vincent had to keep his guard up when Auston was around. The observant little bastard saw everything.

"Just looking for a hot little something to take home with me," Vincent replied.

Auston slapped him on the shoulder and laughed. Auston wasn't a big man, but fairly good-looking as far as men went. He only stood at about five foot eight, but his stocky build and wide smile seemed to attract the ladies.

Vincent was Auston's polar opposite. Auston had fair skin and blond hair with a Nordic look, where he had darker features and didn't stand out in any crowd.

Auston smirked at his friend. "No one wants to go home with your ugly mug." He smiled wide, like a Cheshire cat.

Vincent just smirked and tipped his beer back. He found it helpful to be seen out with people before a kill. He was counting on his friends getting drunk and not being able to recall the time just in case anyone ever suspected him. So far, his plan had worked beautifully.

Vincent sat in the corner, waiting and watching while his friends continued to drink. He nursed his beer, ensuring he didn't drink too much and his mind would remain clear. There was nothing remarkable about him. He was plain and unassuming. He looked like an average Joe you'd see on the street, forgotten as soon as you passed by. He had brown hair that wasn't too dark. It had been called mousy brown, which suited him just fine. He wasn't muscular or fat, not big or small. He didn't think he was attractive, but he wasn't ugly, either. He could simply blend in. Nothing about him was remarkable or memorable except his eyes, which he changed when it suited him.

Once he felt his companions were properly sloshed, he got up and headed to the back of the bar. If anyone cared to pay attention, it would appear as if he had gone to the restroom, but instead, he headed out to the back of the bar. The Seattle streets were muggy and wet from a recent downfall. He didn't mind it here. It was such a big city that no one ever noticed him, which allowed him to hunt undetected.

He enjoyed reminiscing about that night he made his first of many kills in Seattle and the days when he hunted solo. It was enjoyable to hunt with his beautiful wife, but men were meant to track their pray. With her, the victims came too easily.

CHAPTER
THIRTEEN

MAC PULLED up to the Holiday Inn's main entrance to find Alice patiently waiting for her. Alice was a pretty young woman. Mac guessed she was in her mid-twenties with straight black hair and wide eyes that often made her look surprised. Alice had changed into a pair of old jeans and a t-shirt that hugged her small frame. In contrast to Alice's petite frame, she was the same height, but curvier in a good way. Mac hadn't really taken stock of her before, but could see how men would line up for this young lady.

Mac smiled warmly. "Hi Alice, thanks for waiting for me. I hope you weren't standing there long."

"Nope, just got here myself. Your timing is perfect."

"Good to hear. Would you like me to drive?"

"Nah, I can drive. The Black Bear Diner is my uncle's place. I know some shortcuts to get us there without getting on the main roads. This time of night, they're liable to be packed."

Mac wasn't used to all the traffic in the bigger city, so they climbed into Alice's Honda Civic. Sensible, economical, but bright blue for a bit of color. Mac always thought that people bought cars that went with their personality. This seemed right for Alice. They made small talk on the way to the restaurant, but Mac was dying to ask what she knew.

She took a moment to shoot Hudson a quick text to let him know she would call him after so he wouldn't worry. When she looked up, Alice was staring at her.

"Um, so do you guys have any leads yet?" There was hesitation in Alice's voice.

"Nothing concrete. Did you know Airman Collymore?"

"Yeah, we were dating," she said in a low voice.

Mac paused for a little longer than she had intended. This was the exact lead she had been looking for. "I'm sorry for your loss. Is there anything I can do for you? Get you someone to talk to?"

"I'm talking to you," she said pointedly. "I don't need a shrink, if that's what you mean. I need to help you catch the bastard that did this to Ryan."

"If you want to help, please tell me everything you know about Ryan Collymore. His friends, where he hung out, and what he liked and disliked. Even if it seems unimportant, please tell me. Sometimes the smallest details lead to a break in a case."

Alice turned into a restaurant with nicely carved black bears out front. It looked like a welcoming place. As soon as they walked inside, a bear of a man came around the corner and swallowed Alice up in a big hug, lifting her off her feet.

Alice squirmed for a few minutes, smiling up at her uncle. "Put me down," she protested, laughing. He smiled and put her feet back on the floor. "Uncle Don, this is Mac. She's working on Ryan's case."

Uncle Don looked down at her with a weathered face. His eyebrows knitted, making him look a little constipated. Mac smiled back at him but wasn't sure what to say.

"Ryan was a good kid," he said. "Anything we can do to help you catch the bastard that took him out, you let me know." With that, Uncle Don turned on his heels and led the two ladies back to a secluded table where they could chat. "Dinner's on me, girls; order whatever you want."

Uncle Don walked away to attend to other customers while Mac looked at the menu.

Mac looked up. "Do you already know what you want?"

"Yeah, my uncle's sirloin steak is the best I've ever had. He puts this sauce on it that should be illegal." Alice smiled.

"Sounds great." She paused. "So, what did you want to tell me?"

Just then, the waiter came to take their order. It felt to Mac like Alice was stalling, so she tried a different tactic.

"How bad could it really be?" Mac asked.

Alice looked confused. "How bad could what be?"

"Whatever it is that Ryan Collymore was into," Mac said pointedly.

"Well, that's just it. I'm not entirely sure what he had himself tangled up in. He was fascinated by different cultures and subcultures and was going to school to be an anthropologist focusing on sociocultural anthropology."

Mac looked a little perplexed. "Okay, so you'll have to give me some insight. I know a little bit about what you're talking about in theory, but what exactly was he into in the real world?"

"In his off-time, he studied how different subcultures operated in the Tacoma and Seattle areas. He had become fascinated with some of the specific subcultures in Seattle," Alice explained. "He was looking into some of the more interesting communities like vampires, furries—who I guess are people who dress up as animals—cosplayers, bikers, and BDSM. He was working on his thesis surrounding different subcultures that practice and participate in different sensual and erotic play. He was brilliant, and if the thesis went over well with his committee, they would give him a full scholarship to enter his doctoral program. His military education benefits weren't enough to cover it."

"I see," Mac said. "Do you know where he was going the night he died?"

"Just out with his friends, as far as I know."

"Do you know if he participated in any of these subcultures, or just observed?" Mac asked.

"He said he was there just for academic purposes, but said sometimes he needed to blend in, so he would dress like whatever subculture he would go check out. I got the feeling that he did more than observe. Don't get me wrong, I don't think he was cheating. I just think he was really into his research and would participate to get a feel for it."

"What makes you think that?"

"There were a few times when he would come back with marks on his body. He promised me he wasn't cheating, but I still didn't like it. I was actually thinking of breaking it off with him because he was changing so much. He wanted to experiment with some of the subcultures, wanted me to try different things with him," Alice said, looking down at her hands.

"What kinds of things?"

"He wanted me to dominate him, roleplay, dress up, that kind of thing. He even dared to buy me a couple of outfits. I'm no prude, and I'm a huge believer in to each their own, but it wasn't my thing. It was fine when he wanted to study, but when he wanted to join in, I was out."

"Do you know where he would meet some of these people?"

"Not really," she admitted. "He asked me to come with him, but I was a little scared. I'm just your run-of-the-mill, simple kind of person. I always wanted to settle down and have a couple of kids. I'm not very adventurous. Not that Ryan didn't try, but I just wasn't into it."

Their meals showed up. The dinner in front of them looked amazing. Mac took a deep breath in and let out a soft moan. "That smells amazing."

"Wait until you taste it." Alice smiled.

They devoured their food in silence. Mac hadn't realized just how hungry she was, but more importantly, the quiet gave her time to think. She began to run the idea of the different cultures in her mind. There were all kinds of different possibilities. She felt people could lead whatever kind of lifestyle they wanted to as long as they didn't hurt anyone else—but, in this case, people were being killed. She could feel her excitement rising as she processed the new information.

CHAPTER
FOURTEEN

LESS THAN TWO YEARS AGO, Vincent had met his wife at her work, of all places.

"Hey Davis, your next patient is here."

The nurse got up from behind her desk and grabbed her next chart. She called his name, and Vincent presented himself. She led him back into the clinic's hallway and checked his weight. "How tall are you?" she asked.

"About five foot eleven," he answered. He knew he was staring at her, but he couldn't help it. She was breathtaking. She had beautiful chestnut hair that didn't look quite right against her porcelain skin. He thought she would look better as a redhead.

"Excuse me," she said, pulling him from his thoughts.

"Sorry, what did you say? I was distracted."

"I can see that, now please pay attention," she said, offering him a kind smile. "Now, please come with me so we can take your vitals."

I'll go anywhere you want me to, he thought to himself, and followed her to the examination room.

She asked him to sit and proceeded to take his blood pressure and temperature and ask him a battery of questions about his daily habits. "Do you smoke?" she asked him for the second time.

"Um, no, except for an occasional cigar," he finally responded.

"Do you drink?"

"Not often."

"Why?" she asked, catching him completely off guard.

"What do you mean?" he asked with a perplexed look.

She smiled back at him. She liked his eyes. They were a piercing blue that almost matched her natural green ones. She often wore contacts when she went out, but she left them natural here. "Why don't you drink?" she repeated. "Don't you like to have a good time?" She smiled wickedly.

"Oh, I like to have fun. Just not that kind of fun."

He smiled at her again, but there was something animalistic in his eyes that excited her. She couldn't put her finger on it, but he was definitely different, and she liked it.

"Really." She grinned.

Wow, she has a beautiful smile, he thought.

"Maybe you could show me some time," she offered as the doctor walked in, and her demeanor changed completely. "Hi sir, this is your next patient." She handed him the file. "He's in good health, doesn't drink or smoke excessively, and is here for his annual periodic health assessment."

The doctor took a few minutes to look over his file. "Very well, when was your last PHA?"

"About a year or so, I think," he finally responded. He was having a hell of a time paying attention with Davis in the room. Sure, she was stunning, but he had been with and killed plenty of gorgeous women. There was simply something different about her, and he intended to find out what it was—and was he ever right.

So much had happened since he had met his beautiful wife. He couldn't believe how lucky he had been. After meeting her at the clinic, he couldn't get her out of his head. She was so stunning and had those green eyes. There was just something irresistible about her, an animal magnetism that he just couldn't leave alone.

He followed her to a party one night. She had left the base in her little white car and gone to her lavish home on the water. The house had surprised him at the time. She came back dressed in this amazing black leather dress that hugged all of her curves. He'd almost missed her because her hair was different.

At the clinic, she had short, dark-brown hair pulled back in accordance with military regulations. Now, she came out of her house with long red hair. He loved it and couldn't believe she could be even sexier than when he'd first met her. "Simply seductive" were the words that came to mind.

She climbed into her little car and went to a nightclub. He found it interesting when she parked down the road and walked over. The heels she was wearing had to be uncomfortable, but he sure did enjoy watching her sway as she walked.

Eventually, he followed her into the club to see her dancing with one man, letting him grind against her, and then with a woman who wanted to dance slowly. It was intriguing to watch her go from one dance partner to another without missing a beat.

As the night wore on, he slowly moved closer to her. When she turned and caught his eye, he almost thought he had made a mistake. Blue eyes? What the hell, had he been following the wrong woman?

And then she smiled at him.

"Hey, you." She walked up to him. "What brings you to my stomping ground?"

He looked at her nervously. "Nothing, just hangin' out."

"Are you following me?" she joked.

"Yes."

She looked at him with wide eyes at first, but realized she appreciated his honesty. At least he wasn't lying to her the way most men would. "Why are you following me?"

"I find you fascinating and want to know more about you," he said shyly; he thought she'd like him better if he was shy.

"Interesting. Well, what would you like to know?"

"Everything," he replied with a mischievous grin.

"Trust me, you don't want to know everything," she said.

After dating for a few months, she had finally opened up to him and revealed her dominatrix side. He explained that he wasn't interested in being dominated, but would like to watch her during one of her sessions with a client. And he was right, he enjoy watching and the more he found out, the more intrigued he was.

At first, she was reluctant, but eventually, he convinced her that he wouldn't get jealous. It just wasn't his style. She informed him that she rarely had sex with her clients. It was more about her submissive being controlled and giving up control. Many of her clients were high-end executives and some higher-level military members who needed the release. They simply wanted to give up all control. One of her clients felt he deserved to be punished, so she would punish him. In a way, she was a bit like a therapist.

―――

The first time she took Vincent to one of her sessions was a little taboo, but exhilarating for both of them. She had confided in him about Joe, but he hadn't told her about his past—well, at least not in great detail.

She had a client that was willing to allow him to watch. They had discussed it in great detail, and Vincent could tell she was nervous. He was only allowed to sit in a chair in the corner.

"I like you a lot and don't want you to turn and run away," she explained.

"No chance of that," he reassured her.

That night she took Vincent to a hotel room. The client wore a mask because he wanted to disguise his identity. They were in a nicer hotel room on the eleventh floor. It was one of the fanciest places Vincent had ever been. The client came into the room in his mask and looked at the man sitting in the corner, and then she walked in.

Vincent couldn't breathe as he watched her tie her client to a chair in the middle of the room. She had never looked so good and in control. She strapped a ball gag to his face and began slowly torturing him. At first, she teased him with light slaps from a flog. She clipped what looked like mini jumper cables to the client's nipples. This made Vincent flinch slightly from where he sat in the corner, but her client whimpered.

"More, mistress," the client begged.

"How much more?" Without waiting for an answer, she turned up the dial and sent a shock through his body.

The session went on like that for nearly an hour. She would slowly increase the pain, and the client only wanted more. She had even burned his skin a little with hot wax and then let it dry, ripping it from his skin. At the end of the session, the client happily paid her, got dressed, and left.

Vincent had never been so turned on in his life. He took her without asking permission, with animalistic energy. He couldn't get enough of her. He had done some awful things to the human body, but he had never enjoyed one the way he enjoyed hers. He didn't feel the need to kill for the first time ever.

CHAPTER
FIFTEEN

MAC WENT BACK to her room that night after meeting Alice and found a beautiful potted lily plant. She walked up to smell the flowers. Lilies were her absolute favorite flower. There was no card, but she figured it had to be from Hudson. They had only been together for a short time, but he was attentive, caring, and always did nice things for her.

Just then, the phone rang.

"Hey hon, how's everything going out there?" Hudson's deep baritone came across the line.

"Hi back at you," Mac said. "Thanks for the beautiful flowers. I just got back to my room."

"What flowers?" Hudson sounded confused.

"These aren't from you?"

"Nope, but now I wish I had thought of it. Should I be worried about a secret admirer?" A trace of nervousness crept into his voice.

"Nah, I'm sure it's nothing. Maybe they're from the ADC office thanking me for helping on the case. I'll ask them tomorrow," she said, trying to calm Hudson's worries.

No matter how hard he tried, he still had some trust issues after coming home from a deployment to find his now ex-wife in bed with another man. He had been crushed and was still a little gun shy about relationships. Hell, so was she. She hadn't let anyone get this close before, but for entirely different reasons.

"So, how's the case coming along? Will you be coming home soon?" he asked to change the subject.

"Not bad; the case is coming along okay. We have lots of information but very little evidence to point us in any direction. I may have a new lead."

"So, what's the lead?" Hudson asked.

"I just got back from meeting with Alice, the victim's girlfriend. It might be something, but it also may be nothing at all. She said that our victim was into studying subcultures and had been following different groups in the Seattle area."

"What are you thinking?" Hudson asked.

"Well, Collymore's body had evidence of long, deep marks that could have been caused by a whip. His body had already begun to decompose, but some of the marks went all the way to the bone. That takes a lot of anger."

"Could it be that he was trying out some of the cultures he was studying?" Hudson asked.

"Possibly. I know it's fairly stereotypical of me to think that all dominatrixes use whips and chains, but it could be something," she said. "According to Alice, he looked into different types of sexually deviant cultures like BDSM and some other ones, but the BDSM sticks out the most because of the whip marks on the bodies."

"So, what's your plan?"

"Well, I was thinking of going downtown to see if I could get into one of those subcultures and see if there's anything to it," Mac said. "Someone has to know something about what he was into or who he was studying."

"If you need a wingman, I'm all yours," he said. "I'm happy to go kinky with you anytime."

She laughed. "Don't get too excited. I need an in first. Most of those groups don't just let you come waltzing in without an invitation."

CHAPTER
SIXTEEN

IT WAS EARLY in the morning. Vincent watched his wife sleeping next to him. She looked so quiet and at peace. He marveled at how she looked like an angel in some moments, with her hair fanned out on her pillow, purring softly. He wondered what she dreamed about and if her dreams were as violent as his.

He had suffered from insomnia kicks for years. At times he slept without a problem, but other times he would only sleep for a few hours a night. He had a beautiful wife who was as deviant and twisted as he was, maybe even a little more, and just kept upping the ante. Since he had met her, he had slept better than at any other time in his life. It amazed him how time flew by and life couldn't get better.

He loved everything about her. At least, he thought this might be what love felt like. He had never felt for anyone before, but she had to be the closest thing to love that he could imagine. She was the first and only human he had spent time with that he hadn't envisioned killing. *That has to mean something*, he thought.

It was probably because she killed with him, and that was simply delightful. She had a much easier time luring in all kinds of prey. Women and men alike would willingly go home with her. She could get anyone she wanted. Sometimes he would choose, and sometimes she would. They made it a little game, kind of like rock, paper, scissors.

It was a tantalizing relationship, and neither of them could get enough. When they first met, she had revealed her true self to him, but he had held back, knowing she wouldn't accept him for the monster he was, but he was so wrong. They had continued playing with her clients, like the first time.

For a while it had satisfied them, but it got old, and they needed something more exciting until Roni came along. She had been this sexy, petite Asian woman who wanted a little adventure. They had shown her one hell of a time, playing with her for hours until she died. Just thinking about the experience made his erection grow.

They'd had so many adventures together. Interestingly, no one had come across Brandon's body yet, even though he had been dead the longest. Brandon hadn't been their first kill together, but he had been the first one in this region, and their first black man. They had tucked Brandon's body away in a secluded place near Snoqualmie Falls.

It was a beautiful place where they had been hiking and felt it was the perfect location to hide the body. They'd been correct; no one had stumbled upon it yet. He knew people had found some of their earlier kills and a few of the kills he had committed before meeting his beautiful wife, but there was nothing to point back to them.

She rolled over in bed and slowly opened her green eyes. "Couldn't sleep?"

"Nah, just thinking," he grumbled.

"What's on your mind?" she asked, running a finger down his chest.

"The task force, mostly," he admitted.

"We've been cautious. We wore gloves, wiped down the bodies and the rooms, burned their clothes, and then submerged the bodies. I couldn't imagine how they could trace any of them back to us. Could you?"

"No." He paused, staring up at the ceiling for a moment. "It's that woman."

"What woman?"

"The one from Fairchild. I read that she caught a chief master sergeant who was killing women out there when no one else could. I think we should take her out."

"That would bring down too much heat. Think about it. If we start picking off military members, the entire force of the government could come down on our heads…" She trailed off. She was going to have to find out what her informant knew. She had been seducing a man on base who could help with the situation. He had once described himself as being built like a tank, and the nickname stuck. Tank was putty in her hands, and she knew he would give her whatever information she wanted.

She focused back on her husband. "It would heighten the investigation and possibly link us to the military. It was bad enough that Collymore ended up being military. Who knew a military kid would play in our world?"

"Well, we're military, and we like to play all kinds of wicked games." He smiled at her.

"The reason we're safe is that we keep degrees of separation. We work on the base and need to keep our two lives separate. This isn't the time to get sloppy," she said sternly, almost like she was talking to a disobedient child.

He hated when she talked down to him, but she did have a point. "Okay, what do you think we should do?"

"I think we need to change things up a bit and do some investigating of our own."

CHAPTER SEVENTEEN

THE FOLLOWING DAY, Mac headed for the ADC office to figure out their strategy. She intended to interview the two guys Collymore had been out with the night he had died. Kibble said he would get clearance from the OSI liaison he was working on the case with.

OSI typically investigated high-profile cases on base and often worked directly with the FBI, but in this case, Kibble had called in favor of a friend of his, Special Agent Whitlock. They had become good friends at Officer Training School, and Whitlock owed him a favor. The Office of Special Investigation on base was their conduit between them and the FBI.

Kibble hung up the phone. "So, Whitlock gave us the go-ahead to interview the two potential suspects. They were the last people to see Collymore alive, so they're at the top of the list. We can find them at the chapel. They've both been removed from their duty stations pending the investigation."

"Sounds good. Do either of them have representation?" Mac asked.

"No, neither one has lawyered up yet, but I suspect it's just a matter of time."

She left Kibble at the office and headed toward the chapel after asking for directions from Carter. JBLM was much larger than

Fairchild. They only had a few chapels on her base, but on JBLM there were nine, which seemed like a lot, but who was she to judge?

After a few minutes of navigating the base, she found the building she was looking for. She walked in to see a vast open space with multiple small offices off to one side. She found a young airman and asked him where she could find Airmen Wyatt and Lincoln.

"Just down the hall and to the left, ma'am."

"Thank you," Mac replied, following his directions. She came around the corner and down another hall. The place felt like a maze, and she hoped she could find her way back out. Finally, she walked into a large open room where she saw two young airmen wiping down the pews. Both had their outer uniform shirts off, so she couldn't read their nametags. Neither airman acknowledged her when she walked in.

"Excuse me," Mac said, "could you point me toward Wyatt and Lincoln?"

"Well, yes, ma'am, I'm Wyatt, and over there is Lincoln," one said with a sly smile and slight southern accent. He was definitely the dominant one in the room. Lincoln raised his hand and waved at her. "What can we do for you?" Wyatt asked.

"Hi, I'm Mac. I wondered if I could ask you a few questions about Collymore."

This seemed to throw the two young men off-balance. "What do you want to know?" Wyatt, the leader of the two, asked.

Lincoln had yet to say a word.

"I wondered if you could tell me about the night the three of you went out and Collymore disappeared?" Mac asked, sitting on one of the chairs lining the wall. She smiled at Wyatt, the more talkative of the two. She always found that sitting made people relax and want to open up to her.

"We'll tell you anything you want to know as long as we don't get into trouble," he said. "They're already investigating us, and we did nothing wrong."

"Not to worry—I'm not part of your defense team, but I have no intentions of getting you guys in trouble unless you tell me you actually killed Collymore," she said, making direct eye contact with Wyatt and then with Lincoln. "What do you think, Lincoln?" She paused, looking at him. "Will you talk to me about that night?"

"Yes, ma'am," Lincoln said softly.

Lincoln and Wyatt couldn't have been more different. Wyatt had strawberry blond hair and large, wide eyes with a more handsome, chiseled face, a built physique, and almost seemed to be flirting with Mac. Lincoln had straight brown hair with a narrow face and small eyes. He seemed perpetually nervous as his eyes darted around the room, looking for an escape.

"Okay, Lincoln, let's start with you." She lowered her voice. She had a feeling that Lincoln had never been the one to go first at anything. "What can you tell me about that night?"

"Um, well, ma'am—" he began.

"It's okay if you call me Mac," she said, trying to put him at ease. She looked over at Wyatt and noticed him glaring at the other man like he was willing him to say the right thing.

Lincoln cleared his throat and began again. "Okay, Ms. Mac. Um, well, we went to this bar and had a few drinks—"

"Could you please start from the beginning?" Mac asked, maintaining her soft tone.

"Um, yes, ma'am—I mean Mac. We met outside the dorms."

"What was the plan for the evening?" she asked.

"We were going out for steaks and then some drinks, and maybe..." Lincoln looked down at his feet.

"Maybe what?" Mac encouraged.

"Well, maybe to pick up some ladies," Lincoln said.

"Okay, so how did the evening actually unfold?" Mac asked pointedly, watching Lincoln try to disappear into the floor.

Wyatt seemed to be getting more and more agitated, fidgeting with a string on his uniform.

"We went out to dinner at Outback Steakhouse. We ate and had a few beers. It was nice," he offered.

"Okay, so where did you go next?"

"We went to Club Kremwerk," Lincoln said.

"It's this hot little dance club in downtown Seattle," Wyatt offered; he was clearly tired of being ignored.

"Okay, Wyatt, why don't you tell me how things went once you got to the club?" Mac asked, making eye contact with him for the first time in a while.

"We got there about elevenish, I think, and started dancing," Wyatt said.

"Did you all stay together?"

"At first, yeah, but then we started pairing off with women." He actually had the audacity to look Mac up and down.

"Did Collymore pair off with anyone?" Mac asked.

"Oh yeah, he picked up this obscenely sexy woman. It was dark in there, so I didn't get a good look at her face, but she had a body to die for," Wyatt blurted out, and Lincoln blushed.

"Tell me about her. What do you remember?" Mac pushed.

"Well, she was the hottest thing I'd seen in a long time, and way out of Collymore's league," Wyatt offered.

"Describe her for me, Wyatt. Tell me everything you remember."

"Okay, so she had this long red hair that brushed against her perfectly round *aaa*... I mean backside. She was wearing this tight little dress that curved to her body almost like it was painted on. When she pulled away from Colly, you could see she had a nice rack," Wyatt offered without looking the least bit bothered by his description.

Meanwhile, Lincoln was staring a hole through his hands.

"Lincoln, what do you remember about the woman Collymore was with?" she asked softly.

"She was very pretty," he said.

"Do you remember if she was thin with small hips, or curvier like me?" she asked, trying to get a picture of the woman. *Nice ass* and *great rack* didn't tell her much, since those were just preferences.

Lincoln looked away for a minute and then made eye contact with Mac. "She was in the middle. Not as curvy as you, but not tiny, either."

"She definitely had all the right curves in all the right places," Wyatt said. "I could see that her face was attractive, but just couldn't make out the details, you know."

"What could you tell me about her face?" she asked, looking at both young men.

"She looked like a model in a magazine," Lincoln said.

"A *Playboy* magazine, maybe," Wyatt piped up. "She wasn't one of those stick models in the clothing magazines. She looked like a pin-up girl."

"Okay, so this stunning woman came on to Collymore?" Mac asked.

"Yeah, it was crazy. We ordered a few drinks, but the waitress came back to say that someone had bought our drinks. We were scanning the place to see who had bought them," Wyatt explained. "Colly spotted her first, at the other end of the dance floor. She made eye contact with the lucky bastard and beckoned him over." Wyatt demonstrated by bending his index finger at her in a come-hither motion. "We couldn't believe he could be so lucky. I mean, that never happens to anyone."

"Okay, so he went over to her, and then what?"

"She walked up to him almost like she knew him from before and kissed him… I mean, she really kissed him like she meant business. She even put her hand on his ass," Wyatt said, sounding a little excited recounting the events.

"Then what happened?"

"I don't really know, to be honest," Wyatt admitted. "There was this cute brunette in a red dress…"

Mac didn't need further explanation. Wyatt clearly had issues focusing on things, and if there was a pretty woman nearby, he was hopeless. She was hoping Lincoln was more observant. "Lincoln, did you see what happened next?" she asked gently.

"Yes, ma'am, um, Mac. They danced for a little while, and she was all over him, which kinda worried me a little because she seemed overly aggressive. I mean, not like normal where you can slowly get intimate with someone. She looked like she was about to jump him right there on the dance floor, and then she pulled away. He looked a little out of sorts like he couldn't believe what happened, and then she grabbed his hand and headed for the door."

"Then what?"

"Then nothing," Lincoln explained. "They disappeared onto the dance floor. I assumed he was still there. I mean, he would have told us if he was going home with her or something, but he just got swallowed up in all the people, and then we never saw him again." A look of devastation crossed his face. "He just never came back out of the mass of people, and then we found out he died. I mean, we should have done something. I knew something was wrong, and I watched her take him away."

"You couldn't have known, man. Neither of us could have known something like that. Even if we'd told Colly to walk away, would he? I mean, she wasn't the type you walked away from, no matter what kind of man you are," Wyatt said, clearly trying to convince himself as much as his friend.

"Is there anything else you guys can tell me about that night?" Mac asked to redirect their attention.

"No, ma'am," they responded in unison.

Mac dug in her pocket and pulled out two business cards. "Thank you for your help, gentlemen. Please call me if you think of anything else you might find helpful."

Wyatt took the card, and then offered, "One other thing that was a little odd," he said, pausing for a moment. "You see, Colly was dating Alice, and he was crazy about her. He wasn't the type to cheat on his lady. He was thinking of marrying her, not leaving her. It wasn't his style, but I kinda wonder if he knew this woman from somewhere."

CHAPTER
EIGHTEEN

HE WRAPPED his hands around her throat and started to squeeze. She couldn't find air. Her lungs began to burn, and she could feel the darkness surrounding her vision. She tried to fight back, kicking and twisting her body to get free. She sank her nails into his strong arms, but nothing happened. His grip kept getting tighter until it felt like she was falling into unconsciousness.

Mac woke with a start, covered in sweat with her hands clenched tightly on her blanket draped around her neck. The dream was always weird and distorted, and she woke up feeling out of place. She hated not sleeping in her own bed, and the comfort of Hudson's body next to her always made her sleep more soundly.

She glanced at the clock; it was only 0400 hours. The dream—or, more to the point, nightmare—was always the same. It seemed distorted and fuzzy at first, but then it turned into something that felt entirely too real. She knew it was her mentor. The man who'd tried to kill her only six short months ago.

She vividly remembered when she had no choice but to sink her knife into him to protect herself. She still couldn't get the feel of the blade or the sound it made when it entered his body out of her mind. It just kept replaying every time she closed her eyes.

The only way to clear her mind and make her body feel better was a good workout. She chose a different one this time, just to change things up. She peeled her body out of bed, wiped it down with a clean washcloth, and got ready to work out her frustrations at the gym.

She walked in to find the place reasonably deserted at 0500 hours. She preferred to get her workouts taken care of in the morning. Many times she found herself working out in the afternoon due to scheduling conflicts, but when she made her own schedule, it was always the first thing.

It was the best way to start the day. Her head was clearer, and she functioned so much better throughout the day; plus, she didn't have to create time in the afternoon. Her eating habits were better, and she wasn't as hungry if she hit the gym first thing in the morning. Afternoons were dicey because she often found herself hungry at the gym, and being hangry didn't make for a good workout.

Damn hotel beds, she thought as she began with a warmup on the elliptical. She twisted her neck from side to side, and it popped audibly. The earbuds were loud in her ears. She loved a little country music, but she listened to the harder stuff when she worked out. Her thoughts wandered back to the investigation. *How are all the victims connected?* she wondered absently. They were all from different walks of life with no apparent connection.

Her phone began to ring, interrupting her thoughts. Such an excellent start to the day was ruined.

"Hey Mac, sorry to disturb you this early. I hope I didn't wake you up," Kibble's voice boomed.

"No, I'm up. Just at the gym," she said breathlessly on the machine.

"I hate to ask you this, but could you finish up and meet me at the ADC office? There's been another body," he said, pausing to let the information sink in.

"Do we know who it is yet?" She slowed on the elliptical to regain her ability to breathe.

"No, just that she's a Caucasian female with a slight build."

"Okay, give me a few minutes and I'll be over. Have all other agencies been notified?"

"Yes, we're meeting on site. Her body was found on the beach by two early morning fishermen. It appears there's little damage to the body, and it wasn't in the water long, so we may actually be able to get some useful evidence."

"Be right there." Mac hung up and turned off her machine. *Well, at least thirty minutes is better than nothing.*

She quickly ran through the shower and tied her hair up so she wouldn't be out of regs. It would have to be one of those *au naturel* days with no makeup.

Twenty minutes after talking with Kibble, she walked into the ADC office. He was standing in the clients' waiting room with two cups of coffee in hand. She smiled, hoping one of them was for her.

"Thank you very much," she said as he handed her a cup.

"I was guessing, but figured a skinny vanilla latte might be acceptable. It's my wife's favorite drink. She tells me that it still tastes good but has fewer calories. I figured it might be your taste since you're always working out."

"That's perfect. Thank you for thinking of me." She liked her coffee any way she could get it. Generally she just drank it black, but she liked the froufrou stuff as much as the next person. She just avoided it because it usually had empty calories.

Kibble reminded her of one of her brothers. Even though her brother was a professional criminal, he was still nice to her and always tried to think of her. She did appreciate his thoughtfulness.

They went down to his rental car, and she let out a laugh. It was a tiny blue compact car, and his shoulders barely fit. He looked highly uncomfortable. It took him a few minutes to adjust enough so he could drive.

"Are you sure you don't want to take my SUV? It's not big, but it has more room than this thing," she said.

"No, thanks. I'll be fine. Let's just get there and find out what's going on. I don't want us to be the last ones on the scene and get left out of the information. After all, we're the outsiders, so they aren't likely to catch us up unless they need something."

"Fair enough," she said as they made their way off base.

CHAPTER NINETEEN

WHEN THEY ARRIVED, the place was crawling with police, FBI, and reporters. Mac hated reporters. Actually, it wasn't the reporters she hated, but the fact that they might put her in the spotlight. If the story were to go national, her family might find out, which would be very bad for Mac and anyone close to her. She thought of Hudson and her sister.

She cleared her head and stepped out of the vehicle. The entire car shifted audibly and visibly when Kibble climbed out. "Don't say a word," he said with a slight grin.

They made their way through the crowd, avoiding the press as much as possible. One of them caught sight of their uniforms and started toward them. She pushed Kibble on the back lightly. "Time to go. The press is headed our way." Mac mentally kicked herself for not insisting they show up in civilian clothes.

The yellow crime tape was pulled tight around a large portion of the beach and all the way up to the walking path. It was a nice-looking spot under different circumstances. It took them a few minutes to sign in and get cleared to move into the crime scene. Thankfully, they were able to get through before the reporter made it over. She shouted a few questions, but Mac and Kibble ignored her. They knew better.

There were uniformed and plain-clothed people surrounding the body when they walked up. It took a moment to find a break in the wall of bodies, but finally one of the officers stepped aside. The medical examiner was already kneeling next to the body, blocking the victim's face.

Mac tapped one of the local officers on the shoulder. "Who is it?" He was about to answer when Mac finally got a good look.

It was Alice. She was lying in the sand with a sheet covering most of her body.

Mac's eyes widened as she inhaled sharply. All the blood drained from her face, and she felt like she would throw up.

Alice's eyes had turned a milky gray and stared blankly into space when the ME ran her hand over them to push them closed. She looked peaceful, minus the ligature marks across her throat and flies starting to buzz around her.

"You okay?" Kibble asked.

"Her name is Alice," Mac whispered. "I just had dinner with her the night before last," she said, still not fully processing what she'd seen. "She was Collymore's girlfriend. She said she had information for me."

"Did she know anything?" Kibble asked, leading her away from the body.

"Um—" Mac took a deep breath, trying to focus. "Kind of. She said that her boyfriend was looking into different cultures downtown. He studied anthropology but may have gotten a little involved in the different groups. I'm not sure exactly what he was into, but now I definitely think it's worth investigating. Her uncle is going to be devastated."

"How do you know her uncle?"

"We had dinner at his diner. He's a nice guy. I'm not sure how he's going to take the news. Poor man."

"One of the police officers will take care of the notification," Kibble said.

"I'd like to be there, if they'll allow it."

"Why is that?" Kibble asked.

"I just feel somehow responsible. I can't explain it, but I'd like to be there."

CHAPTER
TWENTY

"HAVE YOU EVER NOTIFIED A FAMILY BEFORE?" Officer Keizer asked as he drove Mac to see Uncle Don. He was a portly man with a large stomach that pushed against the buttons of his uniform. She wondered absently if it was hard for him to run after suspects.

"No, this is my first time. I've known people who have been notified, but I've never had to go and tell someone that their loved one has passed away," she said, looking out the window.

"Keep in mind that everyone has a different reaction and handles the news in their own way. Some people just stare at you like you have two heads; others might cry out. I even had one guy take a swing at me after I told him."

"I just hope he doesn't blame me. I'm the last one that saw her alive, as far as we know. He could think I'm somehow to blame." Her forehead creased with concern.

"How well did you know the victim?" Keizer asked.

"Not well at all. She approached me and said she had information about the Collymore case, and of course I wanted to know what that was."

"That makes sense," he said, and then went quiet. Mac wondered if he also thought she had something to do with it, which unnerved her further.

They pulled up to the diner. Officer Keizer unbuckled his seatbelt and looked directly at her. "Are you ready for this?"

"As ready as I'll ever be," she replied, but she just wanted her stomach to stop doing backflips. She didn't kill Alice, but maybe she had put a target on her back by questioning her. Perhaps she was somehow responsible.

As soon as they walked into the diner, Uncle Don came around the corner. "Mac, it's so good to see you," he said with a big grin. "Couldn't get enough of my amazing cooking?" He stopped mid-stride as he took stock of Mac's expression and realized she had a police officer with her.

"Hello sir, my name is Officer Keizer. Is there somewhere we can talk?"

"Sure," Uncle Don said. "What's this all about?"

"In private, sir," Keizer insisted.

They walked through the diner's kitchen, where his staff was preparing for the next crowd. He led them to a small office down a narrow hallway. "In here should be fine," Uncle Don said.

The three of them squeezed into the small, disorganized office space. Uncle Don slipped behind his desk but remained standing to make more room. Keizer looked uncomfortable in the small space.

"So, what's this all about?" Uncle Don asked.

"Um," Mac began, but the words were caught in her throat.

Keizer took over. "We're sorry to tell you this, but your niece, Alice, was found dead this morning. We're very sorry for your loss," he said in a practiced, even tone. He had obviously done this before.

Mac stood there, feeling at a loss for words. "I'm so sorry, Uncle Don."

He looked at them like they were speaking a foreign language. "But how?" was all he could say.

"She was murdered last night," Mac said, finally finding her voice. "We don't know what happened yet, but we're doing everything to find out. Is there anything you can tell us that might point us in the right direction?"

Uncle Don just looked at her with sad eyes and shook his head. "I know she was helping Ryan Collymore research those weird people," he spat, "but I get the feeling they were doing more than just research."

"What makes you think that?" Mac asked.

"Every time I asked her about it, she would blush or change the subject. There was definitely something she wasn't telling me. I feel it in my gut," Uncle Don said with conviction, patting his round stomach.

"Is there anyone else who was close to her that might be able to tell us more about what she was involved in?" Mac asked, looking over at Officer Keizer to ensure she wasn't stepping on his toes.

Surprisingly, he nodded, which she took as a sign to continue.

Don took several deep breaths. "I can't believe she's gone."

"I know. I can't, either," Mac said, giving him a moment to compose himself.

"You know Mac, her best friend might know something. They work together on base. I haven't seen her around in a while, but I'm sure she would be helpful. Let me find her phone number." Uncle Don started scrolling through his contacts on his cell phone. "Here it is." He wrote down her name and number.

"Thank you," Mac said, placing her hand on his arm. "We'll find whoever did this."

Officer Keizer walked in front of her out of the diner. As the door closed behind them, he turned toward her. "You did a good job in there, but you made a rookie mistake."

"What's that?" Mac asked.

"You never promise a grieving family member that you'll catch the bad guy. There are too many cases that go unsolved."

CHAPTER
TWENTY-ONE

"WHAT THE HELL WERE YOU THINKING?" Gennavie screamed at her husband. "I thought you were smarter than this. I know common sense isn't that common, but a man with your IQ shouldn't be this stupid."

He looked at her like she had lost her mind. "What on earth are you talking about?" he said calmly.

"You know damn well what I'm talking about. In what world did it make sense to kill Alice? What purpose did it serve? I thought we had agreed to make these decisions together, and now you go and do this," she shouted, pacing back and forth in the kitchen.

"Lower your voice and calm the hell down," he growled at her. "It would do nicely for the neighbors to hear you, wouldn't it?"

"We don't have any neighbors within earshot, jackass." She took long breaths in and long breaths out, but was seriously struggling to find calm. This would never have happened when she was on her own. She had everything under control, and now she had married a loose cannon that went off on his own. She looked out the window, not knowing what to say. She was entirely too pissed at this point. "Why?" was all she could muster.

"Because she knew too much, and you know it," he said gently.

"She was already talking to McGregor, and Lord only knows what Alice really told her."

"What did you find out from her before you…" She let the words trail off.

"Before I killed her? Is that what you're asking? We've done it together, so I don't see what you're so upset about. I was just taking care of a loose end," he said defiantly.

"It seems to me that the loose end is this Technical Sergeant McGregor. She's already found more in the short time she's been here than any of the other flunkies who call themselves law enforcement. They call her Mac, and she's good, from what I can see. I sent her flowers with a listening device in them, but for some reason it hasn't been working, so I feel like we're flying blind. Why don't we just take her out of the picture?" she demanded.

"We can't; she's too visible. You said so yourself. People will come hunting if she goes missing. Plus, Alice told her that Collymore was looking into different subcultures and studying people like us, but nothing that could be directly connected to us. Mac really doesn't know anything," he said, trying to look convincing. "If she gets too close, we can take her out together."

"You'd like that, wouldn't you?" she teased with a mischievous smile. "I think you have a thing for this Mac woman. I've seen her at the gym. Don't think I'm not also watching all the players in this game. She's stunning, and I think you want her all for yourself."

He smiled widely. "Yes. But I'd like to see you with her first, and then I'd like to kill her slowly." He got up from the couch and came over to where she stood in front of the window. He grabbed a fistful of her hair at the nape of her neck. Today it was shoulder-length and dark, chestnut brown. He yanked her head back and kissed her deeply, with animalistic urgency.

"How would you like me with her?" she teased.

"I want to watch you play with her nipples, sucking and pulling. When she's all hot and ready, I want you to enter her with that big strap-on of yours," he said, getting excited as he spoke.

She was wearing one of his old white t-shirts and a ratty pair of cut-off jean shorts. He pulled the shirt over her head to reveal her bare breasts and squeezed roughly.

"What would you do to her?" she asked, not entirely sure she wanted the answer but feeling excited at the same time.

He hoisted her over his shoulder, walked to the bedroom, and tossed her onto the bed. He pulled her shorts loose with one swift move, revealing her beautiful mound. He climbed on top of her and wrapped his hands around her neck, pulling down his sweatpants and entering her as he tightened his hands around her small neck. He knew she got off on erotic asphyxiation and was rewarded when she started bucking against him, fighting for air and the orgasm he was only too happy to give her.

CHAPTER
TWENTY-TWO

"SO, how did it go with Uncle Don?" Kibble asked as Mac walked back into the ADC office.

"About as awful as expected," Mac said. "What are we planning for the day?" she asked, changing the subject.

"I have some other clients that I need to take care of," Kibble said. "I was wondering if you could follow up on a couple of our leads. Maybe you could head out to the bar where Collymore was last seen. It would be a good place to start. Maybe they know the redhead that picked up our guy."

"I'm on it," she said, grabbing her keys. First, she wanted to hunt down Alice's friend.

"Don't go down there in uniform. We don't want to attract attention," he warned.

"No problem, I was planning on changing. I'll check in after I'm done," she said as she headed out the door, and Carter walked in. She exchanged pleasantries with him and left.

After looking up the club, she realized it didn't open for several hours, so she tracked down Alice's friend at the billeting office on base.

Mac walked in to find a large blond woman sitting at the front desk. "Hi, I'm Sergeant McGregor, and I'm looking for Beth."

"What's it to you?" the woman said.

"I'm here about Alice. I just want to ask a few questions."

"Okay, then ask." She got up from behind her desk and Mac saw her nametag.

"Thank you for talking with me, Beth," Mac said, trying to calm her down a bit. "I was just wondering if you could tell me if Alice had any enemies?"

"No, everyone loved that girl. She was as nice as they came. It was that bastard boyfriend of hers who got her wrapped up with all those people."

"What people?" Mac asked.

"He was looking into different fetishes and stuff, and if I had to bet, one of them got ahold of Alice."

"Okay," Mac said calmly. "Can you give a description of any of them?"

"Nah," Beth said. "I should have asked more questions. It was just shop talk about some of the people Ryan was looking into. You know, when a woman is unsure about her man, we talk."

"Did she ever give you any specific details about who he was looking into or where they were from?"

"No." Beth seemed to calm significantly, and Mac realized she was angry at the situation and not being able to prevent what had happened. "But I should have known."

"This is not your fault," Mac said.

"Then whose fault is it? Ryan was a good guy, but he was looking into bad people, and I think that's what got him and Alice killed."

"Is there anything you can tell me about Ryan or Alice that struck you as odd?"

"Besides Ryan's interest in strange people, no. They were about as normal a couple as anyone else. They were in love and talking about maybe getting married. Alice was a little worried about Ryan's extracurricular activities, but I don't think it worried her enough to leave him."

"Okay, thank you for your help." Mac fished a business card out of her uniform. "Please call me if you think of anything else."

CHAPTER
TWENTY-THREE

MAC HEADED BACK to her room to get changed. She thought she would head downtown to familiarize herself with Seattle and Tacoma's cultures. It was undoubtedly a different cup of tea from Spokane. They had some interesting characters in Spokane, but Seattle had a whole different vibe.

She found parking after circling the block several times and thought she would start near where Alice's body had been found. There were rows of shops, places to eat, and tons of interesting people on every corner. She found the large groups of tents around the city to be interesting. It felt like they had set up their own community with its own unique sounds and smells. She wasn't being judgmental since often it only took a little bad luck for someone to end up homeless. No one set out to end up that way.

Mac was enjoying having a little downtime just wandering in and out of the different shops and people-watching. She loved to people-watch and found humans to be most interesting. Each one was unique, with many of them trying to stand out from the crowd, while others tried to melt into the background.

A pretty young woman looking at a book at a local bookstore caught her attention. A tall, lanky man with a ridiculous mohawk that was rainbow-colored and swayed back and forth on his head crossed her line of vision. He was dressed in black with chains and spikes coming out of his clothes, and a few dangling from piercings on his skin.

She caught movement out of the corner of her eye, but when she turned around, no one was there. It was probably nothing, but she felt more alert and moved on. She went to a resale store at the bottom of a steep stairwell to get a better view in case someone was following her. She figured she could lose someone in a place like that.

The door at the bottom of the stairs chimed as she entered. Racks of knickknacks and collectibles lined every wall. It looked like a higher-end garage sale on crack. Dragula was playing in the background, which was an odd choice of music for a store. *Dig through the ditches and burn through the witches* played loudly overhead. It had a good beat, just a little odd for a public store.

She quickly made her way to the back of the store to get a good vantage point, but she saw no one. *Maybe he or she is waiting for me to come out*, Mac thought—until Carter, of all people, walked through the door. He scanned the store and quickly found her in the back, in front of a wall lined with creepy-looking old dolls. He waved and started toward her. She wasn't sure if she should head toward the exit on the other side of the store or stay.

She had picked this place because it had two exits: one was the front entrance at ground level, and the other was a secondary exit with steep stairs that led up to the main road and lots of people. But she hadn't expected Carter. He seemed really nice. Maybe he was coming to tell her about something with the case—but why didn't he call? She had given him her number, just in case.

"Hey, I've been trying to find you," Carter said breathlessly. "For a small woman, you can get around pretty quickly."

Mac smiled a little uncomfortably. "What's up, Carter?"

"Oh, nothing really; Kibble just told me you would be in this area, and you were waiting for the club to open up and that I should come down and keep you company."

"Why didn't you call me?" she asked.

"I forgot your number at the base," he said a little too quickly. "So, what's the plan?"

"I don't really have a plan. I was going to the club to ask if anyone had information about Collymore and the lady he was with. If we can track her down, maybe she could tell us a little more about that night and if she witnessed anything."

"Sounds good. Would you like to grab an early dinner while we wait?" he asked, and sensed her hesitation. "Just friends, I promise. I'm married, and we're expecting our third baby. I'm just starving," he said with a disarming smile.

"Okay, now that you mention it, I'm pretty hungry. Any suggestions?" she asked, thinking he looked awfully young to be having his third of anything, let alone a third child. Maybe he was older than he looked or had come into the military later than most.

"There's a little place with the best hamburgers just around the corner."

They walked to the small diner, and Carter opened the door for her. They exchanged stories over lunch. She told him about Hudson and their relationship. Carter explained that he had been in the military for five years. He had a line number for staff sergeant and liked being a defense paralegal. He originally came in because his now-wife—his girlfriend at the time—became pregnant, and they needed good healthcare.

"So, tell me, what brings you here?" he asked, looking innocent enough, but she could feel her body tense.

"I was involved in that case back at Fairchild," she said vaguely. "During that time, Kibble was my defense counsel on some bogus drug charges that the guy hunting me tried to frame me with. Anyway, long story short, my boss at Fairchild, Captain Stanton, was singing my praises, and Kibble requested my assistance, so here I am."

"Have you ever worked with Kibble? I heard he pulled some strings to be put on the case."

"I don't know about all that, but he seems nice enough," she said. "They put me in this new position where I'm supposed to be looking into high-profile cases and coming up with different ways to prevent these kinds of things from happening, or at least figuring out how to get an indication that a member has violent tendencies."

"Wow, that sounds like an interesting job. I've always found the criminal mind absolutely fascinating."

"Me too; I'm actually in school for it right now. I'm doing my masters in criminal psychology and can't get enough. It's fascinating to study how people think. The DSM-5 has so many different aspects of human behavior." Her eyes lit up while she talked about it. "I actually need to hit the books tonight because I have a huge paper due."

"You must really have passion for this sort of thing. How are you supposed to see if someone has violent tendencies? Are you a profiler or something?"

"No, I just happened to figure out the case with Chief Deleon last winter. I don't think the Air Force thought it was possible to have one of their own, let alone a chief, commit murder. I mean, there's plenty of crime in the military. If there wasn't, you and I would be out of a job, but it's mostly low-level stuff like drug charges, theft, adultery, and that sort of thing, which can keep us busy. Of course, there are the sexual assault cases and domestic abuse, which is serious, but rarely does the defense land a murder case. Even if there is murder, it's normally a crime of passion or revenge. I had one of those once where a guy came back from Korea and lured his wife's lover back to a hotel and stabbed him thirty times. It was fascinating. In this last case, he suffered from a traumatic brain injury that damaged his frontal lobe and caused him to turn into a psychopath."

"What do you mean?" Carter looked at her with curiosity. "You're telling me he got hit in the head and suddenly started killing people?"

"Not exactly like that, but close. He took a pretty bad blow to the head while he was deployed. An Afghan woman he was involved with placed a bomb in his backpack, blew up half his crew, and sent him to the hospital with serious injuries. He came back home and passed all of his physical requirements and was cleared for duty, but something had changed in him."

"I heard you were pretty close to him before he turned into a monster. What was he like before?" Carter wanted to know.

"It was weird. He was still the same man somewhere deep down, but how he processed information had changed. He thought he was saving people from Sahar, the woman who had planted the bomb. He was hunting down women that looked like her and killing them. It was strange, but he actually thought he was the good guy. I think he was still in love with her in a sick, twisted way, but he also thought she had come back from Afghanistan to kill more people, and it was up to him to stop her. He was delusional and killed innocent women. It was tragic for everyone, including him. He had been such a nice man at one point. He had helped me through my career and some rough points. It was hard to process the difference between the man I knew and the man he had become," she explained. "What about you? Have you had any interesting cases yet?"

"Nothing like that," he said. "We've had several sexual assault cases, which is unfortunate. I never understood that one. How it could be a turn-on to have sex with a passed-out woman? The cases we've had so far are all about women who are too intoxicated to consent. A couple of them have been buyer's remorse, where she has sex with a man and then wakes up the next morning with regrets and cries rape to her friends to make herself look innocent, but I've also had a couple that were clearly raped, and that just makes my stomach turn."

Mac agreed. "Obviously I don't understand it either, but some men feel like they're entitled to a woman for one reason or another. So, are you planning on pulling twenty?" she asked, abruptly changing the subject not wanting to dive too deeply into the subject. Every time they had a case were a woman was abused in some way she always thought of her sister.

"We'll see," he said. "There are definitely pros and cons. I came in for school, but you never know. I need to get through my degree first and then go from there."

"What are you going to school for?" Mac wanted to know. She was enjoying this relaxing conversation. She had felt so guarded ever since she had been betrayed by Chief Deleon. It wasn't just him, though, and she knew it. Several people on base thought she had been involved in the drug trade and had turned their backs on her. People she thought were her friends had just figured she was guilty until proven innocent.

She was still struggling with that. Even with Hudson, who had repeatedly proven how devoted he was to her, she struggled to open up and trust him. She thought she loved him, but her love and trust were complicated, especially after what she had been through in childhood. Her mother had used her as a pawn in business and against her father. That kind of psychological torture was challenging to get past. She was working on it, but last winter had definitely been a setback.

"Criminal justice," Carter responded. "So, what do you think is going on with these cases? Do you have any theories on who did it?"

"Sorry," she said, "I'm not allowed to discuss this one."

CHAPTER
TWENTY-FOUR

AFTER THEIR MEAL, they headed over to the club. It was just after 1800 hours, and they had just opened their doors. Kremwerk looked like an old, rundown building from the outside. The entrance had *KREM* in large black letters encased in chrome plating above the entrance. It wasn't what she'd expected from a popular nightclub.

Inside, the club looked like an old warehouse except for the stage, bar, and dance floor. Not to mention the enormous strobe light hanging from the ceiling among the exposed air ducts, steel beams, and blue lighting. Mac had researched the place before coming; the club promoted itself as an LGBTQ-friendly venue and had some of the wildest shows providing a safe and comfortable environment for all types of people or subcultures, which was precisely what she wanted to discuss.

It was clear why Collymore was attracted to this place. If she were looking into different cultures, this would be a place she would go. He would have been able to study all types of cultures here in a place where they felt comfortable and at ease.

Mac walked up to the bar. "Hi, I'm Evelyn McGregor, but everyone calls me Mac. I was wondering if we could ask you some questions?"

Carter stood beside her but didn't say a word. He was clearly a little uncomfortable with this environment as a man in drag walked past. Mac actually thought he looked really good. It amazed her how people could morph. Mac thought he actually looked better in a mini skirt than she did.

The bartender was a pretty woman with short, dark hair that was buzzed on the sides, and she wore a little red tank top that showed off her trim stomach and cute figure. She was washing glasses and preparing for the night's events. "What ya want to know?" she asked, not offering her name.

Mac pulled out a picture of Ryan Collymore. Alice had given her a picture of him out of uniform. He was a good-looking kid with dark hair and big brown eyes. She could see why Alice found him attractive, but there really wasn't anything that stood out about the guy, so Mac figured it might be a long shot that someone would remember him. "Do you happen to recognize this guy?"

"Yeah, I know Ryan. He sure is an inquisitive type. He's always coming here asking everyone tons of questions about why they do what they do and all of that. Why, is he in trouble?"

"I'm afraid he was murdered last Saturday. He was last seen here dancing with a redhead in a green dress. Do you happen to remember that night?" Mac said hopefully.

"I wasn't working that night, but Joey was. Let me go get him for you. Hey Joey," she hollered into the back.

""Stop bustin' my chops. I'll be there in a minute," came a deep voice with what sounded to Mac like a New York accent.

The bartender turned around and smiled back at them. "Do you want anything to drink while you wait?"

Mac looked over at Carter, who still looked extremely uncomfortable.

"Um, no, I'm good," he muttered.

"Thanks, I'll have a Diet Coke," Mac said.

A tall, thin man came through a door off to the side of the bar. He had blond-and-green spiky hair that stood straight on top of his head. He had Asian features with high cheekbones, and with his unique hairstyle, he was striking and could stand out in any crowd.

"This lady wants to know if you saw Ryan poking around asking all his questions last Saturday," the lady bartender explained.

"Yeah, he was here with a couple of other guys. What do you want with him?" the guy asked.

"Ryan went and got himself killed last Saturday, and these two want to know what you saw," the bartender said.

"Shit Alex, we don't need that kind of attention," he said, looking at the female bartender. Mac made a mental note of Alex's name.

"You don't think I know that, but it ain't like we killed him, or he died here. They just need to know if you saw him with a red-headed chick in a green dress," Alex said.

"Yeah, she was really hot and way out of Ryan's league, but I don't know her. She's not a regular, but I can ask around a bit. I would have definitely remembered that one," he said, winking at Alex.

"You're such a pig." She elbowed him in the side.

"His body had whip marks and some pretty severe damage," Mac said. "The evidence indicates he may have been participating in bondage of some sort before his death. Do either of you know a place around here specializing in those activities?"

They both looked at each other and said in unison, "Lady Carina's Dungeon."

"If Ryan or the chick you're looking for is into the world of BDSM and is from around here, Lady Carina will know about it. She's very popular in that culture and knows everyone," Joey said.

"Nice. Do you happen to know how I would find this Lady Carina?" Mac asked.

Carter had yet to utter a word; he stood next to her looking a little bug-eyed.

"Go on her website and fill out a session request form. I know it sounds formal, but she can't be too careful in her line of work. She'll run a background check on you and then set you up for a session. If it's your first time, you're in for a real treat," Alex said with a smile.

"Have you been to see her before?" Mac asked, intrigued.

"Nah, but I've heard it can be a life-changing experience."

CHAPTER
TWENTY-FIVE

THEY GOT BACK to the base later than Mac had wanted, so she was a little tired the next day after staying up to finish her paper. She had to make her classes a priority otherwise she would never finish.

In the morning, she arrived at the ADC office after her workout. Carter wasn't there yet. He had been quiet the entire way back to the base. Mac wondered if the environment had just freaked him out a little too much. He came across as a country boy who hadn't been exposed to much in his life, though she knew he had seen some just by working cases.

She exchanged pleasantries with Kibble.

"Could you organize what we have so far?" he asked. "There's a whiteboard and printer in the back."

"Yeah, no problem. I just need to check in at Fairchild, and then I'm on it." She dialed Stanton's number and got his voicemail. She had hoped to bring him up to date, but there wasn't a lot to tell. They still didn't have much in the way of a suspect pool, just a few good leads to follow up on.

"Would you like some liquid life? I was going to make a fresh pot," she asked Kibble as she walked back and forth, moving files and her computer into the back room.

He smiled at what she called coffee. "Sure, thanks."

Once she was finally set up, she worked meticulously through the evidence. So far they hadn't found any connections between the victims, though they were still looking. As far as Mac could tell, this guy was brilliant. He never picked the same victim type. It was a clever strategy on the killer's part.

She started by placing the pictures of the victims in death order. The FBI had provided digital copies of all the evidence for each victim to all parties investigating the case. She listened to the old government printer whirl in protest as it spits out pictures, reports, and statements about the victims, crime scenes, and background information.

She placed the last victim up on the large whiteboard. Alice's pretty face stared back at her, demanding justice. In total, there were four women, including Alice, and two men. Underneath each picture, she started listing out the details of each person: where they worked, lived, who reported them missing, where their bodies were discovered, and any other details she thought might be relevant. Above the pictures, she put their approximate dates of death.

Stepping back, she looked at the information she had placed on the huge whiteboard while she waited for the rest to print. This was a gruesome timeline. She found inconsistencies with some of the injuries. Once it was all laid out in front of her, she wasn't convinced that all the murders were connected. The only thing that connected the last three was the unique ligature pattern on the bodies. They were, of course, most pronounced on Alice.

Most killers had a signature and didn't change it, at least not that much. Mac wondered why Alice was found so quickly and didn't present with whip marks or damage to the genitals. It also didn't appear that Alice had been bound by her wrists and ankles as Ryan had.

She sat back, pondering the details. Maybe he had been interrupted with Alice by the early morning fisherman, or possibly the two murders were unrelated. That didn't seem likely, since Alice and Ryan had been dating and were clearly connected in life.

She moved to the left to look at the pictures from a different angle, accidentally knocking Ryan's file to the floor. It was the only complete file provided by the FBI, since they were assigned to focus on his background. They had the most access and resources to investigate.

The contents of the file spread across the floor like a makeshift fan. She went down on her hands and knees, trying to pick up each paper one at a time to keep them in order. If nothing else, the FBI was meticulous and organized. She appreciated that about them.

Kibble walked in to see her picking up each sheet of paper and examining it prior to putting it back in the file in order. "Are you doing, okay?" he asked.

"Sure, just being klutzy." She smiled up at him.

"What's that?" he asked, pointing to the corner of a white envelope sticking out from under a pile of papers.

She carefully pulled it out so as not to disturb the other papers. "I don't know. I didn't notice this was in there before," she said, handing him the envelope and getting to her feet.

Kibble walked over to one of the desks, grabbed a letter opener, and sliced the top. He pulled out a plain white, folded piece of paper. It was a small manila envelope that was still sealed. He opened it curiously, and Mac watched the color drain from his face.

"What is it?" she asked.

He simply handed it over and picked up the phone to call Bardot with the FBI. Mac could only hear his side of the conversation. He explained briefly what they'd found. "Yes, ma'am, it was in the Collymore file. No, ma'am, we had not previously seen the envelope. Yes, the envelope was sealed. I opened it myself." He paused, listening. "Yes, it directly threatens Technical Sergeant Evelyn McGregor." Another pause. "We're on our way," Kibble said, then hung up the phone.

"Looks like we're going in. Grab your stuff; we might be there for a while," he told Mac. "Hey Carter," Kibble hollered toward the other side of the office.

Carter walked in. "What's up, sir?"

"I know I asked you to set up some client meetings for me today, but now I need you to call everyone back and cancel them. Please extend my sincerest apologies, but it can't be avoided. If any of my clients need a delay submitted, could you let my paralegal know so she can get them taken care of?" Kibble asked.

"What happened? Can I help?" Carter asked.

"Not at this time. We just received new information on the Collymore case. It's nothing to worry about. We just need to go meet with some of the others who are investigating," he explained, being purposely vague.

They grabbed their stuff and headed out the door. Mac was quiet until they were safely inside Kibble's vehicle. "Why didn't you tell Carter what was going on?" Mac asked as he started up the car.

"My gut," he said as a way of explanation.

"What does your gut tell you, exactly?" Mac asked, intrigued.

"So, I'm not saying Carter did anything wrong or is involved, but you and I both looked through that file from front to back. I looked at every piece of paper myself, and that envelope wasn't there. The only other person who had access to it was Carter."

"What about one of the clients? Could they have gained access to the file?" Mac asked.

"Not easily. If Carter stepped away from a client, it is possible, but the file was locked in the visiting attorney's desk that I'm using, and the only other person with a key is Carter. Currently it's circumstantial evidence, but I don't want to take any chances with your safety."

Kibble's line of thinking made sense. Mac hated thinking Carter was involved, but she couldn't discount the possibility.

CHAPTER
TWENTY-SIX

THEY WALKED into the FBI office in Seattle to find one of Assistant Director Bardot's men waiting for them. He was one of the same oversized men that had been at the initial case overview. "Good afternoon, I'm Special Agent Lopez. Please follow me."

He led them down the hall through a corridor and into an elevator. Mac was amazed that it looked like any other government building. She'd just assumed that they would have the most up-to-date, state-of-the-art facility. It wasn't bad, but it certainly wasn't as fancy as she'd imagined it would be.

Agent Lopez put them in the elevator and pushed the button for the seventh floor. Mac found herself feeling nervous. In the span of only one day, she'd had her life threatened and was going into the FBI's inner sanctum. She'd always wondered how they operated and looked. She actually thought it might be an exciting career after she retired from the military.

She squared her shoulders, thinking how badass it must be to be an FBI agent. Maybe it wasn't as glamorous as she thought, but it sure would be cool to find out. Her heart quickened as they got closer. She wondered absently if they would accept her at an older age. It didn't even matter if she was an actual agent, but maybe she could just be involved.

The elevator doors opened into a huge room lined with tons of desks, computers, and phones. It looked like their technology was superior to the Air Force's, but they had all the same cheap furniture, or nothing fancy. She was amazed that anyone could focus in an environment like that. She thought it would be highly distracting.

She saw Bardot coming their way with a determined look on her face.

"My office," Bardot said, "now."

They followed her into a large office with a welcoming sitting area; it felt completely different from the rest of the office. Agent Lopez left them at the door, closing it behind them.

Bardot indicated for them to take a seat and put on gloves before holding her hand out so Kibble could hand her the folder and the opened envelope. She looked at the envelope, turning it over to see if there was any indication of where it had come from, but it was blank. She pulled the sheet of paper out and unfolded it. It read, *I know who you are and what you did. Stop, or you will die!* The note was typed on plain paper with no other markings.

"Did anyone else touch this other than the two of you?" Bardot asked.

"Not that we're aware of," Mac offered.

"Who else had access to the file?" Bardot asked.

Kibble explained that Carter had primary access. Carter's defense attorney was TDY to Beale Air Force Base in California, so Carter was the only one with keys to everything.

"Fair enough," Bardot said. "What do we know about Carter?"

"Not much, I'm afraid," Mac answered. "I was downtown with him yesterday at Club Kremwerk. He seemed fine, but we only talked about previous cases, nothing personal. I just met him a few days ago and know very little."

"Do you have any additional information to contribute, Kibble?" Bardot asked.

"Not really. I've been in contact with Carter during this case and a few times pertaining to clients, but have had no outside interactions with him."

"I see." Bardot looked directly at Mac. "So then why exactly do you feel you're being targeted, and what does he think you did?"

"I'm not entirely sure why he's interested in me, to be honest. I'm not even from around here, and I have no connection to any of the murder victims. The only thing that makes a little sense is that he could have heard about the incident at Fairchild last winter," Mac stated, feeling like she was being interrogated.

"Tell me about that case," Bardot pushed. "The killer could be someone from your past. Is there anyone you can think of—related or unrelated to the case—who might want to harm you?"

"Not that I know of," Mac said with a shaky voice, but she did know. Several people would want to do her harm if they ever found her, but she felt convinced that these weren't those people. She tried to reassure herself that her family couldn't find her. She had been too careful. No, this had to be about something else. "Maybe he saw me at the crime scene and just became fixated. It happens when a killer decides he needs to challenge the investigators. He could feel like I'm an easy target. As far as I know, there wasn't anyone else involved in the case at Fairchild except for the chief, but he's gone."

"Gone how?" Bardot asked, raising her thin, manicured eyebrow.

"I, well—I killed him in self-defense," Mac admitted, trying to keep her voice steady.

"I see," Bardot said. "Until we know more, I want you to remain vigilant and check in with Kibble daily. I don't want you running off on your own. Keep me apprised of Carter's actions and keep your files with you at all times. We cannot afford to compromise this investigation or put you at risk."

CHAPTER
TWENTY-SEVEN

"HOW COULD you possibly still be pissed at me?" Vincent asked.

"Because you put us in jeopardy," Mistress Gennavie growled.

"Alice hasn't come back to us at all. Ryan, on the other hand, seems to be the problem. I think you're just pissed because I killed Alice without you," he taunted. He knew better than to poke the bear, but he liked when she was all riled up. There was nothing sexier than a little snuggle with a struggle. He smiled at his own thoughts.

He knew she couldn't get off without a little—or, in most cases, a lot—of violence. They had tried regular sex once just to see, and no matter what he did, he couldn't get her to orgasm, but the minute he let her choke him or slap him, it was like a fire had ignited in her. It was intoxicating to watch her transform like that.

He honestly wasn't sure he loved her or was even capable of such emotions, but he certainly had a lot of fun with her. It was the first time he had ever killed with a partner. Previously, he had always killed alone and never talked about it with anyone. That was how stupid people got caught, but he wasn't stupid. Far from it—he knew he was better than anyone else at his killing game and was just thinning the herd. With her, it was different.

With most humans, he would get bored with them after playing for a while, but with her, he felt invincible and had yet to lose interest. Her explosive temper was sexy as hell. She could be just fine and then explode at the drop of a hat. Man, she was sexy when she did that. Plus, she was as much of a narcissist as he was and deserved to be. She could get pretty much any prey to follow her willingly. She had this way of morphing her personality to fit what other people needed her to be. It was fascinating.

"Are you even listening to me?" She stood in front of him with her hands on her hips, looking down at his growing cock.

"I'm listening to you rant and rave about nothing."

"So, you're not the least bit worried that they'll be able to trace Ryan, Alice, or any of the others back to us?" She looked at him doubtfully.

"Not in the least."

"And why is that?"

"Because we're too careful. Yeah, there might have been a redhead with long hair in a green dress and blue eyes playing with our victims just before they disappeared, but you, my dear, currently have green eyes and short brown hair. If it suits us, we'll just change your look and move on to a different pool of victims. Trust me, we're fine."

"But I miss our hunting. I need a little excitement. I'm bored to death waiting for the stupid investigators to lose interest," she said, showing her pouty lips.

"Not to worry, beautiful, we'll go hunting again soon. Have you gotten any new information from your source?"

"Yeah, he says they have no solid leads and think it's the work of one guy, not a couple or a woman. Apparently, Mac went to Kremwerk and asked some questions, but no one could identify me."

"See, you have nothing to worry about," he soothed.

In actuality, he had killed Alice without her because he occasionally needed to dominate on his own. Sometimes she was entirely too temperamental, and if he was honest with himself, he missed the hunt. When she was with him, there was no hunting to be done. They would just flock to her like moths to a flame. She would just go in and pick one and bring him back. Sometimes they played their little game, and he got to choose, but even then there wasn't any stalking, hunting, or deception. He missed it.

He felt men needed to hunt and couldn't help himself when he saw Alice sitting on the park bench, sobbing for her lost boyfriend. He had been following her for a while, whenever he had time away from his wife and work. He had even spoken to her several times. Just a friendly conversation, but he enjoyed the interactions. She was so innocent and kind and thought the world around her had to be the same.

On the last day of her life, she had looked up from her beautiful view of the park nestled inside the safe walls of JBLM. He had been watching her for about an hour as her shoulders shook with grief. She hadn't even noticed when he came up to her.

"Hi," was all he said.

"Oh, hi," she said, wiping her eyes. "I'm sorry, I look a mess."

"You look amazing," he said, making her blush.

"What are you doing here?" she asked.

"Looking for you, actually. I heard about Ryan and thought you might need a friend."

"That's very kind of you, but you didn't have to come all the way out here. Actually, how did you know I was here?" she asked, tilting her head to the side. She looked like an innocent puppy.

"Oh, I just asked at the Holiday Inn, and they said you liked to come here to think sometimes." He had to focus so he wouldn't show his excitement. He could almost feel her life in his hands. This moment was like no other. They were alone and secluded. It was early evening, and no one was at the park at this hour. Warning bells should have been sounding in her tiny little brain, but she didn't think the way he did. She didn't hunt or think about evil things in the world. She was an innocent. That was what he needed right then.

"That doesn't sound right to me. No one knows about this place but me," she said, shrinking away from him.

Ooh, maybe you have good instincts, little puppet. "Well, if you'd rather be alone, I can leave you to your mourning. I just wanted to make sure you were okay and wouldn't hurt yourself or anything. Plus, it's getting dark, and you shouldn't be out here by yourself. At least let me walk you back to your car," he offered with a charming smile.

Alice hesitated for a moment. What was wrong with her? He was just trying to be nice, but something made her feel uneasy. Maybe she was still reeling from the loss of Ryan. Despite her reservations about Ryan's activities, she had honestly thought they were going to have a life together. She had even told Uncle Don how excited she was that he might propose to her. The thought of all the cute babies they could have had replayed in her mind for the hundredth time. She felt utterly lost and couldn't imagine finding another man like Ryan.

"Yeah, you can walk me back," she said. She knew Vincent was a nice guy and had always treated her with respect. Plus, he was married, and where she grew up, married men did not hit on other women behind their wife's back.

He put his hand out to help her off the bench. Once she was standing, he put his hands back into his jacket. It was actually a little warm to be wearing it, but he needed a place to hide his supplies. He wrapped his hand around the special rope he liked to use. He liked the intricate pattern it left around his victims' necks. It almost looked like a DNA strand when he braided it this way. He had multiple ropes he had created in different patterns. This one was yellow and green. He liked how it looked and thought it would be a beautiful necklace over her soft skin. He wondered if she would fight, kick, or try to scream.

He hadn't been disappointed. They walked through a patch of thick trees, following a little dirt path that brought up plumes of dust as they walked. It has been a relatively dry summer so far. It was darker back here, and he liked it dark. It made his heart race. He had hunted during the day and found it didn't cause the same level of fear in his victims. In the dark, it silhouetted the whites of their eyes. It made their fear so much more real.

Alice walked ahead of him without a care in the world. Why should she worry? He was her friend, and friends didn't hurt friends, right? *Wrong*, he thought as he smashed her in the back of the head with a large black Maglite. It tore a gash through her scalp. He stepped back, watching her fall face-first into the dirt. Her dark hair splayed out around her head, making her look like a fallen angel.

His angel—this one was just for him and no one else. He wanted to savor her and enjoy her before putting her in the water, but not here.

Not on base. Never mix business with pleasure. What was that saying? Don't get your honey where you make your money…or something like that. He smiled as he picked up her limp body and headed for his car.

CHAPTER
TWENTY-EIGHT

VINCENT HAD PARKED RIGHT NEXT to Alice's car. She had unwittingly parked in a place where no one could see them coming out of the woods. She had made it easier for him by parking right along the tree line. He liked it when his prey helped cover up their own abductions.

He placed her in the vehicle's trunk and calmly, slowly drove off of JBLM. That was the problem with killing on base: Washington state's largest police force was actually on JBLM, making this a high-risk game. The damn security forces and military police were everywhere, like an infestation of cockroaches. It was essential to stay at an even thirty miles per hour. You could get pulled over on base for simply going five over, which just wouldn't do.

When she opened her eyes, it was pitch black. At first she thought she had blacked out. She had debilitating migraines that sometimes made her feel off-balance, but she had never passed out before. She could feel rough carpet under her hands. She tried to sit up and hit her head. "What the hell," she muttered, propping herself on her elbows. The throbbing in her head was nearly unbearable.

The all-too-familiar aura spots crossed in front of her eyes. It was an unsettling sensation that typically happened before a migraine, but her head was already killing her this time. She felt disoriented. It didn't make sense that her head hurt in the back. Usually the migraines came right in front of her eyes. They always started with an aura and vision blur, and then the pain. It would normally stop her in her tracks, but this was different.

She leaned to the side and felt the back of her head. It was sticky and warm. She pulled her hand in front of her eyes but couldn't see anything. Panic started to take over. She took slow, deep breaths, trying her best to calm down, but she could feel her heart ramming against her rib cage. She stopped and listened, realizing she was in a vehicle—probably the trunk, she guessed.

It would do her no good if she lost control. Maybe there was a way out of this. She began feeling her surroundings. It was a small, tight spot with no room for her to stretch her legs or turn around. She felt along the floor, praying he had left her phone with her, but it wasn't in her back pocket. The vehicle bounced, causing her to hit her head again. She cried out in pain as they hit another pothole.

The pounding in her head was making it hard to think. There had to be a way out. *Isn't there a safety thing inside trunks just for these types of situations?* She breathed in and out, trying to calm herself and keep the migraine at bay. She methodically ran her hands along the top of the trunk and along the back, looking for anything.

She thought she remembered reading something about the safety lever being a glow-in-the-dark type of plastic, so if a person was locked in a trunk they could see it, but she couldn't see anything. Then she remembered why: Vincent's car was an old Ford Mustang and didn't have a safety latch.

She began searching for tools instead. Her hands searched the space, finding a seam along the edges of the trunk. The spare and tools were underneath her. She pulled at the edges, scrunching her body as tightly as she could against the opposite side. She was finally able to pull the old carpet up and feel around inside.

Her breath caught when she wrapped her fingers around what felt like a crowbar. It was slender, metal, and cold to the touch. At least now she would have a chance. She pulled hard but couldn't get it loose from the strange angle she was at. She yanked her body back and forth, trying to get it loose. Panic began to creep back in as she felt the vehicle slow to a crawl and finally stop. She pulled even harder, twisting her body and smacking her head against the roof of the trunk again, making her see stars.

The door opened and shut, and footsteps scraped against gravel. She steeled herself, getting a better grip on the crowbar, and pulled at the steel handle using all her weight. Just as the trunk opened, she pulled the crowbar loose, blindly striking out at her assailant. She felt the crowbar make contact. The blurry figure in front of her let out a scream and stepped back.

He dove forward, striking her with his fist across her face. He nailed her right in the temple, causing her to lose consciousness. He looked down at her still body, making a mental note to rid the trunk of any weapons before placing another playmate inside. He picked her out of the trunk like she weighed nothing at all, flinging her over his shoulder like a rag doll. His arm hurt where she had made contact with him, but the sensation simply made the experience more exciting. When it bruised, he would remember her fear and how she hadn't wanted to die.

He walked down the narrow path deep into the woods. That was the beautiful thing about this area: there were so many secluded places to hide and play. He had found this one less than a month ago when he and his team had been running an exercise to hone their emergency medical technician and rescue skills during a recent exercise. It was the perfect place, with deep, thick woods and beach access. He couldn't have asked for better if he had gone hunting for the place himself.

Alice's body thunked on the ground as he laid her on an old blanket he had left in a clearing earlier in the day. He lay down next to her, stroking her skin and playing with her dark hair. She was so beautiful. A bruise had started to form on the side of her head where he had hit her. He let his fingers trace around the bruise. "Now, why did you have to go and make me do that? We'd have much more fun if you just followed the rules," he said almost lovingly.

She finally stirred. It was about time; he was getting bored waiting for her to come to. He wanted to play with her, and it just wasn't any fun if she didn't participate. He ran his fingers along her body, softly touching her breasts, running his finger in a figure-eight pattern. She moaned lightly. "Oh, you like that, do you?"

Her eyes shot open, and she screamed until his strong hand clamped down over her mouth. She grabbed at him with her hands, scratching at his flesh. "Now, you can scream all you want, but no one will hear you," he said, watching as the resolve began to leave her face. He removed his hand.

"What do you want from me? If you let me go, I won't tell anyone. I promise," she pleaded.

"Don't worry, I'm not going to kill you; I've just always wanted to have sex with you. Ever since I met you, I've wanted to have you." He smiled like it was the most normal thing in the world.

"If I let you, will you leave me alone?" she asked tentatively. *I can do this,* she thought. If she just closed her eyes and let him do what he wanted, maybe he would let her live.

"Yes, of course," he said, trying his best to sound genuine. "All I want is to have you, and then you can leave. I'll even take you back to your car if you want."

"Okay." Her voice sounded weak and afraid. She didn't want to give him the satisfaction of knowing she was scared.

He began to kiss her neck and roughly tore at her blouse. The buttons began to pop as he pulled. She closed her eyes, not wanting to see. He roughly pawed at her body. His calloused hands ran down her stomach and into her shorts to violate her. He stopped just before he reached between her legs. He was looming over her body, and she could smell his foul breath. She never remembered him having lousy breath before, but now it assaulted her nostrils. What was he doing? *Just get it over with,* she wanted to scream.

He pulled his hand out of her shorts without touching her. "Get up on all fours," he demanded.

She let out a soft whimper but slowly rolled over, getting up on her hands and knees. At least she wouldn't have to look at him while he did it. She didn't want to remember any of this. Her shorts and panties were being yanked down around her knees. She began to shake uncontrollably and tried to put her mind somewhere else, but her brain wouldn't let her block out the violence she was experiencing.

She felt a cool breeze pass across her almost naked body. It felt like everything had stopped for a moment. She could hear him moving behind her. She looked down at the pine needles and dirt between her fingers. She tried to focus on anything except for what was about to happen. *Why is he waiting?* she wondered in terror, wanting the nightmare to end.

Something dropped next to her face. It was yellow and green and looked like a snake dangling next to her head. She let out a bloodcurdling scream. He could hear the creatures of the night scurry away, frightened by the deafening sound. He wrapped the rope neatly around her throat and started to pull back. She reared up against the rope, trying to loosen his grip so she could breathe, but it didn't work. She clawed at the weird material around her throat.

The strange rope tightened even further, which didn't make sense until she realized he had looped it around her like a makeshift noose. The sound of his zipper going down was all she could focus on. She felt him enter her from behind, pulling tighter on the rope as she fought to get loose. Slowly, the darkness began to swallow her vision until there was nothing.

CHAPTER
TWENTY-NINE

IT HAD BEEN a long day already as they left the tall FBI building and headed back to Kibble's car. He looked over at Mac. "How are you holding up?"

"I'll be fine. I want to go back to my room and just decompress. It's been a rough week, and I'm bone-tired," she admitted.

"Not to worry, Mac. We'll get this figured out," he said in a fatherly tone.

They drove back to base in silence. Mac stared out the window. There were too many thoughts running through her head. *Why would this guy want anything to do with me?* she wondered. Maybe he wanted to throw them off his scent and put the focus on her instead. She wasn't sure; she just knew she had to figure it out.

It was Friday, and all Mac wanted to do was shut the world out and talk to Hudson for a while. Sleep would help. As soon as she got back to her room, she shut the door and went to sanitize the bathtub. She needed a good long soak, but thought hotel room bathrooms probably weren't cleaned up to standards, so she did it herself. She remembered her dad's old saying: *If you want a job done right, do it yourself.* This wasn't what he'd meant, but it served her well in almost all of life's situations.

It was what made her a successful airman. She wasn't afraid to get her hands dirty and work or play just as hard as the guys. In the military, it was sometimes tough to be a woman. Not nearly as tough in the legal world as it had been on the flight line, but the military was still predominantly male. She had to give the Air Force credit: they sat at just over twenty percent women, whereas the other services sat quite a bit lower.

The week's stress was starting to wear her down, and her body ached because of it. She sat on the bed, watching the now clean bathtub fill up. When it was about half-full of warm water, she put two cups of Epsom salt in to soothe her sore muscles.

She slipped out of her boots, peeling off her uniform and stretching her legs out in front of her. She stood to head for the bath when there was a knock at the door.

"I don't want anything," she hollered at the rude interruption, not really caring who was outside.

"Are you sure about that?" came Hudson's unmistakable voice.

She looked out the peephole out of habit and couldn't believe her eyes. There stood her boyfriend with flowers and what looked like dinner. She opened the door without even thinking to tie her robe.

He stood there with his eyes wide and a big, goofy grin on his face. "Well, hello. I would have been here earlier if I knew I'd be greeted like that," he said, stepping into the room.

She backed up and looked him up and down like he was a meal to be devoured. The sight of her in all her glory left him speechless and wiped all thoughts from his brain. She popped one of her hands onto her left hip, shifting the robe open even farther. He slowly put down the flowers and food without taking his eyes off her. He was afraid if he looked away, she would disappear. Until that moment, he had no idea how much he had missed her.

His body ached with the need to be touched, to be taken, and to take. Raw desire coursed through his veins, pounding in his chest and other areas. He was already hard with the insatiable need to lose himself in Mac's warm embrace. She smiled at him, backing up a little farther, torturing him, making him wait until she slipped the robe off her slender shoulders. His breath caught despite himself. He had been with her for six months, and he still couldn't get enough.

At first he had been surprised by how deeply he had fallen for her, but now he had grown to enjoy how she made him feel unhinged. He felt like an addict, and she was definitely his drug of choice. The taste of her lips, the scent of her skin, the look of pure ecstasy in her eyes when she reached climax—and he definitely wanted to be the person who did that to her.

He took two long strides, clearing the distance between them, kissing her passionately, devouring her mouth and running his hands down her exquisite body.

Every thought in her head evaporated to focus on the pure pleasure of his touch. She reached down, fumbling with his belt, but her fingers were slipping. She pulled back for air. "I missed you too." She smiled at him. "Now, it doesn't seem fair that I'm the only one in my birthday suit."

He smiled, pulling his blue t-shirt over his head to reveal his perfectly chiseled abs. She couldn't get over how absolutely enticing he was. She seductively crawled up on the bed, propping herself up on her elbows. She was pleased to see how clearly excited he was to see her as his pants dropped to the floor.

He crawled on top of her, wanting to take things slow and easy. To savor every inch of her soft, supple skin. He buried his face in the crook of her neck, sending shivers down her body.

She slipped her hands between his legs and began to stroke softly and whispered in his ear, "I want you now." She dug her nails into his tight ass, wrapping her legs around him, lifting her hips and inviting him in.

Who was he to say no to a request like that? He couldn't even think at the moment. He slipped inside of her, excited by her wet heat. He tried to go slow, but then she moaned, "More," and he lost all sense of control. His strokes became harder and faster as he felt the urgency building inside her. She coiled around him and arched her head back, letting out a loud, primal cry as climax overtook her body, which threw him over the edge, engulfing him in mindless euphoria.

"Good Lord, woman, you're going to be the death of me," he finally said between deep breaths as he rolled his large body off of her.

She snuggled up next to him and kissed him softly. "I missed you too." She grinned.

They lay there in silence for a while, enjoying the moment and being back in each other's arms. "Hungry?" he finally asked.

"Famished." She smiled. "How did you know I hadn't had dinner?"

"Just a lucky guess. It looks like I got in between you and your bath." He raised an eyebrow.

"I think after your favorable performance, you can be forgiven." She grinned at him.

They straightened the rumpled bed sheets and laid out the dinner he had brought. She was hungrier than she'd realized and dug into the French dip sandwich. She didn't say a word until the first half was gone. He just watched as she enjoyed every bite. He'd never known someone could make eating a sensual experience. There was very little he didn't like about her, and it frightened him. At this point, he had no other choice but to hold on for the ride and hope she felt the same.

CHAPTER
THIRTY

THE NEXT MORNING, they woke wrapped in each other's arms. *It just doesn't get any better than this,* Mac thought as she watched him sleep. She knew things like this had to end, but this one would hurt. All of her relationships had looked promising at the beginning. Not that she had a ton to reference, but the few relationships she did have she usually ended up sabotaging, though this one had gone much better than previous ones.

Hudson had proven to be very understanding about her weird tics, fierce independence, and untrusting nature. She had yet to tell him about her past and certainly didn't warn him about her family. Considering that he'd lost his younger brother to drugs and crime, she wasn't sure how he would take it. She just wasn't ready to let go of him yet. If she was having a bad day, she could lose herself in his arms, and the big, evil world would just melt away. His warm embrace and kindness would be missed. Her sister called it the hug factor, and Hudson had it in spades.

He stirred next to her. "Well good morning, beautiful. How are you feeling?"

"Better with you here. I slept like a baby," she admitted, and then looked perplexed. "You know, I never understood that saying. Babies are normally up every couple of hours and rarely sleep through the night."

He smiled at her. "You got me, but you sometimes snore like an old man."

She shoved him playfully. "So, what's the plan? How long do you get to stay?"

"Just the weekend, I'm afraid. I thought maybe I could put a fresh set of eyes on your case and help you investigate a little. I hate to think of you out on the Seattle streets by yourself," he said, trying not to sound too protective.

"You know, I can handle myself," she reminded him.

"I know. I've seen you take down men my size, but I'd still like to help you if you'll let me."

"Actually, I was going to see if you could come down here anyway and help me with a lead. There's a licensed dominatrix in town that may have a good lead for my case, but she'll only see people by appointment. I was wondering if you would go with me to the appointment as a couple looking to explore different sexual avenues. We actually have an appointment tonight," she said, smiling mischievously.

"That's a horrible idea." He grinned. "What time?" He leaned in and kissed her. "Am I supposed to be your sub or your dom?"

"Since she's a female dom, I thought she might open up to another female dom. Kind of show me her ways. Would you be my submissive tonight?" She batted her eyes at him, giving her most seductive smolder.

He laughed. "I thought you'd never ask, but I have nothing to wear to the ball as your submissive Prince Charming. Aren't I supposed to be in a dog collar or something?"

"Well, as a matter of fact, I thought we could go shopping for a little something naughty to wear. Don't worry, you'll be fully clothed—kind of. There's a shop downtown that specializes in BDSM equipment and clothing. Considering your size, I'm hoping they'll have something that will fit you, plus I want to ask if they know anything about our redhead who was the last to see Collymore."

"Nice, I'm in. Now tell me about this case of yours."

They sat on the bed, enjoying the morning and digging a little deeper into the case. She went through evidence, giving him the highlights but not going into great detail. She conveniently omitted that she had received a message from who she assumed was the killer. She also left out the part where everyone suspected Carter. It never ceased to amaze her what people were capable of.

"I see where you're going with the dominatrix theory. Besides the whip marks and the woman that Collymore was last seen with, is there anything else?"

"Not really," she admitted. "Just my gut, and the fact that Collymore was looking into alternate lifestyles. Honestly, we don't have anything on this case now, and it's the only lead that makes some sense. I figure it can't hurt to look into it, and if it is a dead-end, we reevaluate the situation."

"Sounds fair. What do you make out of the weird pattern on some of the victims' necks? Clearly they were strangled, but with what?"

"No idea. I've been looking at different types of rope online and still haven't come across anything that makes sense."

CHAPTER
THIRTY-ONE

GENNAVIE SAT BACK in her perch at the second-floor café, watching her husband watching Mac. It amazed her how absolutely oblivious her husband could be. She often wondered how he hadn't gotten caught before meeting her. After the third time she had caught him watching Mac, she started following him regularly. Her disguise was perfect for the day: oversized sunglasses with a blond wig and a large-brimmed straw hat to block the sun from her fair skin.

She watched over him like a hawk. She wasn't sure if he was becoming obsessed with Mac, but the fact that he was hiding his observations from her had her worried.

Mac came out with a yummy mountain of a man that could stop traffic. *Mmm, I'd like to play with that one. Tame him and make him beg.* The titillating scene played out in her head.

She actually preferred large men. It made her feel powerful and strong when she could dominate them. She loved to watch a huge man beg with his giant shoulders beneath one of her heeled boots as he kneeled before her. She had to focus so as not to get all worked up inside.

Maybe she had been an evil queen in a past life. Not that she really believed in all that shit, but she also didn't believe in heaven or hell. She fancied herself an evil sorceress and actually looked a lot like the kickass Marvel character Medusa with the long red hair. Instead of attacking people with her hair, she liked the whip-and-chains approach, and sometimes administered certain drugs to make her victims hallucinate prior to her killing them. It was extremely fun to play tricks with their minds.

On the other hand, her husband had little imagination, and she was growing bored with him. Apparently the feeling was mutual. He was fun, and they had mind-blowing sex after a fresh kill, but lately he had been distracted and cheated on her. She hadn't forgiven him that indiscretion. That little bitch Alice had nothing on her. All he had to do was ask, and she would have been happy to join him for Alice's kill.

She was an equal-opportunity dominatrix, after all. They had killed men and women of all types and didn't discriminate. Why had Alice been different, and what was it about Mac that was holding his attention? At first she'd thought he was watching her because he was afraid that she was getting too close, but that clearly wasn't the case. He would come back from watching Mac thinking Gennavie didn't know about it. He kept getting angry with her any time she asked questions.

This told her he was up to no good. To be honest, they were never up to any good, but they were normally wreaking havoc together. Now he was straying on her, and no one did that to her. It infuriated her that she no longer seemed to do it for him. She knew she was a complex woman and hard to handle. There were so many layers to her that no man had gotten close to peeling back all of them, but no one had been stupid enough to betray her and live to talk about it, either.

She watched her husband discreetly slip into the bondage store after Mac and her big boy toy. She and Vincent were familiar with the store and got many of their supplies from it. That actually may have been a stupid move; repetition made people predictable, and predictability got you caught. She was not the type to live in a cage.

The couple looked so in love that it was sickening. They held hands and talked almost nonstop, in direct contrast with her and her husband these days.

A tall, good-looking waiter came up to Gennavie. "Is there anything I can get you?" he said, flashing her a megawatt smile.

She had been there for a while, but the café wasn't busy. She ordered another drink so she could keep her table and get him to go away. Though, he was cute. Maybe that was what she needed. Turnabout was fair play. Perhaps she should take a man back to their bed and play with him there. She decided that that would make her feel better, but she didn't make a move. She accepted her drink, smiling at the young man dismissively.

It was a lovely day, but her mood was as dark as the devil's heart. Who did he think he was? He had forgotten who she was, and it was time she reminded him of why he had married her in the first place. He had been fascinated with her, and now he was discarding her like used furniture.

Not going to happen, she thought as she felt her blood boil.

The loving couple finally emerged from the sex shop with big, shit-eating grins on their faces. *What did you find in my world?* she wondered, and then bristled when she saw Vincent following not too far behind. The couple got back in their car and drove away. She half expected her husband to follow, but he didn't, and she wondered why. Did he know where they were headed? It was time she found out what was going on.

CHAPTER
THIRTY-TWO

GENNAVIE WATCHED as Vincent walked away from their favorite sex shop and down a street, disappearing from sight. She waved the waiter over and paid her bill, quickly exiting the second-floor balcony café, cursing the heels she had chosen to wear with her green-and-white floral sundress. She had a thing for the color green, especially emerald. It looked good against her porcelain skin. She thought about mixing it up a bit, but kept reverting back to the same color.

Her heels clicked loudly against the cement, giving up her element of surprise. She figured she had lost him at that point—until she rounded the corner and found him sitting on a bench with his legs stretched out in front of him, people-watching.

She slipped off her shoes and slowly walked up behind him, running a blood-red fingernail across the back of his neck.

He whipped around, not recognizing her until he saw her unmistakable full red lips. "What the hell," he said once he realized it was her. "You about made me shit myself. Why are you sneaking up on me?"

"Who's the one sneaking?" she hissed at him.

"So, you've been following me." He raised an eyebrow.

"Yes, I'm following you. First, you go off and kill Alice without me, then you become all secretive and start blocking me out. We used to hunt together, and now you're here, hunting solo." She actually looked sad.

"Don't be ridiculous; I'm not hunting. I'm doing surveillance to make sure they're not on to us. Mac has clearly called in reinforcements, and I wanted to see what they're up to. With them going to our favorite store, I don't get the warm and fuzzies."

"Okay, if this is only surveillance, why didn't you tell me what you were doing?"

"Because I didn't want you to worry, honey," he said, softening his tone.

"Well, you sneaking around and leaving me out of things isn't making me worry less. It's just pissing me off, so stop it."

"Sure, hon, whatever you want," he said. He would let her believe whatever she wanted to for now. He knew she was a control freak, and convincing her that she was in control was usually his best bet. Even though this time, he was in control.

"What do you know?" she asked, trying to calm herself.

"I know that they've been to Kremwerk and interrogated the bartenders about who you are. I don't think they found out anything since you never got close or interacted with them," he said calmly. "It'll be fine. Your informant seems to be keeping you up to date on all their moves."

"What did they do while in the shop?" she asked, becoming calmer. Maybe he was just trying to cover their tracks. Mac and that mountain of a man still made her nervous, but more importantly, the thought of being in a cage made her skin crawl. For her, it was a fate worse than death.

"That part was intriguing," he said with a mischievous smile. "They bought full leather and lace getups. Surprisingly, the big man is the sub. I wouldn't have guessed those two were into the lifestyle. Do you think they're on to us?"

"Did they talk about where they were going?" She could tell that Mac excited him, but it only worried her. What if they found out who she was through that world? Everyone in the dungeon knew her alter ego. She was reasonably confident that no one knew who she really was, but it was a little too close to home for her liking. She had been using Lady Carina's dungeon for years. "I think we need to keep an eye on them."

"I have to say, that Mac chick sure could stop traffic in hers," he said, making room for her to sit next to him while they discussed the situation.

"Are you planning on tailing them tonight?"

"Unfortunately, I have to be out in the field tonight," he said. "They're pulling weekend exercises, and I need to keep up appearances, and so do you."

"I know perfectly well why appearances are important," she snapped. "I'll track them tonight, and then we can compare notes when you get back from the field."

CHAPTER
THIRTY-THREE

MAC AND HUDSON went out for a wonderful dinner at a steak house in downtown Seattle. It was a little higher end, but the meal was to die for. They figured it was better to have a good meal before exploring this new world. There was no telling how long it would take. Neither one of them had ever seen a professional dominatrix before.

Lady Carina's website was very interesting—they had watched the virtual tour of her dungeon—but didn't quite prepare them for the real thing. They walked up to the Queen Ann-style house that sat slightly elevated on a hill. It was a beautiful old place, but the exterior gave away none of the secrets it held inside. They both felt a little exposed, all dressed up for the occasion.

Mac had gone for an elegant dominatrix look, or at least that's what she thought the outfit made her look like. She wore a lace mask around her eyes and nose, a black leather corset, and had pulled her dark hair high on her head in a sleek ponytail. She had on a short leather skirt that made her feel a little more comfortable, with a classy pair of lined thigh-highs and bright-red heels. She had to admit that there was a certain excitement to being in disguise. Not that she was hiding from anyone, but she could see the appeal. It would allow people to go further than they would if their identity was known.

Hudson stood next to her, looking quite dashing—she thought, anyway—minus the mask. "Are you sure about this? I feel ridiculous," he said, looking down at himself. "I mean, you look amazing, but are we sure we know what we're getting into? I feel like I'm suffocating in this thing." He was wearing a leather mask with a zipper for a mouth, a collar around his neck for Mac to lead him around with, no shirt, and tight leather pants with his biker boots to finish the ensemble. His large chest and trim waist looked exquisite, almost like he was chiseled from stone. He kind of reminded her of Henry Cavill in *The Witcher* without the white hair.

The door was opened by a middle-aged man in a tuxedo. He was no taller than Mac in her heels, and very formal. "Good evening," he said, opening the door. Mac felt panic, thinking they could be in the wrong place. "I am Lady Carina's assistant, and you are her eleven o'clock appointment," he said casually, noticing Mac's hesitation.

"Yes," Mac said.

"Very well, follow me, please," he said, opening the door wide for them to enter.

They walked into the main entrance that opened up to sprawling marble floors and high cathedral ceilings. A large chandelier hung from the side of a winding staircase that led to the second floor. The home was decorated in Victorian style with a medieval flair. Instead of flowers or vases as accents, she had decorated them with skulls. In her China cabinet, there was no China but rows of what looked like torture devices, sex toys, and leather goods for sale.

Mac looked down into the main dining room to find several more cabinets filled with similar offerings. She could see several women milling about on the first floor. Most of them were dressed similarly to how she was, in leather and lace. One woman led a man around wearing nothing but a G-string and a dog mask. He was crawling behind her on all fours. Mac tried to look away, but all she could do was stare.

"This way, please." The assistant led them up the long staircase and into a decorated sitting room in the same elegant Victorian style. "Please have a seat, and Lady Carina will be with you momentarily. Would you like a beverage while you wait?"

"No, thank you," Mac said.

Hudson remained quiet with his eyes down, playing the part of the submissive.

Lady Carina's assistant left them sitting in the small room. It looked almost like a waiting area in a high-end hotel. It was decorated a lot like the Historic Davenport Hotel in Spokane. She liked going there because it almost felt like she was royalty. Just a little bit of spoiling never hurt anyone.

CHAPTER
THIRTY-FOUR

FINALLY, Lady Carina appeared in the doorway. She was the most classically exquisite woman Mac could ever remember seeing. She had jet-black hair pulled into a severe ponytail. Her eyes were almost catlike with dark makeup, and she had blood-red lips. She looked like someone out of the 1920s with short-cropped bangs that accented her high cheekbones. Colorful floral tattoos ran down the right side of her body, and more ink peeked out above her thigh-high boots. She was wearing a red corset cinched tight around her tiny waist, elbow-high gloves that partially covered her tattoos, and a short black skirt much like Mac's.

At first they both stared, until she broke out into an infectious smile with huge dimples popping out on her beautiful cheeks. "Well, look at the two of you," she said, her grin actually spreading farther across her face, which Mac found intriguing. "Stand up and let me take a look at the two of you." They stood, and she circled around them, slapping Hudson's ass as she passed. "Well, aren't you a big one?"

Mac smiled at her, trying not to laugh at Hudson's apparent discomfort. "We were wondering if we could ask you some questions," Mac asked, watching Lady Carina run her red fingernail down Hudson's chest.

"I figured something was up when I reviewed your request form.

You're not my normal clientele. All talk and no action, huh," she said, pursing her red lips into a pout.

"Afraid so," Mac said. "We came this way so as not to alarm your staff or other clients. We're military and investigating the death of one of our airmen."

"I had nothing to do with a murder," she said, immediately defensive.

"I never said you were, but we have reason to believe you know someone who might be involved, or at least has information for us. We would really appreciate your help," Mac said.

"Murder is bad for business. I don't want anything like that associated with my place. Follow me so we can talk privately. I don't want anyone to get spooked. It's one of the reasons my place is so popular—we ensure the safety of our employees and clients. No one gets hurt here except for the whippings they pay for, and everyone leaves satisfied," she reported with pride in her voice.

Mac and Hudson followed her into a room with chains hanging from the wall, various types of whips, flogs, rods, straps, crops, electrodes, and other crazy-looking devices that Hudson wasn't sure he wanted to experience. There was a suspension cage hanging from the ceiling and a bondage table in the middle of the room.

"This room is soundproofed for obvious reasons. Sometimes our clients scream, and we would hate to scare off new customers," she explained, taking a seat on a high-backed red Victorian chair in the far corner and indicating for Mac and Hudson to sit opposite her. "It's always important to interview my clients prior to a session. I'm here to please them and fulfill their darkest desires. Yes, they submit to me, but ultimately they're in charge. If I abuse them beyond their comfort level, they won't return, and eventually I could go out of business."

It was a strange setup. Hudson sat stiffly in the chair next to her. He leaned over to her. "Can I take this thing off? I'm sweating like a pig," he grumbled.

"Of course," Lady Carina answered for Mac. "We always want everyone to be comfortable. The masks take a little getting used to, but some models are more comfortable than others. You happened to choose one that does not breath well."

"I see," Hudson said, pulling the sweaty mask off his head.

Lady Carina handed him a cool, wet wipe to clean off his face. "Handsome and strong. Boy, you're one lucky woman," she said. Mac simply smiled. Lady Carina sat back and stared at them. "So, what would you two like to know?"

"We're investigating the murders of several people that we're not entirely sure are related," Mac said. "Some victims have whip marks across their chests, buttocks, legs, thighs, and genitalia. The ligature marks are quite unique, and the whip marks are fairly deep."

"Interesting. How deep are the whip marks, and how close together are they?" Lady Carina asked.

"On one of our victims, the whip marks cover most of his body and overlap in several areas. There are places where the whip marks cut through the skin, leaving deep gashes. Do you know what kind of whip would do this?" Mac asked.

"The most common whip that would leave that type of single, long wound is a bullwhip," Lady Carina explained. "What they're made of will determine what kind of damage they cause. Obviously, softer leather material will cause less damage, but most whips are made out of stiffer leather straps. But they can also be made out of nylon parachute cord. The reason these types of whips cause the most damage is the velocity at which the tip of the whip strikes the skin. The person inflicting the damage stands far away from their victim, lashing out and making them bleed."

"That's good information, thank you. We also wanted to know if you had come across a woman with long red hair. She's petite and drop-dead gorgeous. She may have been the last one to see one of our victims. They were last seen together at Club Kremwerk."

"Let me see, I work with several redheads who enjoy dominating. Can you be more specific?"

Hudson spoke up for the first time. "This woman has waist-long hair and was last seen wearing an emerald-green dress."

Lady Carina's eyes showed recognition, but then she looked away.

"You know who we're talking about," Mac said.

"I can't be sure, but she's one of my best, if it is her. I actually don't know her real name. She refused to reveal herself to me, but she's been so popular that I made an exception and let her stay. She rents space in my house to see her clients, and I get ten percent of her earnings. I couldn't let a woman like that just walk away."

"What can you tell us about her?" Mac asked.

"She's stunning and always in control. She changes her appearance, but prefers the long red hair for her Mistress Gennavie look. Her clients just can't get enough of her. She was formally trained in Amsterdam and has a completely different style, like no one I've ever met. She gets into her clients' minds and makes them eat from her hand."

"Isn't that the whole idea," Hudson asked, "to get her clients to submit and do what she demands?"

"Not necessarily. If a dom makes it all about themselves, the sub won't return. Most submissives want to be dominated for a reason, and those reasons are diverse. Sometimes they crave the loss of control because their daytime lives require them to be in control at all times. Imagine a CEO of a company who's always in charge and never loses control. For a small amount of time, they want to be controlled, to step away from that high-pressure life and submit.

"Other clients feel they deserve to be punished because of some misdeed they did in their past. This allows them to live with whatever they happened to do. Most people are surprised to learn that this lifestyle is more about the submissive's wants and desires than the dominant's. Mistress Gennavie was exceptional at figuring out what her clients needed. Not necessarily what they wanted, but what they needed—even if they didn't know what that was when they first came to see her." Lady Carina sounded almost in awe of Mistress Gennavie.

"Can you tell us a little more about the lifestyle?" Mac asked. "For instance, I notice that you're called 'lady,' but she's called 'mistress.' What's the difference?"

"This place is about roleplay and escaping from the big bad world. Mistress, lady, goddess, princess, queen, and dominatrix are interchangeable terms depending on the fantasy and each person's role. In many cases, we change roles depending on our sub's fantasy, how they wish us to dress, and how they're dressed. This is all worked out during the planning meeting. After we're done, there is an after-care session to see how the submissive felt about the session and, of course, to care for them. Some of our sessions can be quite intense, and others can be less. Open communication is essential."

Lady Carina paused, focused now on Mac. "A professional dominatrix never takes their submissive further than they're comfortable with. Yes, it is about pushing the limits, but it's not about breaking those limits. That's why we have safe words or some indication that says we're on the verge of going too far. I consider myself a woman of many talents"—Lady Carina gave her a wicked smile—"but reading minds is not one of them."

"Do you think Mistress Gennavie is capable of killing someone?" Mac tilted her head to the side, absolutely intrigued.

"Oh yes, we are all capable of great violence. No one is exempt from this, but knowing that and learning control, especially in our line of work, is very important. Mistress Gennavie seemed to have mastered that control. I never personally witnessed her losing control with any of her clients. She was always professional. With that being said, I have no information to offer you about her life outside my dungeon."

"What did she tell you about her time in Amsterdam?" Hudson asked.

"I asked her where she had learned her technique. I've been in this business for a long time. As you know, I am a very public figure in this world and am openly a professional dominatrix. Many people keep this life and their normal"—she made air quotes when she said *normal*—"world separate. Anyway, she told me that she was in Amsterdam for about four years and had learned her techniques from a world-renowned goddess during her stay. A while back, we actually teamed up on a client. It was quite exhilarating to watch her work."

Her lips curled, eyes wistful. "We offered a 'heaven-and-hell' package. She played the devil with her bright-red hair, and I played the angel for once. In a nutshell, it was about her taking the client to their absolute limits, and I was in charge of bringing him back down so he could handle the abuse she was inflicting." Lady Carina saw the look of concern on their faces. "Keep in mind, this is all consensual and agreed to prior to the session. There's never a time when the client is forced to do anything they don't want to. They are very willing participants, and they pay very well for a nice whipping," she said with a smile.

"Just out of curiosity, how much do you charge per session?" Mac asked.

"A two-hour session is approximately eight hundred dollars, but can fluctuate depending on what the client wants. I, of course, charge extra for same-day bookings, overnight stays, and so on. Sex is never part of the package. I don't run that kind of place here. It's simply about dominating and being dominated. Some clients just want to be my live-in slave for the day. They sleep in my cage and obey my every whim." She clapped her hands together and grinned.

"Aren't you ever worried about your safety?" Hudson asked.

"No, I'm never here alone. There are always other dominatrixes and masters running about, playing naughty games. Plus, I have a panic button in every room that notifies Andre if there's a problem."

Mac smiled. "Who's Andre?"

Lady Carina pulled her phone out of a small pouch hanging from her waist and showed them a picture of a huge, barrel-chested man with a bushy beard. "He watches over us. No one messes around in my house, and everyone knows about Andre. He completes all my background checks prior to meeting with new clients, takes care of the transactions, and accompanies me to events. He provides much more than just protection."

"Has there ever been a problem involving Mistress Gennavie?" Mac asked.

"No, she keeps to herself. She just rents the space and runs her own show. She has never had anyone disobey her. I pity the fool who would try. She can be vicious at times."

"Thank you for your time and all the information. Would it be okay if we reach out to you in the future if we have more questions?" Mac asked.

"As long as you're willing to pay my fees, you two can come back anytime you want," she said, smiling.

They stood to leave.

"Are you sure you don't want to try a session?" Lady Carina said. "The things I could make the two of you do…"

"I think we're good, but thank you for the offer and your time," Hudson said.

"Suit yourself. Maybe next time. Stop by and see Andre on your way out to complete payment," she instructed as she walked them to the door of her dungeon.

CHAPTER
THIRTY-FIVE

AS THEY WALKED BACK into the well-lit and elegant waiting room, Lady Carina's assistant appeared. "Follow me, please," he said in the same even tone.

Mac and Hudson fell in line behind the assistant. "Can we ask you some questions?" Mac asked.

"No," he said without hesitation.

"What's your name?" Mac pressed.

"Assistant," he responded. He kept walking without saying a word until they arrived at a door on the first floor that sat between two cabinets filled with all kinds of naughty toys. "Andre will be with you in a moment." He knocked on the door lightly three times, turned, and walked away.

"Interesting guy," Mac commented.

The door opened slowly, and out walked a huge man with a long, grizzly beard and bushy eyebrows. He was about the same height as Hudson—Mac guessed six foot six inches—but he was enormous. He was the first person Mac had come across that made Hudson look small. She glanced over at Hudson; he clearly felt the same way.

"Credit card," Andre grumbled at them. Mac took out her credit card and handed it to the man. He swiped her card with his meaty hands. "You can go now," he said, moving them toward the door.

The assistant was waiting for them with the door wide open. Mac and Hudson quickly left the dungeon.

"That was weird," Mac said. "Once we were done, it was like we were no longer welcome. I wonder if they've had problems with people trying to stick around or just being creepy."

"Who knows. We came, we saw, we got a little weirded out. Now let's go back to your hotel for a little normal time," he said with an encouraging smile.

"Yeah, that isn't exactly my cup of tea, either. Do you mind if we drive around for a bit? I just need to clear my head."

"Sure," Hudson agreed as they headed to Mac's little SUV.

———

Mistress Gennavie couldn't believe these two. How in the hell had they tracked her here? It was like Mac had taken wild guesses, and somehow they'd ended up right. Other than the whip marks on the bodies, there had been nothing to lead her directly to Lady Carina. She was stewing in the car, wondering what they had learned about her. She'd used Lady Carina's house to see her clients for almost two years now. She could feel her temper flaring as she watched Mac and Hudson leave the old home.

No one else had a clue except for these two. She needed to see Tank and find out what was going on behind the scenes. But then she thought about it.

The answer was simple.

They looked like they didn't have a care in the world, but Mistress Gennavie was going to make them care. One of the things they'd drilled into her brain in the military was KISS—keep it simple, stupid.

It was simple: eliminate the threat, then walk away.

She fell behind Mac and Hudson, keeping her distance so they wouldn't notice her. At first they just drove around town. She patiently followed them, hoping they would stop somewhere and give her an opportunity to strike, but she had no such luck. They were headed back into Tacoma and back toward the base. Gennavie's heart sank.

Her disappointment was stronger than she had anticipated. She hated to worry, and these two were messing with her plans.

Mac was behind the wheel, and she could see Hudson's large frame in the passenger seat. Gennavie began to resign herself to coming up with a different way to solve the problem. Maybe she could poison Mac somehow. That should be easy enough, since she had access to plenty of drugs at the clinic. She pondered the idea as she drove behind the two.

Her heart began beating wildly in her chest as she watched Mac's vehicle turn off I-5, headed to the Port of Tacoma. *This night might not be a waste after all.* It was very secluded this time of night, so she hung back even farther. She would hate to alert her prey.

CHAPTER
THIRTY-SIX

"WHERE ARE WE GOING?" Hudson asked.

"I just thought it would be nice to look out over the water and talk for a bit," Mac said, pulling in next to an old gray building that sat on the edge of the water. It was peaceful as they looked out at the dark waters lapping against the dock. Mac rolled down her window to let the fresh breeze in. It smelled a little like fish, but she welcomed it anyway. She eased back in her seat, took a deep breath, and slowly let it out. She knew Hudson was watching her, waiting for her to talk.

"Penny, for your thoughts," he said.

"Just thinking about this case. I feel like it's my fault that Alice is dead. I should have seen it coming. Of course, the killer would go after her if she talked with the cops. I should have made sure she was safe. You think I would have learned after last time with Ali," she said in a pool of self-loathing.

"For one thing, Ali wouldn't accept protection, and she's still alive because you saved her life. If it hadn't been for you, she would be dead right now and not dating our good friend Joe. Alice came to you and really didn't have any profound leads, so how could you know that she was in danger?" he said, lacing his fingers through hers.

"I just feel..." She stopped mid-sentence as a loud truck engine roared to life. It sounded like it was right behind them. Before she could process the information, blinding lights from a large truck bathed the inside of the SUV. They sat frozen in suspended animation. "Just the Port Police wondering what we're doing out here this late," she said with a hopeful glance at Hudson.

The moment was shattered when the huge, dark truck with a large grill slammed into the back of Mac's little SUV.

"Son of a bitch," she screamed, slamming her foot down on the brake, but it did nothing. The massive truck looked like a semi behind them and pushed her SUV with little effort toward the edge and the water. "Put up your window," she screamed.

"No," Hudson said, "leave it down."

She stopped midway and lowered her window back down just as they slammed into the black, inky water with a sound that exploded inside the vehicle. Her head lurched forward, slamming into the steering wheel, surprising her; the airbag hadn't deployed.

It took her a minute to get her bearings. She could feel a trickle of blood running down the side of her face. Her finger ran across the cut; it didn't feel too bad, but it hurt like hell. She looked over at Hudson, who was still gripping her hand a little too tightly.

"Are you okay?" he asked, breathing hard.

She took several deep breaths. "I think so. As far as I can tell I just hit my head."

"That's good. We'll float for a minute before it starts filling up with water. Likely whoever dropped us into the drink is still watching. Stay very still and don't move until we're fully submerged. Your body will want to panic, but just take deep breaths. I'm right here with you, and we'll be fine."

"Okay," she said, responding mostly to the tone of his voice. It was so black inside the vehicle that she could only make out faint lines on his face. "There's something you should know about me," she said as the water began to rise around their legs.

"We can talk about whatever you want once we're safe. There's nothing to worry about. I've done this before," Hudson admitted.

"You've done what before?" Mac asked.

"Gotten out of a sinking vehicle. It's a long story," he said. "Now try not to make any large movements. Slowly release your seatbelt."

"What happens when we go under?" Mac asked in a shaky voice.

"The pressure inside the vehicle will equalize, and we'll be able to slide out of the window undetected. It's crucial that we swim away from the vehicle and remain hidden in case we're being watched. We want him to think we didn't make it out," he said. The water was now up to their waists. "Steady your breathing; you'll need all the energy you have to swim out."

"Hudson, listen to me. I need to tell you something."

The water was creeping up to their chest. She shivered as the cold water slid under her armpits. It still had a ways to go on Hudson since his head reached the top of the vehicle. She clicked the seatbelt open, floating up slightly to have more air.

"What is it you need to tell me?" he asked, tilting his head toward the car's ceiling to get more air.

"I'm not a good swimmer," she admitted as they both took deep breaths in and the vehicle dropped under the water. They were suspended for a moment, floating in the blackness. She couldn't see him but held tightly to his hand. Once they were fully submerged, he led her out the open window and away from the quickly sinking car.

Shit, that'll cost me, she thought as she watched it drop away from them.

Her head stung where she had struck the dashboard. *If there's too much blood in the water, will it attract unwanted company?* she wondered. *Are there even sharks in this area?* She had no idea, but certainly didn't want to find out.

Hudson was pulling her away from the car and toward the shore, or at least she hoped he knew which way that was, since she couldn't see anything. She held on tight and kicked her legs, feeling her red heels slip from her feet and drop down to the dark abyss.

She felt disoriented and couldn't tell if Hudson was dragging her up or down. She silently prayed he was going up, because her lungs were burning and she wasn't sure how much longer she could hold her breath.

Relief washed over her as their heads slid above the surface. She gulped air, filling her starving lungs.

Hudson gently put his hand over her mouth to keep her quiet.

They were near the large pillars that held up the pier. Thankfully the water was relatively calm, so they weren't getting knocked around like pinballs.

They floated there for what seemed like hours before slowly making their way to the ladder on the far side of the pier. The ladder was worn and had barnacles that scraped along their hands.

"Do you think he left?" Mac asked.

"I think it's time we take our chances," he said. "We can't stay here too much longer, plus we need to call the authorities. Do you have any contacts you've been working with?"

"Yeah, I can call Bardot," Mac said.

"Who's that?"

"She's the top FBI lady leading the joint task force. She'll know what to do."

CHAPTER
THIRTY-SEVEN

THEY CAUTIOUSLY CLIMBED up the old ladder. Hudson had gone first, and his wet clothes were dripping on top of Mac's head, which usually would have annoyed her, but at this point she was just happy they were alive. Hudson surveyed the area to ensure there weren't any threats and saw nothing.

They both took a deep breath once their feet were on solid ground. They were chilled to the bone. Even in summer, it still got cold in the early morning hours. Dawn was just starting to break, and they needed to find a way to get help. They walked down the pier to the old gray building and knocked on the door, but no one answered.

"No one is here for another hour or so," a raspy voice said from around the corner. They rounded the corner to find a small, weather-beaten elderly man sitting in his sleeping bag. "Now stop making so much racket. I'm trying to get some shuteye 'fore the boats start rolling in."

"We need a phone," Hudson said. "Do you know where we can find one?"

"If it'll make you two go away," he wheezed. "There's an old payphone down between those two buildings. Not sure if it works, but you give it a try and leave me be."

Mac stepped from behind Hudson. "Thank you."

"Well now, pretty lady, you can stay as long as you want." The man raised a crusty eyebrow at her and then grumbled and rolled himself back into his sleeping bag without another word.

They moved as quickly as their stiff, cold legs could carry them. Their phones were wet. Mac's purse had gone down with her car, and it had everything in it. She hoped they could get it out of the water and recover her identification. That would suck to have to replace everything. Thankfully, Hudson had his wallet in his pants—and a very soggy phone, but they could deal with that later.

The payphone was just where the homeless man said it would be; surprisingly, it worked. After many attempts and finally getting through to a helpful operator, they were connected to the FBI. Unfortunately, that was just the beginning. Since all of Mac's contact information went down with her vehicle, they had no choice but to find Bardot the roundabout way.

Finally, after shivering at the payphone for almost half an hour, a very groggy and pissed-off sounding Bardot came on the line. "Who is this?"

"Ma'am, this is Technical Sergeant Evelyn McGregor, and I need help."

"What's going on, McGregor?"

"My vehicle was forced off the Tacoma Pier tonight. We were hit from behind by a large vehicle that felt like a semi-truck, and our car fell into the water," Mac said, her voice shaking partially from the cold.

"You said we. Is someone with you?" Bardot asked.

"Yes, ma'am. My friend is here, Master Sergeant Gavin Hudson. He's visiting me from Spokane."

"I see. Give me your location," Bardot said.

Mac did her best to describe where they were. The pier was just big enough that it might take time to find them.

Within the hour, the entire area was lit up by flashing red-and-blue lights. It was one of the nicest things Mac had seen. She felt shaken by the incident and wasn't sure what to think.

A young policewoman had brought them blankets and warm coffee, which was a relief since Mac wasn't exactly dressed appropriately. They had been checked by paramedics, and Mac's head had been bandaged. It wasn't anything serious, just a deep scratch.

Bardot walked up to them with a concerned look across her birdlike features. "What the hell were you two doing out here?"

"I was just looking for a quiet place to talk," Mac said.

"And what exactly are you dressed up to be?" Bardot asked.

Mac pulled her blanket around her, embarrassed. They had both taken off their masks after their encounter with Lady Carina, and Hudson had put on a hoodie. However, Mac was still wearing her outfit, which was uncomfortable, wet, and much more revealing than she would have preferred when surrounded by the task force. "We were chasing the lead about the whip marks on the victims. We wanted to know if there was a link between the whip marks and the red-headed woman last seen with Collymore."

Bardot listened intently. "What did you find?"

"Actually, Lady Carina—" she began.

"Who's Lady Carina?" Bardot asked.

"She's the professional dominatrix that we went to see tonight," Mac said.

"I had no idea there was such a profession," Bardot commented. "Go on."

"Anyway, Lady Carina knows a woman that matches our description who rents space from her. Unfortunately, she doesn't know much about this woman except she's a fantastic earner, and Lady Carina gets ten percent of her earnings," Mac said. "She let us know that this woman was formally trained in Amsterdam and keeps her Mistress Gennavie persona separate from her regular life. She said that was fairly common in the business."

"I see." Bardot thought about it for a minute. "You've done some amazing investigative work, but I've put a call into Captain Kibble, and he agrees with me that you should be sent home until this gets solved. Obviously, this guy has a hard-on for you."

"But ma'am, this is personal. He just tried to kill us, and I'm not so sure it is a guy. I think it may be this red-headed woman. All leads seem to point to her," Mac said with more force than she'd intended.

"I like your instincts, Mac, and I'll keep you posted on the case as things progress. We can track down the leads you started looking into. I want you to debrief Kibble and then get back on the road," Bardot said, leaving little room for argument.

"What about my car and my purse? It had my military ID in it. I can't even get back on base," Mac said.

"I see," Bardot said.

Bardot's nonchalant attitude was starting to unnerve Mac. She felt Hudson lace his fingers through hers to calm her. Bardot held up her finger and stepped away to make a phone call.

"I can take you home with me for now, and we can start working on replacing everything in your purse," Hudson offered.

"Thank you, but there was something special in there that can't be replaced," Mac said.

"What is it?"

"It's a necklace my dad gave to me before he disappeared. It's the only thing I have left of him," Mac explained as she saw Bardot making her way back over to them.

"Okay, I have a team coming out to drag your car out of the drink. Kibble will meet you at the base. He made arrangements for you to gain entry to the base and your hotel room through his OSI contact. You two go back to the hotel, get a warm shower, and stay put. I'm posting a man outside your door for protection."

Hudson raised an eyebrow.

"Don't think you're not in danger as well, Mr. Hudson," Bardot said. "Your life was just threatened, and I'm not having either one of you killed on my watch. If this is a woman, then she's extremely strong and resourceful. Personally, I think it may be a team. There are several indications that we may be dealing with two killers."

Mac let the concept roll around in her head. There was very little information about serial-killer couples that she knew of, but it had happened. Usually they fed off each other. Sometimes there was a dominant-submissive relationship, and sometimes two dominants tried to one-up each other. She would need to do some research to try and get inside their heads. That was a piece of the puzzle she hadn't yet considered.

CHAPTER
THIRTY-EIGHT

BARDOT STAYED BEHIND at the crime scene, assuring Mac and Hudson that she would let them know as soon as she had something. She was apprehensive about this case, if she was right about the killers. There had been another similar case where a husband-and-wife team had spent their time trying to up the ante until it all came crashing down around them. They had gone out playing the deadly game of suicide by cop. She sincerely hoped this case wouldn't end the same way.

The huge crane dipped its thick cable into the water, where a professional police diver waited. He led the cable down and was gone for what seemed like too long. Bardot wondered if he couldn't find the car until the diver surfaced and gave the crane operator a thumbs-up.

While they were pulling Mac's SUV out of the water, the FBI's evidence response team was processing the large black diesel flatbed truck that had been used to push Mac and Hudson off the pier. Clearly, they had struck a nerve with the killer or killers. Bardot retraced the places they had looked into: Kremwerk, the Lady Carina angle, and Alice had definitely been involved somehow.

Alice didn't feel like a random killing to Bardot.

Most killers had an agenda or purpose for killing. This seemed almost purposefully random. The victims were different in about every way possible. The only two who'd been linked were Alice and Ryan. The rest of the victims seemed to be all over the map. It just didn't make sense.

"Ma'am"—one of the technicians from the evidence response team came up to her—"there are no prints in the truck, but we did find a synthetic piece of hair that looks like it came from a wig. The truck appears to have been hotwired. According to the Port Police, it was parked just down the way next to that old gray building."

"Any witnesses?" she asked the young tech.

"No, ma'am. There was a homeless man, but apparently he passed out and didn't see anything until, and I quote, 'a hot wet lady and her mountain man came and woke him up with all their racket.'"

"Very well, thank you for the update. Let me know if you find anything else," she said, dismissing him as the bumper of Mac's now soggy, broken SUV crested the water's surface. Gallons of water flowed from the vehicle as it dangled from the crane. The damage to the back of the vehicle confirmed Mac and Hudson's story. Not that Bardot didn't find the two credible, but after years in her line of work, she believed in "trust, but always verify."

Once they got the SUV safely back on solid ground, Bardot walked over to the car to see Mac's purse soaking wet but still in the front seat. She had been lucky; the purse had been closed, and the strap had latched onto the gear shift, keeping it inside the SUV. She put on gloves and asked one of the technicians to hand her the purse. She walked over to a flat stone bench and dumped out the contents.

Mac didn't keep much in the way of personal items in her purse. It only contained a simple wallet with her identification and some credit cards, but no cash or makeup. Bardot felt through the purse and looked for anything out of the ordinary. It didn't sit well with her that the killer had targeted Mac out of everyone else working the case. What was the link between the suspect and Mac?

She headed back to her office. There had to be something that intrigued the killer, and she was going to find out what it was.

CHAPTER
THIRTY-NINE

MAC AND HUDSON returned to the hotel, exhausted. They peeled off their still damp clothes and slid into a nice hot shower together. Mac held on to Hudson silently, losing herself in his arms, and began to cry. He held her, not saying a word until she had gotten it out. "We're okay," he finally said.

"I know, but we could have died. If you hadn't known what you were doing, we would have been at the bottom of Puget Sound. I've survived too much to die just because some asshole has a vendetta," she said with venom in her voice.

"Well, it looks like it's time to walk away." He wanted to ask exactly what she had survived, but she hadn't opened up about her past, and he didn't think this was the time to ask, but he was very curious. "What do you intend to do?"

"I don't know. Maybe do what I'm told for once…" she said with a mischievous smile on her lips.

"Yeah right, Mac. I'm serious. I don't want a repeat of last winter. It's time for us to pack up and go home. Let's leave this one to the local experts and the FBI. I'm sure they can handle it, and don't forget about Kibble. I'm sure he'll keep you posted, but that's it," he said, looking at her sternly.

She stuck her bottom lip out at him like a pouting child.

He grinned back at her and kissed her pouty lips. "I love you, Evelyn McGregor, and I don't want to lose you."

She kissed him back hard, letting him know what she thought about his last declaration. She hadn't told him she loved him yet. She was sure she did, but she was terrified of what he would think when he found out about her past and family. She had trusted a few select people with that information over the years, and inevitably they had turned their backs on her.

He sensed her hesitation and let out a sigh. He already knew about her sister Lola, but the rest of her past was a bit of a mystery. Lola had helped him find Mac after she had gone after the last killer they had been tracking. Mac was a bullheaded woman and had gone off to find Chief Deleon, a serial killer who had lost his marbles and decided to take out women who looked the same. Mac had tried to hunt him on her own and stop him from killing Ali, who was abducted as his last victim. She had succeeded in finding Ali and saving her, but almost got herself killed.

Lola had helped Hudson track Mac down. He would have never found her on his own. Lola was a wicked hacker and tracker. She could find anyone in the world and had some scary skills. Hudson hoped he never ended up on her bad side.

The whole situation with Lola had him questioning Mac and her history. At the moment, he was content to give her some space, but if they were going any further with their relationship, he wanted to know what he was getting into. He was already head over heels for Mac, but he was smart enough to go in with his eyes wide open, especially after last time. He silently wondered what he would have to do to truly earn her trust.

Hudson's ex-wife had an affair while he was deployed, leaving him devastated and very off-balance. Mac was the first woman he had ever let get this close, which scared him to death. He wasn't willing to walk away, but they never talked about the future or how that looked.

Then the military factor always put an interesting twist on relationships. She had been stationed at Fairchild for a while and would make rank soon, which usually meant she would have to move. He tried not to think about it, but it gnawed at the back of his consciousness.

He had never met a woman like Mac. She was strong, bullheaded, and could fight and handle a gun, but then she was also sweet, vulnerable, and caring, with serious trust issues. It was a lot to handle, but also intriguing and sexy as hell. Seeing her in that dominatrix outfit had almost sent him over the edge. He still couldn't get over how crazy he was about her.

After they were done getting clean and dry, he scooped her up in his arms and laid her on the bed. He simply couldn't get enough, taking his time exploring every inch of her soft skin. She was exquisite and always smelled delicious. After they were done, lying in each other's arms, panting after another mind-blowing orgasm, he looked at her and said, "So, what's the plan, beautiful?"

"I'm not sure yet," she admitted, "but I'm not done. I feel responsible for Alice and want to get justice for her and all the other victims. I think we're on to something; otherwise, the killer wouldn't have dumped us into the ocean. I know they're kicking me off the case, but that never stopped me before. What do you think?"

"Well, for starters, I think you might be a little crazy." He smiled at her. "But aside from that, I'm not convinced that all the victims are linked to this one killer. There are several variables that don't match up. That's not to say a single killer couldn't be responsible, but some of the victims are heavy men, and the woman in question is described as petite. How on earth could she overpower men and kill them with such force and then drag their bodies into the water to dispose of them?"

"You have some good points. She could have subdued them with drugs or restraints to use other objects to inflict the damage. The marks appear to be caused by a bullwhip, but we aren't sure what caused the ligature marks. Those are weird."

"Yeah, she could have subdued them, but how could she possibly transport them? Let's say, for argument's sake, she's your size or maybe even a little smaller. Even if she could transport the bodies in her car, how would she ever get them out of and into the water without help?" Hudson pointed out.

"I see where you're going with this. So, you're saying she has to have an accomplice?" Mac asked.

"It's the most likely explanation, and you know how I feel about Occam's Razor."

"Yeah, I know. Usually the simplest answer is the correct one," Mac said. "Do you think it's one of her submissives helping her with her deviant wants and needs, or do you think it's another killer she's teamed up with?"

"That's hard to say; it could be a number of combinations. Everything we know about this woman says she's self-confident and dominant in every sense of the word, but what else? Do you think she would allow someone to share her kills with her, or is her dominatrix act all a show and she's being controlled by a male killer?"

"It's hard to tell," Mac said. "When looking at the victimology, it almost appears that they're sometimes killing together, and sometimes they kill separately, which is weird. Almost like they're competing with each other. It happens when two dominant personalities feed off each other and have to one-up each other. It would almost be easier if it was a single person or a dominant and submissive, because there would only be one person in control, and there would be consistency. In this case, they're all over the map, and we may not have even scratched the surface on the body count."

"Do you think there have been other victims?"

"I definitely think they've killed before. Who knows how many? It could be a lot more than what we've found. I'm actually focusing on sexual sadism in my thesis. There are lust murderers, also known as erotophonophilia, which means that one or both of our murderers get aroused and, in most cases, get off by killing someone. It could also be a case of hybristophilia, which means that one of the people has a sexual attraction to the other because they commit crimes and is willing to help them carry out the murders. Either way, there's clearly a sexual component to this. The bodies all showed levels of sexual mutilation and, in some cases, sexual penetration."

"You said in some cases there was sexual penetration. Are the women the only ones being sexually penetrated?" Hudson asked.

"Not in all cases, which is a little strange. There's evidence of anal penetration with some of the male victims, but since they were all in water, there's no way to tell what they were penetrated with. If we have a male and female team, she could be having sex with the male victims prior to their death.

"Of course," Mac continued, "we can't rule out the man having sex with the men, whether on the receiving end or doing the penetrating. There are definite signs of genital mutilation in some victims, but not in all. For instance, according to the medical examiner Alice was raped prior to her death, but otherwise there was no mutilation. She was just strangled and killed. There were abrasions on her knees indicating that she was forced into a doggy-style position during the rape, and he may have strangled her at the same time."

"So, what do we know for sure?" Hudson asked. "It's great to speculate, but we have nothing without evidence."

"Well, we know that Mistress Gennavie was the last person to be seen with Collymore. Unfortunately, we don't know very much that we can call fact. We know there are differences in the way they kill—if, in fact, we are dealing with a couple. There's a lot of circumstantial evidence that may or may not link the bodies together. Just because they were found in water doesn't mean they weren't the product of different killers."

Hudson lay next to Mac with his hands laced behind his head. He stared at the ceiling, thinking about the case and the potential ramifications of staying on it. Mac was good at what she did, but her fascination with serial killers' demented and twisted minds worried him. He wondered if this line of work would lead to the end of her one day, or possibly the end of both of them. "Mac, what would you say if I asked you to leave this one alone?" Hudson asked tentatively.

"Why, don't you think I can solve this one? I know it's a tough case, but…" She let her voice trail off.

"I have no doubt that you'll go to the ends of the earth to catch this killer or killers, and then there'll be another case, and another. I'm just wondering what our future looks like with this type of career path."

"Well, first of all, I wasn't exactly asked to do this. The Air Force decided to put me on a task force, and you just don't say no to something like that. It would be career suicide. Also, I like to think we're making a difference here. What if we're able to stop this and save lives?"

"I'm not saying you're not doing good and important work, but you seem to be a serial-killer magnet. Every time we get close to a whack-job, they home in on you. I'm just not prepared to lose you," Hudson admitted with a pained look.

"I'm not going anywhere. Plus, you're here to protect me," she said, grinning.

"If only I could handcuff myself to you, then maybe I could keep you safe, but you're the most stubborn, bullheaded woman I know. Can you at least lie to me and tell me you'll be very careful?"

"Scout's honor," she said, holding up two fingers.

She knew she'd be in deep trouble for not staying off the case, but she just couldn't stop. Not yet.

CHAPTER
FORTY

THE NEXT DAY, Hudson and Mac headed home in his truck. They had met with Kibble and brought him up to date on everything they knew. He promised to keep them posted about the case. Kibble was upset when she explained what had happened. He seemed angry about the entire situation, and her insurance agent was at a loss.

This was her second totaled vehicle in the last two years. She hoped her insurance wouldn't drop her. She planned to pick up a rental vehicle and finish the paperwork when they got home. At a minimum, she hoped they would replace her little SUV. She still owed money on it and hoped they would appraise it high enough to pay off the loan, at the very least. Hudson offered to help in any way he could. He was so good to her. She wasn't sure how she had gotten so lucky.

On the ride back to Spokane, Mac was extremely quiet, lost in her own thoughts. She had promised Alice's uncle that she would find her killer, and it didn't sit well with her that she wouldn't be able to keep that promise. Anger rose in the pit of her stomach. She had a nagging feeling that she was seriously missing something.

The incident where Carter, the defense paralegal, may or may not have warned her to stay away from the case didn't sit right. What she knew about Carter didn't fit with violence or threats. She didn't even know if the case had to do with the military other than Ryan Collymore being an airman and Alice working on the base. They were the only links she was aware of. She hated a puzzle where the pieces didn't fit together.

Hudson was right—she would have a tough time letting this go, especially since she had nothing pending back home. This had been her main focus other than school and now she was left floundering. At least she would have time to replace her car and maybe take a vacation. She knew she couldn't make any hollow promises to let the case go but the thought stuck in her head. She hadn't gotten away for a long time. Actually, she couldn't remember when she had actually taken a vacation last.

Then it came to her. They really did need a vacation. *Is it normal to vacation in Amsterdam?* she wondered to herself. Maybe while they were overseas, she could see Lola. It had been years, and they had just now started to reconnect. They had to be very careful to ensure the family didn't catch wind of the reunion, but it could be done. She thought about that for a while. *Is it worth the risk?* She wasn't sure, but she definitely knew she missed her sister, and quite honestly, her sister could help with the case.

As soon as Hudson and Mac got home, she called her boss and told him she needed to take some leave and get away for a bit and then proposed her plan to Hudson.

"What do you mean you want to go to Amsterdam?" he asked.

"Is it too expensive?" she asked. "Or are you short on leave time? Is your passport expired?"

"No, nothing like that, but I thought we were going to leave this case alone," Hudson argued.

"Really, you can't leave it alone any more than I can. These people—or person—tried to kill us. Can you really rest easy knowing that killers are on the loose? Are you going to be fine just watching the body count go up?" Her face turned red, and she started to raise her voice.

"Don't get too excited," he said, lowering his voice to calm her. He would have been one hell of a hostage negotiator. He was always so cool under pressure. "Let's think about this first. We can't just let everyone know we're running off to Amsterdam. People aren't stupid, they'll know why we're going, and we're in the military. It's not like we can go overseas without a briefing from our leadership and OSI. There are threat assessments and things to be concerned with."

"I see your point," she said, taking several deep breaths, trying to get herself to relax. She loved that he could calm her down. She had always been driven and determined and when things weren't going well her temper would sometimes flare. She wasn't a hothead or anything, just passionate about certain subjects and stubborn as all get-out. "But it's the best lead we have right now. How else can we figure out who this woman is?" Mac argued.

"I'm not saying we can't go; what I'm saying is that we should probably plan a European vacation that just happens to have a stop in Amsterdam. We could stop off to meet my mom and fly out from there, if you want. With your sister being somewhere overseas, it would just make sense that we would go over to visit her, right?"

"Right," she replied, feeling nervous at the thought of meeting his mom. It wasn't that she didn't want to meet her, but the more people she brought into her life, the more people could potentially be in danger from this killer and her family. "Tell me about your mom," Mac said, coming over to sit next to Hudson on the couch.

"She's a wonderful woman, fiercely protective of her family, bullheaded, and she reads minds as a side hobby."

"What do you mean, she reads minds?" Mac asked, smiling.

"She always knows when something is going wrong or what I'm thinking. She was the same way with my brother. She knew how it would go down before anyone else did." Sadness settled into Hudson's eyes.

"I'm sorry about your brother. How about your father? Where is he?"

"I don't like talking about him. He left us when I was just a kid. My mom was left to raise us and pay off the mountain of debt he had left behind. He ran off with a woman half his age. It devastated my mom. She never really recovered from it and still hasn't remarried."

"Did she ever date anyone?" Mac asked.

"She has a partner, or at least that is what she calls him. We put that man through hell when we were younger. He came around a few years after our father left. No one was good enough for our mom, but he stuck it out. I really think he's the main reason my mom survived my brother's death." Hudson paused, thinking for a moment. "What about you, Mac? You rarely tell me anything about your family except the little I know about Lola."

"That's fair. I don't talk about them because it's complicated, and you'll never meet them no matter what happens between us," she stated with conviction.

"Are they in some kind of cult or something?" Hudson asked.

"Nothing like that. I'll just say that they're not healthy people, and it's not an environment you want to be in. I came into the military to get away from them, and keeping them and my sister's location a secret is imperative to everyone's safety."

The look that crossed her face scared Hudson. "What are they?" Hudson pushed. "Are we talking the Mafia?"

"No, but you're not far off. Now, please drop the subject. Are you coming to Amsterdam with me or not?" She looked him in the eyes, not leaving much room for argument.

"Mac, I'll go to the ends of the earth with you. I've saved over sixty days of leave and need to burn some or lose it. I owe my mom a visit, if you're up for it. She's in Kentucky, and we can fly overseas from there. What do you think?"

"Deal."

CHAPTER
FORTY-ONE

"WHAT DO YOU MEAN, you got rid of Mac?" Tank was seething at her.

"She was getting in the way," Gennavie said. "You said yourself that she was getting close, and that little note you left for her did nothing to dissuade her. It just made her come after me even more. That woman has balls; I'll give her that."

"But what if they track the note back to me or think I'm involved with this mess?" Tank asked. "I have a lot to lose."

"Well, you don't actually think I killed any of those people, do you?" she said, stroking his cheek. "I wouldn't hurt a fly."

He raised an eyebrow at her. "Really."

"Okay, so I like whips and chains and a little bit of torture, but I never take anyone further than they want to go. You like where I take you, don't you, lover?" She swooned, running one of her long, nylon-clad legs across his lap.

Her body was more than he had ever dreamed of. She looked like something out of *Playboy* magazine, dressed in her sheer red teddy that cupped her large, round breasts with red straps that pushed them up to full attention. The outfit showed off her taut pink nipples with matching thigh-highs attached to a garter cinched around her pretty little waist.

He lost all train of thought for a moment while she ran her nails through his hair. "Yes, I like what you do to me very much. Actually, more than I should because it makes me do things I shouldn't. But what about your husband?"

"What about him?" She looked at him like he'd asked about an insignificant issue.

"You're a married woman now. What if he finds out?" he asked, seriously questioning what she was doing with a man like him. He wasn't exactly *GQ* material. He wouldn't consider himself disgusting, but he certainly wasn't what most women would consider sexy. Well, except for his wife—she seemed to like how he looked, but they had been together since high school. She had loved him through thick and thin. She had sacrificed so much, giving up her career to follow him, and this was how he'd repaid her. All the growing pains and finally making a decent living, and now he was going to go screw it all up.

"He won't find out as long as you don't tell him." She ran her fingers through the hair on his chest. "You won't tell him, will you lover?"

"I'm not sure if we should keep this up," he said hesitantly. He had never intended to get involved with her. He was married, and so was she. The only difference was that it didn't seem to bother her but, it was really messing with him. Every time he talked with his wife or kids, he felt like the most horrible human on Earth. On the other hand, she was so damn irresistible, it was like a drug he was highly addicted to. He wondered if this was what a cocaine addiction felt like. He promised himself just one last time, and then it would be over.

"Oh, sure you can, sugar. You don't want to give little ol' me up and go back to that boring life with your boring wife." She smiled, running her tongue along his neck and nibbling on his ear.

"Um—" He could no longer think straight and closed his eyes. He wanted to be pissed about her comment about his wife, but she was right. They had become more like roommates than husband and wife. They rarely made love, and he had been so busy with his career that they had grown apart. He didn't blame her, but after having the kids and being a stay-at-home wife, she had gone from a sexy, confident cheerleader to a slightly overweight housewife. That had been okay with him until he had met his mistress. He could no longer remember how he had gotten here. He had once been a normal good man, husband, father—and now she had reduced him to... His mind wandered as she moved down his chest.

"All I need you to do is keep your ear to the ground. Tell me what you find out. Clearly this Mac chick has a hard-on for me, which just won't do," Gennavie said with a pout on her bright-red lips. "Now for your punishment for being such a bad boy." She smiled wickedly at him.

He thought, *What in hell is wrong with me*? until his cognitive thinking abilities left him all together.

CHAPTER
FORTY-TWO

AGENT BARDOT WAS SITTING in her office going over case files and figuring out what was happening with the bodies. She had come across some very interesting information about Technical Sergeant Evelyn McGregor, or Mac, as she was called. It was intriguing, considering the killers they were hunting. Mac was either involved or very good at being in the wrong place at the wrong time. She certainly had the resources to pull this off if she worked for her family.

"Ma'am." A lanky young agent with dark hair and a chiseled face walked into Agent Bardot's office. "We have new bodies."

"How many?" was all she asked Agent Weidman.

"Two, a man and woman. These may be unrelated murders. It was outside the normal MO. This couple was killed in their apartment, and it appears to be much more brutal than previous murders, but there are also similarities."

"Run me through everything you know so far," Bardot said.

"The couple was well-known and liked in the BDSM community. It appears that there was some discrepancy as to whether they're a couple or employer and employee. The woman was known as Lady Carina, and she catered to people who wanted to explore alternative lifestyles. She worked with single people and sometimes couples.

According to her assistant, she was known as a sex therapist who helped people get past their inhibitions and open up to a different way of communicating."

"She was busy enough to have an assistant?" Bardot looked intrigued.

"Yes, she was actually a world-renowned professional dominatrix," Weidman said.

"Isn't this the same woman that Mac and Hudson went to see a few nights ago, right before they got pushed off the pier in Tacoma?"

"I'm not sure. I was unaware of a meeting."

"Interesting, yes. Mac told me that she met with this Lady Carina the night they took a swim in the drink, which leads me to believe they're connected. What are the discrepancies?"

"Well, for starters, the bodies weren't submerged in water. They were left in the apartment, and there was rage in these murders. The other murders seemed to have more of a sexual component, but this one was different. The killer lost control, or at least it appears that way," Weidman offered.

"You said it was a couple. Who was the man?"

"Well, that's the interesting part. There's no way our suspect took them down by herself. The guy is Andre Wallace." He pulled a picture from his file and handed it to her.

A massive mountain of a man stared back at her. He was bigger than Hudson, Mac's partner. *Could Hudson have subdued this man?* She pondered the idea. Not many people could.

"What did the woman look like?" Bardot asked.

He handed her a photo of Lady Carina. Alive, she had been a striking beauty with classic features. She looked like someone who should have been on the cover of a high-fashion magazine, minus all the tattoos and the outfit. "Those are the pictures of them prior to the attack, and here are the crime scene photos," Weidman said, spreading both sets of photos in front of her on her desk.

The bodies lay on a plush gray carpet that was sprayed with blood. Both bodies were bound at the ankles and wrists, but the overkill was impressive. The blood splatter made crazy designs against the cream-colored walls. There was blood pooled under both bodies, lying next to each other in a *V* pattern with their heads touching. The big man had his head smashed in, but the woman had taken the worst of it. The slash marks were long and deep across her body. Her flesh was torn open along her stomach, legs, and arms. The killer had taken a blade and disfigured her face. It felt like the killer was making a statement about the woman. The man was just in the wrong place at the wrong time.

"Do you think our killer is tying up loose ends?" Bardot asked.

"Looks that way, but why change their MO and be so very obvious about it? There's definitely something wrong with this picture," Weidman observed.

"Almost like someone is leading us to the red-headed woman, or maybe she's just getting sloppy," Bardot theorized.

"It's possible but doubtful unless she somehow thinks she's invincible. The killer or killers went to great measures to clean the bodies and get rid of the evidence. The bodies were cleaned postmortem, and the cleaning supplies were found under the sink. We hoped to find evidence on the wet sponge but realized it had been put in the microwave to kill any bacteria or lingering DNA. The killer had also worn gloves or maybe a full-body suit, since we couldn't find even skin follicles."

She decided to try out her theory on Weidman. "What do you think about Mac?"

"Well—" He paused thoughtfully. "The Air Force sergeant who's working the Collymore case doesn't fit. As far as I'm aware, she's been forthcoming and helpful in the investigation. Plus, how do we explain someone else pushing her off the pier?"

"I don't know, but something doesn't feel right about her involvement in this case. It seems like she's in all the wrong places at all the right times."

"I don't know, we've been staring at the few pictures we have of the redhead, and the body types are different. The Air Force woman is curvier and certainly isn't a redhead. What makes you think she might be involved?" Weidman asked.

"I pulled Mac's military security clearance and background check. It felt odd to me that the killer would suddenly make contact with Mac."

"Makes sense. So what did you find?"

"She's changed her name, but if the documentation is correct, she has family very high up in the Mexican drug cartel, and part of their operations are active here in Seattle. I have some calls to the DEA to see if they know of any contact between Mac and her family. Her security clearance said there was no evidence that she had contact with the family, which was why she was allowed to remain on active duty. Contact or not, I've heard rumors that her mother is a brutal sociopath who will take out anyone who gets in the way."

Weidman whistled. "Damn."

CHAPTER
FORTY-THREE

THEY BOARDED a plane at the butt crack of dawn. Mac was far from a morning person and had yet to consume her full pot of required coffee before functioning for the day. She stood behind Hudson, waiting to get to their seats in the back of the plane. She felt terrible for him, with his back hunched and his head cocked to one side to fit inside the small sardine can of a plane.

It was actually an average-size Delta Boeing 747, but Hudson didn't quite fit. Mac thought there were definitely benefits to being small. On the other hand, she envied Hudson's ability to reach just about anything in the highest cabinets in her kitchen. He never needed a stool or had to climb up on the counters.

They finally got to their seats. Mac slid in first so Hudson could have room to put his legs out into the aisle when the stewardess wasn't passing by. Mac was feeling very fidgety. She figured she would have all day to calm down before they arrived in Lexington to meet his mother.

Hudson was squirming next to her, trying to get comfortable and having a hell of a time doing so. She was looking out the window, getting her nerves in check. It wasn't like she didn't want to meet Hudson's mom. She sounded like a pleasant enough woman. She was just fearful of getting close to people. It was bad enough that she was falling in love with Hudson, which put him in danger, but what if they found out about his mom and went after her to get to Mac? She would do anything to protect the people she cared about. All she wanted was a normal life and maybe kids one day, but that just wasn't in the cards.

Mac was lost in thought as the plane started to pull away from the gate. When she finally looked over at Hudson, his face had gone ashen, and he had a white-knuckle death grip on the armrests. "What's the matter?" she asked, suddenly alert to danger.

He grumbled under his breath, "I hate flying."

"You're in the Air Force and you've deployed overseas. How could you be afraid of flying?" She looked perplexed.

"I just am, okay? I've worked on aircraft before and know how many things can go wrong with them. It's a very healthy fear, okay?" he said through gritted teeth.

"Okay, okay, I didn't mean anything by it. We all have our fears. Is there anything I can do to help?" she asked, giving her voice a calming tone.

"Nope, just have to get this death trap in the air, and then I'll be fine," he grumbled.

"Give me your hand," she instructed right before they took off. He slowly released his hand from the armrest, leaving a large indent behind. She took his hand and started running her finger over his palm in a circular motion. "Now, close your eyes and breathe. Just focus on the sound of my voice and breathe in, hold, and breathe out."

Surprisingly, he did as instructed. She thought he would fight her on it.

"Okay, now let all the air out of your lungs and breathe in again." She could see him tense as the plane began to lift off the tarmac and into the air. She kept talking to him in her most soothing voice, and eventually, he calmed once they were at a cruising altitude.

"Thank you," he said as they settled in for their five-hour flight. He was thankful for the layover in Atlanta, but was not looking forward to taking off again, and the landing was even worse. He felt ridiculous being afraid of flying, but he couldn't help the panic attacks. He had tried different ways to get past it, but nothing had really worked, though he had felt better for the first time with Mac by his side. It was weird how much of a calming effect she had on him.

They finally reached their destination after a very long day. They both looked exhausted. Mac's hair was a little wild, and Hudson thought she looked cute that way. They worked their way down to baggage claim to pick up their luggage. She knew she was in the south when she saw a sign for Blue Grass Airport. "My mom should be waiting on the main level," Hudson said.

She had no idea what to expect. Mac felt the nervousness rise in the pit of her stomach as they rode the escalator to the main floor. There was a mass of people in and around the baggage claim area. Mac had no idea who she was looking for. He had described her as a kind woman, but they hadn't gotten into physical descriptions.

Hudson released her hand and left her standing there as he walked over to a tiny woman. She couldn't have been any taller than five feet. She had dark-brown hair and a slightly weathered face. She had the same high cheekbones, olive skin, and large eyes that Hudson had, but in a much smaller package. Mac couldn't help but smile at the scene unfolding in front of her. Hudson had dropped his bag, bending in half to engulf his mother in a huge bear hug, lifting her slightly off the floor. "Put me down," she said with a wide smile on her face.

Hudson carefully placed her back on the floor as she adjusted her glasses. Her son was smiling, showing off his dimples. "Mom, I want you to meet Mac." He looked over at the woman he loved, still standing frozen in place. He took a few steps over to her, grabbed her hand, and pulled her over to his mother. "Mac, meet my mom."

Mac finally snapped out of her daze and extended her hand.

Hudson's mom smiled and pulled her into a warm hug. "It's very nice to meet you, Mac. I've heard a lot about you," she said. "Now, let's get you two out of here and feed you. You look like you've lost some weight, Gavin. Have you been eating enough?" she prodded.

"I'm fine, Mom. I eat plenty."

Mac simply smiled and walked along as the two caught up. "So, tell me all about yourself," Momma Hudson said. "I want to know everything."

"Oh my, where do I start?" Mac said to avoid the question.

"I have a good feeling about you," Momma Hudson declared. "Always listen to your gut is what my momma always told me, and it has never steered me wrong."

Hudson rolled his eyes. "Give her a little time to get to know you, Mom."

"Oh yes, of course, we wouldn't want to scare her off. Lord knows when you might find another like her." Momma Hudson beamed at Mac.

Mac couldn't help but like her spirit. They drove back to Momma Hudson's house. She had moved after her husband had left with her younger son. Hudson had never lived in the house, but he had taken leave and helped her move in. Unfortunately, he had overdosed on drugs, leaving Momma Hudson to live alone.

They walked in to find a cozy little cottage tucked back into a lush forest with towering trees surrounding the property. Mac could hear the sound of a creek running somewhere near the house. She absolutely loved the place and wished she could find something like it for herself. Her little house was not nearly as secluded and didn't have the beauty. *Maybe one day*, Mac thought.

"Isn't it nice here?" Hudson came up behind her and wrapped his arms around her, engulfing her in his warm chest.

"One day I'd like to settle in a place like this, far off the grid, where we can enjoy the sounds of the forest," Mac said.

"You, settle down? I never thought it would be possible," he said, smiling.

"There's a lot more about me than you know. One day, it would be wonderful to escape from everything and maybe have a couple of kids."

Hudson stood behind her without moving, realizing he was holding his breath. "Mac"—he finally released the air trapped in his lungs—"would you really be happy with that life? I know there are things I don't know about you, but would you ever be willing to have a life like that with me?"

Mac spun around to face him. The look in his eyes was genuine and a little fearful. "Hudson, I would love that more than you could know, but there are reasons why I can't, at least not right now. I'll tell you all about it one day, but right now, I just want to catch these killers and stop them from hurting anyone else."

"I'm trying to be understanding, but there will always be bad guys out there, and it isn't your sole responsibility to stop them all."

"I know. I just need you to be patient and give me time. Do you think you can let me work through this?" Mac looked at him with pleading eyes.

"If it means I get to be with you, I'll give you anything you need," he said warmly. She loved it when he smiled and showed his dimples.

"Are you guys almost ready for dinner?" Momma Hudson called from the kitchen.

"Absolutely starving," Mac responded. "Can I help?"

"Oh no, it's almost done. Gavin, honey, could you set the table for me?" Momma Hudson asked.

"Sure, Ma," he responded as he busied himself getting the plates and utensils.

Mac stood to the side, feeling a little out of place and very envious. She had grown up with a very different mother who had never cooked her a meal, especially not one that smelled like the amazing aroma coming from Momma Hudson's kitchen. She envied Hudson for having such a wonderful family. Even though it was a little broken and they had suffered a significant loss, they still had each other. Mac felt very alone in the world at that moment.

"Oh, Mac honey, what's the matter? You look like you saw a ghost." Momma Hudson came up and patted Mac's cheek.

"Nothing, everything's fine. The food smells amazing. Can I help you bring things to the table?" Mac asked hopefully, needing the distraction.

"Sure, hon. Can you grab the bread and that jug of sweet tea over there?" Momma Hudson said in her southern drawl.

They sat down to a wonderful meal. Mac thought her pants would burst if she ate another bite, but the food was so good. *This must be what people mean when they refer to good southern cooking*, Mac thought. It was mouthwatering, and Mac found herself wanting to stay as long as possible.

The two days they had to spend with Momma Hudson flew by. Mac had learned so much about the mountain of a man that she was with. He had been an adorable child and had been six feet tall by the time he reached middle school, full of mischief and wonder. He and his brother used to get into all kinds of trouble together.

Momma Hudson sometimes slipped into a conversation as if her younger son was still alive and out having an adventure somewhere. Mac understood and thought it was likely easier to cope with the loss that way. She couldn't imagine losing a child. If the world was a just and right place, parents would never outlive their children.

Hudson hauled their luggage out to Momma Hudson's Ford Taurus. It was a cute little vehicle with a glass butterfly hanging from the rearview mirror. It fit Momma Hudson perfectly, but didn't quite fit her oversized son.

They all piled out of the car at the airport, exchanging hugs and goodbyes. "Now, you two keep me posted on wedding plans. I want me some grandbabies soon," Momma Hudson said.

"Wow, Mom. Mac and I haven't gotten that far yet. Slow down," Hudson protested.

"Don't tell me to slow down. I'm not getting any younger, and I need to be able to spoil me some grandbabies," she responded stubbornly.

Mac just smiled. She had picked up on the "yet" in Hudson's statement. She was going to miss Momma Hudson and hoped she would get the chance to see her again one day. She liked that he was hopeful for their future, even if she wasn't so sure.

CHAPTER
FORTY-FOUR

BARDOT COULDN'T SHAKE the feeling that Mac and Hudson were somehow involved. Maybe they'd staged the incident at the pier. *Is that even possible?* she wondered. She didn't believe in coincidence, and the evidence pointed back to those two. Once Mac and Hudson had left town, the murders stopped cold.

The deaths of Lady Carina and her bodyguard Andre had happened around the same time that Mac and Hudson had left town, but there was no telling if they had made a quick, murderous stop on their way out. She had talked to Kibble about it, and he hadn't been able to confirm Mac's whereabouts at the time of the murder.

What bothered Bardot the most was what Mac or Hudson had to gain. There was no way Mac had killed Lady Carina by herself. Not with Andre there. He could have easily overpowered her or anyone else, for that matter. On top of that, she had just been notified that Mac and Hudson had left the country together. Thankfully, her contacts told her they were headed to the Netherlands, where the US had an extradition treaty.

She had contacts in Amsterdam on alert to keep her eyes on the couple. She wanted to know what they were up to and who they were meeting with while they were there. She suspected it might be people in her family, though she had problems gaining intel on the elusive cartel. If Mac was involved with her family, they hadn't found evidence of it, but they were still looking.

Agent Weidman walked back into the office. "Ma'am, the evidence response team didn't find any prints, fibers, or forensic evidence on Lady Carina or Mr. Andre Wallace. It appears that both bodies were cleaned, and the assailants wore gloves. We found synthetic red hair that came from a high-end wig. It may match the hair found in the truck that pushed Mac and Hudson into the water. We're trying to trace where the wig came from. We have people interviewing the shop owners of everyone in the area that sells these types of wigs."

"Good work," Bardot said. "Did anything come back from building surveillance or traffic cameras?"

"No. Apparently they had to have entered from either the service elevator or the fire escape. The only cameras are in the apartment complex's lobby, but not on the outside."

"That's frustrating."

"Agreed. So what's our next step?" Agent Weidman asked.

"Unfortunately, we're still at square one on this. Keep looking into Lady Carina and Andre's backgrounds and keep me posted. There has to be something that leads us back to the woman renting space from her and how she's connected to Mac and Hudson. There has to be a record of her somewhere. Find her clients or someone willing to talk about her. Even if it was a cash-only business that she was running, there has to be someone that knows who this phantom woman is. Find the redhead, and we find the key to unraveling this mess."

"On it, ma'am."

CHAPTER
FORTY-FIVE

AFTER OVER ELEVEN hours of flying, Mac and Hudson finally landed in Dusseldorf, Germany, and then boarded a train to Amsterdam. They were both wrecked. It wasn't the first time either of them had been overseas, but it certainly had been a bit stressful with Hudson's lack of love for flying and his large body. The international flight had roomier seats and fit his body better, but they were both stiff and exhausted under the circumstances.

It was only 1100 hours when they arrived and made their way downtown for some food. They had read about a place called the Pancake Bakery that travelers had raved about online. "Can you believe they have bacon-infused pancakes?" Hudson said with a tired grin.

"I know, I'm starving," she said, forcing her eyes open.

As promised, the food was terrific.

After filling their bellies, they headed to the Radisson Blu Hotel in the Amsterdam City Center. The buildings were tall and historic-looking, surrounded by water in almost every direction. The city was enchanting, but they were both way too tired to appreciate it. Check-in wasn't until 1500 hours, but they figured they might be able to convince the staff to let them in early. Even if there was a fee, it would be totally worth it. They were worthless; neither one had slept well on the airplane.

They walked up to the front desk to inquire. Behind the highly polished dark wood counter, a young, thin blond woman welcomed them in almost flawless English. "What may I do for you?" she asked.

"We have reservations for tonight. Is there any way we can check in early?" Mac asked hopefully.

"Let me see what I can do," she said with a polite smile as she typed on her computer. "Your room will actually be ready in about twenty minutes. Would you like to sit in the café until it's ready?"

"That would be wonderful," Hudson said, feeling as if he would fall over at any moment.

It only took ten minutes before they were in their room. It was a simple, elegant suite and resembled most hotels they had stayed in in the US. Mac had been able to use some of her points to upgrade to a suite during their stay.

"I'm going to grab a quick shower and knock off the travel grime. Would you like to join me?" Hudson asked.

"Sure. You go get started, and I'll be right there," Mac said, stifling a huge yawn.

He went into the bathroom and started the oversized shower. It was a beautiful walk-in with high double showerheads, which he really appreciated. He hated staying at places where he had to crouch just to get under the shower's spray. They had even supplied shampoo, conditioner, and body soap. *Nice*, he thought, not wanting to scrounge through his bag for supplies.

He went out to check on Mac and stifled a laugh. She was spread out on the bed, sound asleep with one of her boots half-untied and dangling from her foot. The lights were still on, and she was purring softly. He walked over, shut them off, and slipped her boots off, tucking her under the covers. He figured they would both do better after a good night's sleep. He just hoped they wouldn't wake up at 0300 hours and be completely messed up.

He went back into the bathroom, shut off the shower, gave up on the idea, and lay down next to Mac. He was out cold as soon as his head hit the pillow.

As predicted, he stirred at 0200 hrs to find the spot next to him empty. He opened his eyes to find Mac sitting on one of the oversized chairs thumbing through her computer. "How long have you been up?" Hudson asked.

"Not long. Sorry for passing out on you. I was too exhausted," Mac said, looking back at her screen.

"I was right there with you," he said. "What are you looking at?"

"Well, I put in a call to Lola. She's doing some research about the underbelly of the Amsterdam Red Light District. She actually said she might be able to meet us here. Apparently she's on assignment somewhere in Germany and may be able to get to us. It would be really wonderful to see her. It's been too long."

"That would be great. I'd like to meet your family," he said.

"We just have to be careful. We can't go running around making any noise, especially where she's concerned. Remember, she's in hiding for a reason."

"I know there's this huge secret about your family, but really, how bad could it be?" Hudson asked.

The SAT phone rang, interrupting their conversation. Mac held up her finger, indicating that he should be quiet. "Hi Lola, what are you doing up at this hour? How are you doing?"

"I have my reasons. And I'm doing the same as the last time we talked," Lola said.

"Okay, is there something wrong?"

"Only that the FBI is looking into you and seems to know your location and pretty much everything about you. It appears they know about me, but not where I am," Lola said, sounding irritated.

"But I thought you were working for the FBI in some capacity," Mac said, sounding confused.

"Yeah, but I'm one of their unknown assets. Mac, what the hell have you gotten yourself into, and what have you gotten me into?" Lola huffed.

"Lola, the last thing I wanted to do was blow your cover. I had no intentions of that. I have no idea why the FBI is looking at me. It has to be about the killer who has a hard-on for me."

There was silence on the line. "What the hell do you mean a killer is interested in you? I thought he was dead," Lola said.

"No, that guy is dead. This is a new case. That's why I wondered if you could look into the BDSM scene in Amsterdam, and it's also why Hudson and I are here. I hoped I could see you for a little while as a side benefit."

"What are you, some kind of a killer magnet? I know you're cute, but come on," Lola said, sounding completely bewildered. "I know I'm a bum magnet who likes to date men that are really bad for me, but this is a whole different level. What does Hudson think of your little love affair with these killers?"

"He took me home to meet his momma, so I guess he's okay with it."

"Well, well, is it getting serious between you two?" Lola teased. "Might I have a brother-in-law sometime soon?"

"You know very well how impossible that is," Mac shot back, trying not to give away what she was talking about with Hudson in earshot.

"Oh, hon, live a little. You can't fear her for the rest of your life," Lola said.

"Oh yes I can, and so can you. It doesn't do either of us any good to get sucked back into that life or, worse yet, get killed for what we know. Nope," Mac said with determination. "If I were to do what you suggest, that puts him and his family at risk. It's bad enough I have him tangled up with this case and almost got him killed."

"What do you mean, you almost got him killed?" Lola asked, a little startled that her sister was in this kind of a mess again. She figured that her sister would want to run away from monsters, not hunt them down, considering their family history.

"We were in Tacoma, talking at the pier, and someone put my little SUV in the drink. Thanks to Hudson, we got out of the vehicle just fine, but my almost-new vehicle was totaled. Of course, the FBI still has it as far as I know."

"Okay, so you've got me. Tell me how I can help with this case, but this is the last time. I'm out of the business of saving your ass, especially if there's a possibility that you could lead our family back to me," Lola said.

"You've got a deal. Is there any way we can meet?" Mac asked. She really missed her sister. If she could just see her one more time before they both had to go back into hiding, she would consider that a win.

"Yeah, I'll be in touch," Lola said, and hung up before Mac could reply.

CHAPTER
FORTY-SIX

VINCENT PACED THE ROOM. They had fought yet again about what to do next, and Gennavie had stormed out.

He actually did love his wife and wanted to protect her, but she was being reckless. If she would just listen—but no, she thought she was invincible. He was, without question, the more level-headed of the two. Maybe he could talk some sense into her.

He had no idea where she was at the moment, and he was worried she would go out hunting to blow off steam and get caught. He had thought he was tired of her, but he missed her terribly now that she had disappeared. She was the only one who understood his evil side and the first person he had ever been able to talk to about his darkest thoughts, needs, and desires.

Where the hell is she? he wondered, slamming his fist against the wall. He knew they only had circumstantial evidence against them at best. They had gone a little far with Lady Carina and Andre. It had been a long time since he had killed for rage and left the body on dry land. That could come back to haunt them. He wondered if it would one day.

He took comfort in knowing that his beautiful bride couldn't possibly be impulsive enough to go AWOL from the military. A charge of absence without leave from the military could be severe and could land her in a court-martial. That wouldn't be good for either of them, and could lead the authorities to take a closer look at the two of them.

At least, he really hoped she wouldn't leave. He really wasn't sure what she was capable of. He knew his limits, but wasn't entirely comfortable with hers. He grabbed his keys and wallet; it was time to find her and knock some sense into her before doing something really stupid. He tried her phone for the hundredth time, but it went straight to voicemail.

On the beach, Gennavie's toes sank into the soft sand as she sat lost in thought. She had found this place when she first got here and, thankfully, had never revealed its location to anyone. She knew he wouldn't find her unless she wanted him to. It was her thinking spot, and she really needed to get this one figured out. Her enlistment would be up soon, and she could just walk away into the night with an honorable discharge and everything.

She had really enjoyed being Mistress Gennavie, but there was nothing wrong with reinventing herself again. Maybe she could become someone else entirely. Her uncle had made her disappear once, and she knew he could do it again, but to where? Was it even necessary to disappear, or could she just get rid of her alter ego?

Vincent searched for hours, going to all of their favorite haunts, hoping she would materialize somewhere. Her phone was still off, and he was getting worried. Not because she couldn't handle herself; on the contrary, he pitied anyone who tried to mess with her. He had seen her take down Andre without much effort. It had impressed him and excited him to watch how she used her body as leverage to sink the syringe into his neck. Most people underestimated her, and it was a huge mistake when they realized she was capable of anything.

CHAPTER
FORTY-SEVEN

MORNING FINALLY CAME with the most beautiful sunrise Mac could remember. The Netherlands was certainly stunning this time of year, with rays of sunshine reflecting off the water. They walked out of their hotel to find the streets had impressive hanging baskets of flowers and gardens at every turn. It was nothing shy of breathtaking. She wished they could take some time to explore the area.

Mac had done some previous research and found that most people spoke Dutch but were also fluent in English, which was a good thing since Lola had texted her the name and location of a contact that could help them navigate the city and possibly open some doors.

They walked down the street, ate breakfast at a local café, and waited for the time to pass. Their contact was supposed to find them at the café within an hour. They sat back and people-watched as the crowds strolled by. It felt relaxing and almost wrong that they were there in order to find out about a murderous woman, or at least that was what they suspected she was.

A bald man with a large nose and slightly crooked teeth came over and sat next to Mac at the table. "You must be Mac," he said by way of introduction.

"And you are?" Mac asked, watching Hudson bow his back defensively.

"I'm Finn. Your sister sent me. Boy, you two look a lot alike, but you're polar opposites." He was staring at her, making her feel uncomfortable. Finally, he grinned broadly. "I must make you uneasy, yes. Excuse my staring. And you are?" he asked, looking over at Hudson.

Hudson extended his hand. "I'm here to help Mac."

"Does Here To Help Mac have a name?" Finn asked, sounding a bit like a smartass.

"Hudson," he said, sounding slightly irritated.

"Okay, Hudson, what would you and the beautiful Mac like to know?" he asked, focusing on her. "Has anyone told you that you and your sister could be like that dark and light, yin-yang symbol thing? You are both equally beautiful, but she is light, and you are dark. It is quite striking, no?"

"Yes, Lola and I do look a lot alike. So, what can you tell us about the Red Light District and how we can find someone who might train a professional dominatrix?" Mac asked.

Hudson couldn't believe this guy was blatantly hitting on Mac right in front of him. He knew it was a different culture, but he wasn't very fond of this part. The guy wasn't very big but had a massive set of balls. He actually almost looked homeless. He wore old jeans and a ratty sweatshirt and was sporting an impressively bushy beard with a bald head.

"I work undercover in the Red Light District. It is my job to know what happens there and to who," Finn said simply.

"Very nice; remind me to thank Lola. What can you tell us about the BDSM industry here in Amsterdam?" Mac asked.

"Well, it is vast. You can get anything you want at a price. The sky has no limits in the RLD. Are you looking for something or someone in particular?" Finn asked, raising one of his bushy eyebrows.

"No, this isn't for us," Mac said. "We're looking for information about a woman who's now in the United States. She was trained here as a professional mistress and now operates in Seattle. She has unique features that we hope will shed some light on who exactly she is."

"I see," Finn said thoughtfully. "Well, Ms. Mac, the one and only Goddess Z is the woman you seek. She is like the godfather or, in her case, the godmother of the sex trade. Nothing happens in the RLD without her knowledge. You should meet her."

"Can you introduce us?" Mac asked.

"Well, yes, of course," Finn said with a slightly creepy grin on his face.

"Um, okay, so when can we meet her?" Hudson interjected.

"Tonight should do. There is a party. Do you go undercover?" Finn asked with a goofy grin on his face.

"Yes," Mac replied. "We can go undercover. What would you suggest we go as?"

"Well, a dom and sub, of course," Finn responded like it was an everyday affair.

Mac looked over at Hudson, and he rolled his eyes. He hadn't been a fan the last time they had done that, except of her outfit. If Mac showed up in that outfit, this guy wouldn't leave her alone. In his opinion, it should be illegal for her to wear it, except maybe when they were alone. The problem was that Finn would also be there, and he was already hitting on Mac.

CHAPTER
FORTY-EIGHT

THEY MET Finn that night in the middle of the RLD. Mac had purposely dressed more conservatively for the occasion—which still elicited a lewd comment from Finn, but at least he wouldn't be ogling her breasts all night long. She still wore the leather skirt and a pair of knee-high boots, but had on a top that covered her ample chest. The last thing she wanted was to draw too much attention, but she still needed to fit in with the crowd. Hudson took it down a notch; he'd left his leather mask and dog collar back at the hotel and came to the party with a leather jacket and worn jeans, looking no less the badass.

They had never seen anything like it. Finn stopped in front of the Moulin Rouge, which blatantly advertised erotica and sex shows. There were large windows advertising peep shows, and some of the windows had naked or half-naked people standing in them. They passed by the Casa Rosso, the oldest live sex theater in Amsterdam.

Mac found it interesting how in the United States, they viewed sex as somewhat taboo or at the very least hid it away, but in Amsterdam, they put their sexuality on full display. Prostitution was legal and seemed to be a booming industry. There was no shame in anyone's game as they walked into the Moulin Rouge. She didn't know what to expect and was attempting to keep an open mind.

Inside resembled a strip club in the States, except the woman on stage had a young man tied to a chair in the middle of her platform and was using him to enhance her show. According to Finn, you could go up to the bar and order anything you liked, and most likely you would receive it. If not, the bartender would make you a counteroffer. This would go on until both parties were satisfied with the arrangements. Mac found it fascinating that they were negotiating for other people to do things. She wondered if there was free will and if the woman and men involved agreed to do certain things. She wondered if the bartender kept a list detailing what services each person was willing to provide.

Mac's interest was seriously piqued. She loved studying human behavior and had the desire to start asking thousands of questions, but she knew she had to stay focused.

Finn headed up a back stairwell with Hudson right behind him and Mac trailing behind. She was still busy looking around her captivating environment when she felt a hand on her ass. Two men had come up behind her.

"Hey sexy, where do you think you're going? My friend and I want a lap dance," a tall blond man said, his hand still planted firmly on her backside.

"Back off," she growled.

His friend grabbed her arm and turned her around so she was facing the blond man. He wasn't very big, but he still had a firm grip. The man who was now standing behind her had his shaggy brown hair pressed against the side of her face as he slid his body behind hers and pressed his flat chest against her back. She could smell cigarettes and booze on his breath as he wrapped his hands around the front of her waist.

The tall blond man stepped into her space and dipped his head down. "I said we want to party."

"And I said back off if you know what's good for you."

"I don't think so," the tall blond man said with a sneer.

"Don't say I didn't warn you." She lifted her heeled boot off the ground and smashed it into the man's foot.

He howled in pain but didn't take a step back. "You bitch. How dare you," he screamed as he lifted his hand to strike.

Hudson and Finn turned around, realizing Mac was no longer with them. "Oh shit," Finn muttered.

"Don't worry, she's got this," Hudson said with a smile.

"Shouldn't we help her?" Finn said, sounding worried.

"Just watch; you won't believe what she can do," Hudson said, putting his hand on Finn's shoulder to keep him from interfering. He knew he had a little bit of a sick side, but he loved watching her fight. He had to admit it was the biggest turn-on he had ever experienced.

Mac grabbed the man's hand before it struck her face and twisted his wrist back to a very uncomfortable angle. The man hollered in pain. The guy behind her didn't seem to know what to do, so he lifted her off the ground by the waist, trying to get her away from his friend. This gave her just the right amount of distance to smash the toe of her boot into the man's genitals, watching the man crumble to the ground.

The man behind her set her back down, allowing her the leverage to slam the back of her head into his nose, feeling the satisfying crunch as his cartilage broke. He let go, stepping back to grab at his broken face. Blood was gushing through his fingers.

A third man stepped forward. "Hey, what the hell do you think you're doing?" a large biker asked, growling down at her. He looked to be almost twice her height, which wasn't exactly uncommon.

Finn started down the stairs again, and Hudson grabbed his shoulder and shook his head no. Mac whirled around to face him with a wild look in her eyes. She positioned herself in a fighting stance with one foot in front of her and the other squared at an angle to give her the best leverage. She knew this one would be hard to take down.

She could feel her heart pounding in her chest as she looked the man over for vulnerabilities. He had a large, soft stomach that hung over a giant belt buckle. She thought the kneecaps might be her best approach since there was no way she could reach his head or face, and he'd already seen her take the other guy out by kicking him in the balls.

"Not you. Them," the biker said, pointing at the two men on the ground. "It's forbidden for anyone to assault our ladies," he said as he grabbed the two men on the floor by their shirt collars and dragged them out of the establishment.

Mac stood there for a moment, feeling relieved that she didn't have to fight the biker. She turned to find both Hudson and Finn grinning at her.

"Damn, girl, that was hot," Finn said, voicing what Hudson was thinking.

"Shut up."

CHAPTER
FORTY-NINE

MAC PASSED the two men on the stairs with their mouths still slightly open and took the lead. She walked to the top of the stairwell and looked back at Finn, who pointed his finger to the left. She followed the hall to the left,

where they were met by a large bodyguard who took up over three-quarters of the hallway.

"State your business, Finn," he grumbled.

"Hey dude, how you been?" Finn asked the oversized human.

The mountain of a man just stared back at him. Finally, he asked, "Who are these two?"

"These are just some friends of mine looking to do some business with Goddess Z," Finn said like it was an everyday occurrence.

"You know damn well that she doesn't do drop-ins," the mountain said, broadening his chest even further, which didn't seem possible.

"Oh, come on, she'll like these two. They'll be fun for her," Finn argued.

Mac and Hudson looked at each other uncomfortably, wondering what they were getting themselves into.

"You stay here, no funny business. I'll go check," the mountain said, and walked down the hall to the door at the very end. He knocked three times and waited, holding a parade-rest stance with his hands firmly laced behind his back. Mac wondered if he had served. A soft voice beckoned him into the room, and he disappeared. Moments later, he came back out with a slight smirk on his face. "She will permit you five minutes, and that is all," Mountain declared.

"We'll take it," Finn declared, and started forward with Mac and Hudson on his heels. Mountain stopped them at the door and patted everyone down. No one was armed. The Netherlands had stringent gun laws, and it was nearly impossible to get one into the country, so Mac and Hudson had agreed to leave theirs in the States. Mountain took a little too long patting Mac down, so Hudson growled at him. Mountain raised his hands in defeat and stepped aside.

The room they walked into was by far the classiest thing in the place, and inside sat the goddess. She was draped from head to toe in a light cream color. Her stockings had an almost invisible line up the back with matching heels, and she wore a skin-tight mini dress with a plunging neckline and a gold design running through it. Mac wondered exactly how she kept herself in place without exposing her breasts. The look was topped off with a sheer, floor-length shawl. It was quite the stunning statement and gave her the appearance of royalty.

"I understand you would like to see me," she said, strutting toward the trio with her large blue-gray eyes painted in beautiful shades to match her ensemble. Her blond hair had a tinge of blue-gray laced through it and was braided on either side and swept down her left shoulder. She was quite striking with her flawless porcelain skin, light colors, and her bold red lips and fingernails. Mac found herself staring at this woman.

Mac finally found her voice. "Yes, we wanted to ask you some questions."

"Ah, I see. You two are curious. Would you like a session with the goddess?" she said as she circled Mac and Hudson, admiring her next playthings.

"Not exactly," Mac said.

"Well then, why are you wasting my time? I am a very busy woman."

"We wondered if you could help us find information on a woman who used to work here," Mac explained.

"Oh, well, that is disappointing," Goddess Z said with a slight pout.

"What's disappointing?" Mac asked.

"That you will not play with me. It is an experience you will never forget," she said.

"I'm sure it would be, but unfortunately, we aren't able to at this time," Mac said, trying to stroke her ego so she would cooperate.

"Fine. What do you wish to know?" Goddess Z said in her thick Dutch accent.

"We're looking for information about a woman who was trained here in Amsterdam to become a professional dominatrix. She has a small build, and either has long red hair or wears a long red wig," Mac explained.

"I know no one like that. When was she last entertaining in my playground?" Goddess Z asked.

Mac dug out the picture that had been captured at Club Kremwrek. It didn't show the woman's face, but maybe it would give Goddess Z an idea. She handed over the picture. "We aren't sure exactly when, but it's been a few years, and she went by Mistress Gennavie."

Goddess Z took the photo from Mac's hand and studied it. "Yes, I know this woman. I trained her myself, and she is very good. Not as good as me, of course, but good nonetheless."

"What can you tell us about her?" Hudson asked.

"Well, my dear, I can tell you she is American, and she lived a double life while here. She had a very professional job that sometimes got in the way of her coming to play. I did not like this, but her customers were willing and happy to wait for her if she was not able to come."

"Do you happen to know where it was she worked?" Hudson asked.

"No, I do not, but I think it had to do with the military installation. What do you call it—Spangdalem, I believe?"

"Why do you think she was from there?" Mac asked.

"She would come for the weekend. Her train arrived on Friday late, and I would send someone for her. It took her over three hours to make the trip, and she would be exhausted when she arrived. She often stayed with me, and she always brought along that ugly green duffel bag that left her things wrinkled and a mess." Goddess Z made a disgusted face. "My thoughts were that she was military with a wild side, and I always wish to keep military happy. They bring great business to me, and Mistress Gennavie was one of my best earners and much fun to play with," she said with a wicked grin.

"Is there anything else you can tell us about Mistress Gennavie?" Hudson asked.

"She was different," Goddess Z said.

"Different how?" Hudson asked.

"She was very good at"—Goddess Z paused thoughtfully—"compartmentalizing, I think you would call it."

"What do you mean?" Mac asked.

"There was a time before she left when a body was discovered. He had been mutilated and hung in his room. The police thought it was a suicide because he was dangling from his bedsheet, but the marks on his body and the weird marks on his neck made me think he was killed and staged. I am not sure all of what happened, but I feel she may have been involved."

"Did you see her the night the body was discovered?" Hudson asked.

"Well, yes, that is what I am telling you. She was off, but just slightly. She was never frantic or out of sorts, but on this night, she was, well, different. There was never a time when she was not in control except that night. She seemed distracted and not herself. She looked"—Goddess Z thought about it for a moment—"scared."

"Did you see her after that night?" Mac asked.

"No, it was the last time I saw her. I still miss her. She was one of the few people I could really talk with. If you see her, could you please tell her I want her returned to me?" Goddess Z said.

"We'll pass along the message. You wouldn't happen to know her real name?" Mac asked hopefully.

"No, it is my belief that she had several," Goddess Z said.

"What do you mean, several?" Hudson asked.

"No one in this world goes by their real name. It is just not done, and it is to protect," Goddess Z explained.

"Protect who?" Hudson asked.

"Protect yourself, of course. I would not wish to have my clients show up at my home and meet my family. That would just not do, would it?"

"No, I supposed it wouldn't," Mac agreed. "Do you happen to know what other names she went by and about how long ago she left?"

"I believe she went by Davis, which may have been her military persona, but it is a very common name. I believe she had another name or two, but I do not recall them. Sadly, she left me over two years ago," Goddess Z said.

"Is there any way to get your real name and a number to contact you if we have any additional questions?" Hudson asked.

"No, that is not possible. You know where to find me, and so does Mistress Gennavie. Please ask her to come back to me. I would very much like her company again," Goddess Z said.

"Thank you for your time. You have been very helpful. We'll pass along your message when we locate Mistress Gennavie," Mac assured her.

"Yes, thank you. Now my friend will show you out," she said, tilting her head toward Mountain, who was standing at parade rest in the corner.

He walked to the door and opened it, indicating that they should leave. "Will that be all, madam?" Mountain asked.

"Yes, leave me now. I must rest," Goddess Z said.

CHAPTER FIFTY

MISTRESS GENNAVIE finally allowed her husband to find her. She turned her phone back on after spending the day and most of the evening contemplating her next move. She knew he would be on edge and worried since she was the only person on earth that truly knew who he was, and she didn't want him going off and doing something stupid.

They relied on each other for better or for worse, bound by the secrets of what they had done. Gennavie had concluded that the only real threat was Mac and maybe her sidekick. She was actually looking forward to playing with him and was kicking herself for getting them to leave. It would have made things much easier if she had been able to kill them the first time. Clearly, they were much harder to take out than she had initially thought.

"So, what's the plan?" her husband asked over dinner.

"Not sure, but I'm itching for a fix. Maybe we should go on a trip somewhere. Get away for a while and get into a little trouble," she suggested.

"Sorry, hon, I can't. We have that big inspection coming up, and all leave has been canceled by the commander. Aren't you guys involved as well?"

"Yeah, I know, but I don't think I can wait that long," she pouted.

"Think of it this way: if we get caught, you'll be waiting a lot longer."

"I know, but that doesn't mean I have to like it. I feel like the best way to resume our favorite activities is to eliminate Mac and Hudson. I heard she's from Spokane and is stationed at Fairchild. Maybe we could meet them on their home turf where their guard is down. What do you think?" She tilted her head to the side, waiting for his response.

"Not a bad idea. They wouldn't be expecting us. The element of surprise could actually work. The Fourth of July weekend is coming up soon, and by then, the exercise will be over. Maybe we could take a couple of extra days and go hunting. Would that make you happy?"

"Yes, that would make me very happy," she said with an evil grin.

He loved to see her smile and marveled at how she could compartmentalize just like he could. It was interesting how well they were matched. He had always found other women complicated and mushy, but with her... she was just as much a predator as he was. Her mind was animalistic in nature, and the only thing that kept her going was the next kill. At the same time, she could operate in the military as a model airman that no one would ever suspect. She could come across as kind and caring. He'd once thought he was good at emulating other people, but honestly, she was a genius.

She sat back, wondering what her husband was thinking, as she assumed most women did. Maybe it was time to split up and go their separate ways. Unfortunately, no matter how careful they had been, the murders of Lady Carina and Andre clearly indicated a team effort. There was no way just one person could have subdued the giant and the lady.

It had been quite erotic to play together again. It had simply been too long since they had murdered. In actuality, it had been less than a month, but still, she hated the thought of going back to killing solo. There was just something about having a partner in crime who understood her deepest desires. Plus, there was no way he could rat on her without turning himself in.

So, it was settled: she would set up Mac to take the fall and then kill her and Hudson together in a lover's quarrel. It would be simple—all she had to do was plant a little evidence from the previous victims, then tip off the authorities so that they couldn't help but think Mac and Hudson were involved. She knew she had to be careful and calculating, but that was something she was very good at.

Her informant had kindly let her know that the FBI was already looking into Mac and thought she was somehow involved. Why else would the killer want to track her, after all? It was a juicy piece of information that she intended to exploit.

CHAPTER
FIFTY-ONE

"HER NAME IS ZOE VAN DIJK," Lola said. "She's been running the sex trade in the RLD for a little over ten years. She's well-connected and ruthless. Her willingness to take down anyone that stands in her way reminds me of someone we know."

"Yeah, I know. Is there anything else you were able to dig up?" Mac asked.

"Well, there were forty-three military members with the last name of Davis who were stationed at Spangdahlem over the last five years. It's hard to pinpoint with over five thousand military members coming and going. Are you sure she's military and not a dependent or a civilian employee? If so, that could really widen the search."

"I'm not positive, but she carried a military duffel bag, according to Goddess Z. She said it was old, ugly, and made all her clothes wrinkled-looking, which made me think of the one I was issued in basic training. It's a huge bag that loads from the top, and there's no way to keep your stuff nice and neat since things shift around. I think we should start there. Out of the forty-three, how many are female and left the base approximately two or more years ago?"

There was a light tapping on the other end of the line. "There are three airmen with the last name of Davis who fit your criteria," Lola reported back.

"Hang on." Mac set the phone down, searching for a pen and paper. The hotel room was nice and had left them a complimentary set on the small desk. "Okay, give me their full names."

"I can do you one better—I can run a full background check and profile on each one," Lola said.

"You never cease to impress," Mac said. "When can we meet?"

"I don't know, sis. Are you positive you're not being followed?"

"I'm positive. If it makes you feel any better, we could meet someplace of your choosing. I'll follow any cloak-and-dagger instructions you have in order to have the opportunity to see you again. It's just been so long, and I miss you."

"Okay, meet me at the Hoxton Hotel tonight at eighteen hundred hours. Walk into the lobby and take a left down the hall. Go to room 127 and knock three times and wait," Lola instructed, and then hung up without saying a word.

CHAPTER
FIFTY-TWO

DAISY WAS EXCITED to go on her hike with Noah. He was the quarterback at their high school, and Daisy was the lead cheerleader. He had been dating that skank, Bridget, for the past few years, but they finally broke up, and now she had her chance. It only made sense that they should be together.

It was expected that the soon-to-be prom king should be dating the soon-to-be prom queen, if she had anything to say about it. She wanted him to chase her and to think she was hard to get. She had waited all week for Saturday to finally roll around. She put on a semi-conservative top that showed a small portion of her trim waistline but covered enough not to make her look cheap. She slid on her favorite jean shorts and sneakers and put her hair in pigtails to give her that innocent look.

Noah arrived right on time, looking dashing in a tank top that showed off his nicely formed muscles. *This has to be right*, Daisy thought. "I brought a picnic for today," Noah said. "I hope you like what I packed."

"That was very nice of you," she said as they drove toward the falls. It was a perfect day. The sky was a majestic blue with a slight breeze in the air. She was happy that it wasn't too hot so that her perfectly applied makeup wouldn't melt as they hiked up to the romantic spot near the falls that she hoped he would take her to.

Noah pulled his Jeep into the dirt lot where the little hidden trail started. Few people had known about until recently—it had become a popular makeout spot for teenagers in the summer months, but was way too cold to mess with in the winter.

Noah climbed out of the Jeep and walked to the other side to open the door for Daisy.

"Thank you," she replied.

"Of course," he said. "Are you ready?" he asked, retrieving the picnic basket and blanket from the back.

"Absolutely." She laced her fingers into his, and they started up the trail. After a short hike, they ended up in the very spot she had hoped they would. He carefully moved some rocks and a few pinecones out of the way before he laid the blanket on the ground. It was a beautiful spot with the falls just off to their left, and their private little picnic was hidden from view among the towering trees.

He laid the contents of the basket out on display for her. "What would you like?" he asked. "I have ham and cheese or turkey."

"Turkey would be great." She sat close to him on the blanket so he would smell the expensive perfume she had borrowed from her mom without permission.

He handed her the sandwich with a bottle of water and began eating his. "So, what would you like to do today?" he asked with a suggestive boyish grin.

"What did you have in mind?" she asked, knowing all too well what he'd brought her here for.

"I have a few ideas," he said, running his hand down her bare arm. She didn't move away, so he took that as an invitation. He moved in for a kiss, and their lunch was soon forgotten. He started kissing her neck.

"What a minute, what's that?" she asked, getting distracted by a noise.

"It's nothing," he said, sliding his hand up the back of her shirt.

"Stop it, Noah, something is out there." Panic crept into Daisy's voice.

"Fine," he said, sounding more irritated than he had meant to. "I'll go check it out." He stood, doing his best to hide his erection, and headed back to the trail to see what was interrupting his attempts at seducing one of the hottest girls at his school.

He heard the sound as well, and this time it came with a growl. That certainly got his attention. He felt Daisy's hands wrap around his arm as she followed directly behind him. "What do you think it is?" she asked as a shiver ran up her spine.

"No idea, but stay behind me," he said, trying to sound brave.

They slowly made their way to the falls. Branches were biting at their bare legs as they walked through the brush until they came upon what was making the sound. A powerful cougar had his back to them, eating something. At first they thought it was another animal, until Daisy let out a bloodcurdling scream behind him.

He jumped. "What the hell?"

"That's a human arm," she said in a high-pitched, hysterical voice.

"No, it's not," he tried to protest, but took a closer look and all the color drained from his face. There was a dark-skinned, waxy-looking human arm that looked half-eaten next to the large cat.

Noah turned away and vomited into the bushes.

CHAPTER
FIFTY-THREE

BARDOT STARED at the whiteboard in front of her. Mac and Hudson had been eliminated as suspects in the murder of Lady Carina and Andre. They had been caught on a traffic camera heading toward Spokane at the time of the murders. Since their departure, they had found nothing new. They had gone over everything with a fine-toothed comb and had come up with nothing.

The killers had gone dormant, and without new evidence, they had little choice but to wait for another body to surface. She thought about bringing Mac back into the fold. She had more than a thousand questions to ask her about her family. It appeared she hadn't been in contact with them since she entered the military, but her insider knowledge might be valuable and still relevant.

She paced the room, trying to look at it from all angles. She couldn't just stand by and wait for more bodies to surface. Many killers went through a cooling-off phase over the span of their killing career. Maybe this was the case for these killers. At this point, she had concluded that at least two killers were involved in most of the murders, with the evidence leading her to believe that sometimes they killed together and other times they killed separately.

Most killers had a narcissistic side and thought they were somehow better or smarter than the rest of the population, especially law enforcement. There were many cases where a killer or killers would toy with the police to make themselves feel superior to everyone else. Bardot could only hope that one of them would slip up along the way or they'd turn on each other.

A knock at her office door pulled her back from her thoughts.

"Yes," she said.

Weidman stuck his head in the door. "Ma'am, we have another body."

"Dammit," she said, balling up her fists. "What do we know?"

"Two lovebirds stumped upon a body up near Snoqualmie Falls. A cougar was making lunch out of the remains. It appears the body sat frozen in the water. It was covered in adipocere, the waxy substance that preserved most of the body. We think the cat dislodged the body from its hiding place. Before that, the body was well-preserved in the snow runoff. Most of the water in those parts freezes for a good portion of the year, and even if it's not frozen, the temperatures would be low enough to preserve a body. We've seen multiple hypothermia cases in those parts due to swimmers not realizing how low the temperatures are. We're still waiting for the medical examiner to analyze the body."

"What makes you think this body is related to our killers?"

"There's preliminary evidence of the same type of body mutilation as the previous bodies. What was left of his flesh had what appears to be whip marks, and a portion of the neck shows those strange ligature marks found on a few of the other victims."

"Is there anything else we know about the victim?"

"Only that he's a black male estimated to be in his mid-twenties."

Bardot lowered her head in frustration. "Very well, let me know as soon as you identify the body and have the ME's report."

"Yes, ma'am, we'll keep you posted," he said, and turned for the door.

CHAPTER
FIFTY-FOUR

THE HOXTON HOTEL looked like an old historic Victorian castle with ornate brick architecture, and the canal running in front of it reminded Mac of a moat. She and Hudson walked in to find it decorated with dark wood, leather, and copper accents with a blend of old-school features. They followed the hall to the left down the Escher-style carpets until they reached room 127.

Mac knocked three times and waited. The strangest things brought back memories of their childhood. When they were younger, their mother wouldn't allow them to enter her office without knocking three times. This was her code for the children to announce themselves so they wouldn't interrupt her business. Mac had gotten into a lot of trouble and sustained some severe beatings when she was very young because she would get excited about something and rush into the office to tell her mom without first announcing herself.

She remembered one time when she was four or five. The memory stuck with her vividly. Her brother and her mother were standing over a man who was being tortured. She walked in just as her mother had broken one of the man's index fingers. It had taken her a long time to go to sleep without the sound of breaking bones seeping into her thoughts.

The discipline learned in her mother's fortress had served her well in the military. She had done very well throughout her military career because she was able to maintain bearing and discipline regardless of the circumstances. She always felt she had to announce herself anytime she entered a room when the door was closed. She had been praised for such behavior, but Mac knew it wasn't healthy.

The door in front of them swung open, and Mac jumped. A short, thick man with bulging muscles and a large bald head stood in front of them. "Please step inside," the guard said. They both stepped into the room.

Hudson immediately took stock of the man's SIG Sauer P365 tucked into a holster inside the man's jacket. Another guard stepped around the door. This one was equally armed, but compared to his partner, he was tall and lankly with a long face and goatee. "Your sister apologizes for this," he said as he tossed two black hoods at Mac and Hudson.

"What are these for?" Mac asked, but she had a pretty good idea.

"Just put them on, and I'll take you to your sister," he said, trying not to sound too threatening. They placed the masks over their heads, and the entire world went dark. Rough hands flanked them on either side and led them outside. Mac could feel a cool breeze against her skin and smell the canal nearby. "Step down," one of the men instructed on her left side.

She hesitated, feeling like she was suspended in midair. "I can't," she said.

"It's just a boat," the man said, and before she knew what was happening, she was being lifted onto the boat. She let them move her, hoping that her sister was actually waiting for her on the other side. "Okay, now for you," one of the men said, tugging at Hudson's arm. "You're too big to lift onto the boat, so you'll have to help us out."

Hudson put his hands out in front of him to maintain his balance. He stepped down tentatively and was relieved to find a solid platform waiting for him. He felt off-balance but trusted that it would be okay. If Mac had faith in Lola, then so would he.

They were led to a soft bench with thick cushions and instructed to sit. The pair sat and waited as the boat roared to life. Mac half expected the wind to blow off her mask but realized they must be inside. She could feel the movement of the boat and knew they were on the water, but they weren't in an open boat. She felt for Hudson's hand and laced her fingers with his when she found it.

"Are you doing okay?" he asked.

"A little freaked out, I have to admit, but clearly Lola has good reason to go to these great lengths to hide her location," Mac said, trying to sound reassuring.

"I hope you're right," he said, squeezing her hand.

It seemed like they were on the water for a long time. Mac hoped they would be there soon. She really shouldn't have had so much coffee and water, but in fairness, she didn't know they would be on a boat. She drank around a pot of coffee a day and then tried to counterbalance it by drinking approximately a gallon of water. She figured if she was going to have a vice, she would balance it out a bit.

Now she was regretting her ritual of drinking so much. Her bladder was screaming at her every time they hit a bump in the water. *Lola, come on, where the hell are we going?* she screamed in her mind. Her resolve to hold it was about over, and she was about to ask to use the bathroom when the boat finally slowed and eventually stopped. "Thank goodness," she muttered.

Hudson chuckled next to her. "You have to pee, don't you? I think you have the smallest bladder of anyone I've ever met. How on earth did you make it through basic training?"

"It was rough, let me tell you. My TI thought I had some kind of medical issue."

Strong hands clasped their arms and pulled them up on their feet. They felt disoriented as they were led off the boat. It was certainly easier to get up and out of the boat than it had been to go down. At least it didn't feel so imbalanced. They were led down the street, and Mac guessed probably down an alley since the sound of the wind changed like it would if she had entered a tunnel.

They were led through a door and then placed in an elevator. "Almost there," one of the guards said.

"That's good news. I have to pee," she responded, which got a chuckle out of the guard to her left. She wondered why that was so funny to him. She was starting to find it not funny at all.

The elevator kept going up. *Where the hell are we going?* Mac wondered as the elevator finally dinged, and she heard the doors open. The men guided them into a room and removed their hoods.

"Lola," was all Mac could manage.

CHAPTER
FIFTY-FIVE

HUDSON STAYED where he was as the two sisters embraced. Finn had been right: the two looked identical as far as facial features were concerned, but Lola had fair skin and a pixie look with red hair, and Mac had darker features with olive skin, long, dark hair, and a slightly curvier body. It was weird looking at the two of them together. Both women were stunning in their own right. He smiled at the exchange.

"It's so wonderful to see you again," Mac said with a huge grin. "Can I use your bathroom?"

"Why am I not surprised? It's right over there." Lola pointed to a closed door on the other side of the room.

"Thank you," Mac said, disappearing into the bathroom.

"You must be the infamous Hudson I've been hearing so much about," Lola said as she walked over. "It's nice to finally meet you in person."

Hudson stretched out his hand, and Lola walked right past it and wrapped him in a hug. "Thanks for rescuing my sister," she said, not entirely fitting her small arms around his large frame.

Mac walked out of the bathroom, looking a great deal more comfortable. "I see you've met Hudson."

"I was just thanking him for saving your ass last winter," Lola quipped.

"That's not exactly what happened, and I would have never found her without your help," Hudson said.

"Nice place you've got here," Mac observed, changing the subject.

"Yeah, it's not mine. It belongs to my employer."

"I thought you were working for the government," Mac said, a little uneasy.

"Something like that. Actually, my current employer is a subcontractor for the government and is much better funded, as you can see," Lola said, extending her arm toward her plush surroundings.

The bedroom door to their right opened slightly, a tiny hand appearing. "Mommy, I hungry," a little voice said from behind the door.

Lola jumped up and opened the door to reveal an adorable little girl with red pigtails sprouting from her head. She looked exactly like Lola in miniature size. Mac guessed she couldn't be much older than two, maybe three years old.

"Hey sweetie, I asked you to stay in the room while Mommy has her meeting," Lola said.

"Mommy," Mac said, staring at her. "You weren't going to tell me?"

"The fewer people who know about her, the better," Lola responded sternly as she sat her little girl on the plush carpet.

"What's her name?" Mac asked, unable to take her eyes off the girl.

"This is Olivia. We call her Olive for short. Olive, come meet your Auntie Mac," Lola said to the little girl.

"Annie Mac," she repeated in the sweetest little voice. She almost sounded like she was singing every time she talked. She toddled over to Mac and put her hands in the air.

Mac lifted her up and sat her on her hip as she sank into one of the overstuffed chairs. "It's very nice to meet you, Olivia. How old are you?"

"I two years old," she said with a toothy grin. She had to be the most beautiful child Mac had ever seen.

"Who is her daddy?" Mac asked, still amazed that she had a niece and didn't even know about her. At first, she was pissed at Lola for keeping her a secret, but she couldn't stay mad for long, and if she had someone this precious to protect, she would do anything to keep her safe.

"He's my handler with the FBI. He got me this gig so that she and I would be safer and away from some of the riskier assignments I was getting," Lola explained.

"I see," Mac responded, but didn't entirely understand. Conflicted feelings were running through her mind. If she was being honest, she felt betrayed by her sister. She'd thought they were close.

"Come here, honey, let me get you a snack," Lola said. Mac put Olive down, and she followed her mother into the small kitchen and sat on the booster seat at the table. She was a beautiful, angelic child with large brown eyes, not unlike Mac's. Lola looked over at her sister. "I know you don't understand, but I have to protect her. No one knows about her except for my employer and her father."

"I understand the need to protect her. Don't think I forgot about what happened to Tia." Mac dropped her eyes. Tia was the oldest of the siblings. Their mother had forced her into marrying the son of a prominent drug supplier. The man was cruel and cold and beat their sister daily. She was not a wife but a prisoner in his home. He did vile things to her. They had heard rumors that he had shared her with his friends in exchange for drugs and power. She had eventually become pregnant and could not live with the thought of bringing a beautiful baby into the world she was held captive in. Tia had gone to their mother asking for permission to divorce the bastard and come home. Unfortunately for Tia, the merger between the two families had brought their mother into a high level of power.

Their mother was now one of the most powerful women in any drug cartel. She had partnered with a man who supplied high-grade cocaine and heroin in the United States and overseas and their mother ran the distribution side of things. Together they built an impressive empire using each other to make gains in the industry. Their mother wasn't willing to break the partnership to save her daughter. She told her to go back to her husband and be a good wife. "I just thought you could trust me," she said, sounding more pitiful than she had meant to. Tia committed suicide forty-eight hours later.

"Trusting you was never the issue." Lola looked torn. "I'm so much more worried about the lines of communication. I know we use a SAT phone, but that doesn't mean people aren't able to get intel. I mean, the FBI is looking at your security clearance, which could easily lead back to me. You not knowing about Olive was helping to keep her safe. Now, I simply ask that you don't reveal her to anyone."

CHAPTER
FIFTY-SIX

LOLA MOVED to a small desk area on the other side of the room partially to avoid any additional questions about her daughter or her employer, and also because she was short on time. If she was being honest with herself, she loved the lavish lifestyle her new employer had provided. When she was working directly for the government, it had been very sterile and often uncomfortable. She had been provided accommodations but nothing like this, and she felt Olive was safe here.

She had grown up with this type of lifestyle, and so had Mac. It didn't seem to bother Mac to live like a commoner, but Lola had missed the fine clothes, the overly comfortable beds, soft leather seats in high-priced vehicles, and all the other luxuries that came with the super-rich. She knew deep down there was a price to everything, and one day she would have to pay whatever price her new employer wanted, but for now she was living in luxury, and the most important person in the world was safe.

Lola cleared her throat, trying to focus on the task at hand.

Mac was still looking at her strangely with obvious questions in her eyes. "You haven't gone back to the family, have you?" Mac wanted to know, not trusting her sister's new situation.

"Of course not," Lola said. "You couldn't possibly believe I'm that stupid."

"I don't think you're stupid at all. On the contrary, I think you're brilliant, but you have always had a weakness for this type of lifestyle, and I would hate for that to be your undoing."

"You have nothing to be concerned about, I assure you," Lola said, trying to sound more convincing than she felt. "Now, do you want to see what I found or not?"

"Of course. Thank you again for helping us. I don't mean to question you; I just worry about you."

"You have absolutely nothing to worry about," Lola reassured her again.

Famous last words, Mac thought, and then tried to push it out of her head. "So, what did you find?"

"As you know, thousands of people were stationed at Spangdahlem Air Base during that timeframe. There were several men, but the female-to-male ratio in the military is low, so I reduced it to three women with the last name of Davis." She pulled out the first file. "I believe we can eliminate the first woman simply by nationality and skin tone. You said the woman you were hunting was a redhead with fair skin like me. This woman has a darker complexion."

Mac opened the file anyway and reviewed its contents. Lola was right—this woman didn't meet the physical description. She set the folder aside. "Okay, what else do you have?"

Lola produced the next file, which contained a fair-skinned woman with blond hair. This could be the woman they were looking for. She met the general body type and skin tone of the woman in the green dress that was seen at Kremwrek with Collymore.

"What do you think of this one?" Mac asked Hudson.

"She's certainly a possibility, but we're leaving something else out entirely," he said.

"What would that be?" Mac asked.

"Lola, you said there were several men stationed at Spangdahlem during our window of time. Is it possible that the woman in question could have been the wife of a military member rather than the service member?" Hudson asked.

"That's possible, but if that's the case then our suspect pool just got a lot bigger," Lola said.

"It is possible, but there was no mention of Mistress Gennavie showing up to Goddess Z's playground with a man. If she were married, where was her husband the entire time?" Mac asked.

"Deployed, a night-shifter, a pilot..." Hudson said. "There are many reasons why a military member's spouse might have a lot of time on her hands to travel back and forth to Amsterdam. Plus, Goddess Z said she disappeared sometimes. We assumed it was because she was being sent out in the field or had to attend to her military duties, but it could have been her husband coming home."

"What about the military bag?" Mac asked.

"It easily could have been her husband, and she just used it out of convenience," Hudson pointed out.

"I hate it when you go all analytical on me," Mac said, feeling frustrated.

"Let's take a look at the last folder," Hudson suggested.

Lola handed over the last folder. This woman could also be a viable suspect. She had fair skin and a slight build with dark-brown hair. They had evidence that the red hair was a wig or extensions, so either woman could fit the description.

"Did either of these women have a follow-on assignment to Joint Base Lewis-McChord?" Mac asked.

"I wasn't able to pull PCS records from the base, but I was able to see if either of these women were now stationed at JBLM and found that the blond woman is. I'm not sure about the other woman. It's possible that she's in Seattle, but has a different last name due to marriage or divorce or some other reason."

"Sounds like a needle in a haystack," Mac complained. "At least we may have a lead. Even if this isn't our woman, maybe she remembers other people with the same last name stationed with her during that time."

CHAPTER
FIFTY-SEVEN

IT WAS time to finally head home. Both Hudson and Mac felt defeated and a bit frustrated that they hadn't found better information. It had been wonderful to see Lola, but now she had a sinking feeling that Lola was involved in something she shouldn't be. There was little Mac could do about it unless Lola wanted her to intervene. She just hoped her sister was being careful.

They had every intention of following up with the Davis that had been stationed at Spangdahlem and was now at JBLM. The limited information they had could hold promise, but Mac had her doubts. The woman was an officer, which didn't exclude her by any means, but she had nothing in her past to indicate she was into this type of behavior.

There were entirely too many factors to consider. They clearly were headed down the right path when it came to BDSM and professional dominatrixes. She was thinking about the information they had received from Goddess Z. What an interesting world to live in, where a woman was hired to dominate other people, and those people not only liked it, they paid for it.

Mac had done some additional research on the lifestyle and found that couples who practiced BDSM often had more trust. She couldn't imagine enduring the pain associated with some of the things they do while roleplaying, but she could see how it could increase the bond between a couple. She was still a little stuck on the relationship between a professional dominatrix and a submissive who paid them. It felt a bit like prostitution, but with the roles reversed.

It was probably the same thought process that went with a person who hired a sex worker. They had forbidden desires that could never be revealed to their partner, so they'd go elsewhere to fulfill those desires. She had actually read a fascinating article about a therapist who was also a professional dominatrix. Her clients would come to her for various reasons.

One patient came to her because he had severe control issues. He could not seem to let his guard down and allow people to have any control over his life. He suffered from a debilitating case of OCD. It controlled his life. Most people thought of a person with obsessive-compulsive disorder as a clean freak, but there was so much more to it than that.

It was fascinating how she'd taught him to slowly give up control of his environment and accept the fact that sometimes things happened that a person simply couldn't control. After years of therapy with her, his compulsive behaviors began to wane, and he reported that he was able to reconnect with his family and friends. They had all distanced themselves from him because of his violent outbursts. He reported that the woman had saved his life and his marriage.

It was quite a case, with plenty of compelling reasons why losing control at the hands of another person in a safe environment could be beneficial to a person's psyche. Even though the lifestyle was different, she could understand how and why people might find it intriguing and exciting. The only problem was that the killers were taking it to an unhealthy level by breaking their submissive's trust and eventually killing them.

That brought up an interesting question. How long did they keep their kills alive? Was it just during the event, or did it depend on the victim or the mood? There were more questions than answers. Did they have prior relationships with their prey?

Mac followed Hudson onto the airplane and headed back to the States. She thought about how she would approach Bardot when she returned. If she was doing background checks on Mac, it wasn't welcome. Her family had people in high places that could easily find out about it. If Lola knew, then they could easily find out, which put both Mac and Lola, not to mention everyone around them, in grave danger.

They settled into their seats. Mac looked over at Hudson; the knuckles on his large hands were already starting to turn white as the large Boeing 747 jumbo jet pulled away from its spot. She pulled down the window shade, hoping it would calm him a bit. "Tell me what you're thinking about the case," she said to distract him.

"I'm not sure what to talk about. Our only solid lead is that this mysterious Mistress Gennavie seems to either be the killer or is being stalked by the killer. It's entirely possible that someone is obsessed with her and is killing off her clients," he said.

Mac laced her fingers through his as she felt the jet getting ready for takeoff. She couldn't help but think it was cute that such a big man was afraid of anything, let alone flying, since he had entered a service that was based on air superiority. The plane taxied, and the color drained from Hudson's face.

"What do you think our next move should be?" she tried again.

"Um," he said, closing his eyes and trying to focus. "For right now, we need to get back home and go back to normal life." He squeezed her hand a little too tightly as the jet lifted off. "I know I'm going to have a ton to catch up with at work. We recently had a suicide, and you know that can cause a lot of issues. The guy was well-liked, and apparently the member's wife has three kids and one on the way. On top of that, there's some evidence that the guy had a mistress on the side."

"I'm sorry to hear that. Those cases can be very tough," she said, thinking about the situation. "So, you're saying we should just leave the case alone?"

"No, not at all. I just feel like we've been banging our heads against the wall and not finding anything. I'm just saying that sometimes if you step away for a moment and then come back to it, things will look a lot clearer."

"That makes sense," she said, closing her eyes to rest. "Okay, so let's talk about your case. What evidence is there that he was having an affair prior to his suicide?"

"I'm not sure if it's conclusive evidence, but there was rumor that he was sleeping with a higher-ranking military member in the squadron. If the rumors are accurate, then the woman who's been assigned as the liaison in charge of helping the dead military member's wife is the same woman who has been sleeping with her husband."

"Yikes, that is a nasty twist on things. What's the difference in ranks?"

"The guy is a tech sergeant like you, and the woman in question is a senior master sergeant and was in his chain of command."

"Interesting," Mac said pondering the information. "I wonder if the people or person we're hunting are hiding in plain sight inside the safety of the military?"

"I mean, it's possible. Military members are people just like the rest of society and are capable of anything. Why do you think they're military?" Hudson asked, trying not to think about the plane's upward motion.

"Well, we have two victims that had direct ties to the military, and it would make sense how they've been able to get away with it for so long."

"What do you mean?" Hudson asked.

"Well, think about it. They're highly trained and would have a place to escape to. If they kept their military lives and their civilian lives separate, then it would be the last place most people would look. Military members are inherently trusted members of society."

"What about Collymore? Why would they kill him knowing it would lead back to the military?"

"Maybe they didn't know he was military until after they killed him," Mac suggested.

CHAPTER
FIFTY-EIGHT

VINCENT KNEW he needed to keep his wife calm. This was the exact reason he had never shared his dark secret with anyone. He had been so careful over the years to murder people who weren't connected to him in any way. He had gone to great lengths to change his victimology and stay off the radar, but now she was trackable. She insisted on wearing that distinctive red wig each time they went out to hunt, and she always played her persona as Mistress Gennavie.

He wondered if she liked being Mistress Gennavie much more than her normal life. He knew he liked her that way, when she was unhinged and released into the world to show her true nature. He understood how she felt; one of the only people on Earth who had ever understood him could also be the person that took him down.

The thought made him stop for a moment. He was mindlessly walking down the Seattle streets, looking into shops, just thinking. He stopped cold in his tracks. A man bumped into him and apologized as he walked past. Would he be willing to kill her in order to save his own skin? He really wasn't sure. He had been alone and realized he had been lonely for so long that he hated going back to a world where he had to hide his darkness from everyone.

At least with her, he could be himself. His true self, the killer who found it sexually arousing to see a person take their last breath. He had tried to have previous relationships with other women but found he couldn't perform when the time came. If they were willing and not struggling or thrashing about, he simply wasn't able to perform.

He wasn't sure why he was that way. Well, not entirely, actually. His mother had a lot to do with it. She had been a stage five alcoholic as far back as he could remember. She would start her day with Kahlua in her coffee and would often be inebriated before lunch. It was an interesting childhood, to say the least.

He remembered times when he was only five or six, and he would be left to sit out in the car while his mom got tanked, and then she would drive them home. He remembered the truck redlining because she would forget to shift. One night, he had wet his pants when she had driven them off the road and down a ravine. She had beaten him severely for having an accident in her truck. She didn't seem to understand why he was frightened.

In the first grade, she showed up drunk at his school without any clothes on. He had been mortified, and the other kids teased him mercilessly. The principal had run out into the hall, wrapping a blanket around her body as his mother fought her off, screaming at the top of her lungs that it was perfectly natural.

By the third grade, his mother had been arrested several times, and he had become a loner. He was placed in foster care when she was arrested for trying to light her boyfriend on fire and then driving down the sidewalk on a moped in her birthday suit. Most of his original friends had distanced themselves from him because of all the bullying. They didn't want any part of it, so he found himself alone.

His time in foster care had actually been his fondest memory. The bullying continued, of course, but he was able to sleep at night without worrying about being attacked by his drunk mother. When he returned home, she blamed him for the situation and shaved his head because she was convinced he had brought home lice from the filthy establishment.

When he finally hit puberty, he began to have dark fantasies about killing his mom and other women. He hadn't acted on his fantasies until prom night. His date had been a little odd like him. She was into goth and wore dark-black everything, but was still a striking slip of a girl. They had been dating for almost three months when he shyly asked if she would go to prom with him.

She reluctantly accepted his invitation after acknowledging that the event was overrated and stupid, but that she would go if it made him happy. He thought if he could get her dressed up and make her feel pretty, then maybe he could get lucky. It did make him happy.

That night had gone better than he'd thought it would. He showed up at her rundown trailer where she lived with her father, who was a drunk like his mom. Her dad didn't even acknowledge his daughter as she left the house, but her date thought she looked stunning. When they got to prom, he thought she was the prettiest one in the room. She didn't look like the other girls who were dressed in pretty pastels with conservative makeup, but she certainly turned heads in her tight, floor-length black dress.

She smiled brightly at the attention she was receiving from him and many of the other teenage boys at the dance. She had been invisible most of her life and hadn't stood out because she normally wore boys' clothes. He knew it was because her dad didn't know what to do with a daughter, so he treated her primarily like a boy. She had worked on a neighboring farm for the past few years, trying to save up enough to start college in the fall.

After the dance was over, he convinced her to go back to a hotel room that he'd rented using a fake ID he had acquired from one of her mother's drinking buddies. He found some of her boyfriends to be quite resourceful and would do things for him in order to spend more time with his mother. He really didn't understand what they saw in her. His mother was pretty and all, but she was a mess, not unlike his prom date.

He took her back to the hotel room and offered her champagne to toast the evening. She accepted with a little giggle. He remembered how her skin had looked in the low light of the cheap hotel room. He could see her pulse beating in her neck. They started making out, not for the first time. She had let him play with her nipples before, but hadn't let him go between her legs.

"Tell me you love me," she had whispered. He didn't, but he said it anyway because he thought she might let him have sex with her. He eventually talked her out of her dress and was excited about his first time. She put a condom on him like a pro, and he wondered if this wasn't actually her first time.

He was rock hard, but something was wrong. He entered her and tried all kinds of different positions in order to cum. Nothing seemed to be working, and eventually he started to lose his erection. He grew frustrated until his penis dangled between his legs with the condom slipping down, and then she laughed. Actually, she just let out a tipsy giggle, but it felt like a slap across the face to him.

He became enraged and grabbed her by the throat, pushing her onto the bed. He climbed on top of her. "You're hurting me," she gasped, which did it for him. The rest of what happened was a bit of a blur in his mind. He remembered getting very excited and the blood pumping hard in his temples and between his legs. His vision narrowed to her bulging eyes. She was thrashing around and turning a cool shade of purple. Her pretty lips turned a strange shade of blue, and the veins on her neck started to swell.

The release came furiously, like an explosion. He had never felt anything like it. For the first time in his life, he was satisfied. He collapsed on top of her, breathing heavily, thinking that she was going to be pissed at him for being so rough, but nothing happened. He laid there on top of her, almost afraid to look. Eventually, he worked up the courage.

It was much worse than he could have imagined. She wasn't moving at all. He grabbed her wrist and felt for a pulse, but there was nothing. He laid his head on her small chest, listening for breathing or a heartbeat, but there was nothing. At first he began to panic, but the more he stared at her body, the more relaxed he became. She was so pretty this way. Her silent mouth wasn't complaining. It was just parted slightly with her cold, dead eyes staring back at him, asking why.

"Well, to tell you the truth, I don't really know why," he said to her dead body, "but I certainly like you this way." He lay next to her, stroking her hair. "Plus, now you won't have to deal with your drunk daddy doing whatever he was doing to you. I'm sure it couldn't have been good," he explained to the dead body.

Then something weird happened. He began to get aroused again. At first he felt disgusted, but then disgust turned into fascination. He started examining her corpse, and the more he touched her skin, which was still warm, the more excited he became. He had always wanted a woman who wouldn't complain or laugh at him and, most importantly, wouldn't reject him because he was a little weird.

He found that he liked being able to do what he wanted with the body. It was also why he had connected so well with his beautiful wife. She was stunning and understood him. She would also allow him to strangle her. Autoerotic asphyxiation was the only way he could get her to an orgasm, and her thrashing allowed him to cum. It was a match made in heaven.

He had perfected his technique so he wouldn't hurt her badly. They had to be extra careful because she couldn't have marks on her neck while in uniform, which was hard with her porcelain skin. The marks were easy to cover up in civilian clothes with a simple scarf or choker, but that stuff wasn't allowed in uniform. They had finally found a yellow concealer that would neutralize the appearance of the purple-and-blue bruises. She would cover them with stage makeup, and it had worked beautifully so far. No one noticed except for him. He could tell, but only because he knew what he was looking for.

What she didn't know, and he hoped she would never discover, was that he did things with the bodies prior to disposal. He often had sex with them after they killed them. He couldn't figure out why that did it for him; it just did. He got off by killing with his wife and then having sex with her afterward, but nothing compared to the times he was alone with a fresh corpse.

CHAPTER
FIFTY-NINE

THEY ARRIVED home from Amsterdam completely exhausted. The jetlag and time change were hard to recover from. Mac half expected Hudson to go back to his house and had not quite gotten used to him practically living with her. Somehow, he had just slowly started incorporating himself into her daily life. She liked having him around and enjoyed his company immensely, but she was still reluctant.

There was a small box on the porch that seemed a little damp, but Mac was too exhausted to worry about it. She just dropped it on the kitchen counter and headed for the bedroom with Hudson right behind her. She only had the energy to get into bed and pass out. She slipped into the bathroom to wash her face and brush the scum off her teeth.

She truly enjoyed traveling and seeing new worlds, but this was the part she hated. There was nothing she could do to make herself feel better except for lots of sleep and hydration over the next few days. She felt even worse for Hudson, who had been tense for most of the flight and looked even more tired than she felt.

She came back out of the bathroom in one of his old t-shirts to find him fast asleep in her bed. The rise and fall of his chest were comforting to watch after she had almost lost him last winter. A serial killer had sabotaged his truck and tried to kill him to get to her. Ever since that day, she found herself on edge whenever he wasn't around. It had broken her heart to see him attached to all those machines in the hospital.

To her, he seemed invincible, and she felt safe with him. Knowing that he could be taken down like that had really put her off-balance. Now when they slept in the same bed, she found herself resting her hand on his chest just to make sure he was okay. It seemed silly, but it still made her feel better and helped with the nightmares she kept having.

The next morning, the phone was ringing in the other room. It took Mac a few minutes to wake up and realize she had left it in the kitchen in her purse. She couldn't believe it was already after 1000 hours. Her body was stiff as she stretched, reaching toward the ceiling, and she felt Hudson come up behind her and wrap his arms around her waist, giving her a warm embrace. "Please tell me you're not going to get that?" he pleaded.

"I have to report in, and so do you," she said softly. "And then we can play." She padded toward the kitchen, smiling back at him. Her smile vanished as she got closer to the kitchen. There was a stench assaulting her nose. "I think something is spoiled in here," she said to Hudson, who was behind her.

"That smell wasn't there last night," he said, grabbing her shoulder to slow her down. "It might be dangerous."

"How could spoiled meat be dangerous?"

"We don't have any food in the fridge, remember?" Hudson approached cautiously.

They came into the kitchen at the same time and tried not to gag. The box on the counter was swarming with flies, and the wetness Mac had registered from the night before looked like blood seeping out the bottom and onto her counter. The smell was a horrid and unmistakable stench of decomposing flesh. Mac and Hudson retreated from the kitchen. Mac grabbed her purse along the way and dialed 911.

CHAPTER SIXTY

DISPATCH CRACKLED over the radio in the small confines of the police cruiser. Most of the officers joked that the dispatcher had missed her calling as a sex operator. She had a smooth, sultry voice that made most of them smile when it filled their patrol car. "We have a possible body part scare in your vicinity. Can you two check it out?"

"We're on it," the older officer behind the wheel responded to the handheld radio.

"Great, the address is loaded into your system," the nice voice said back.

Officer Monroy was getting close to retirement and had seen everything he had ever cared to see. He was training up a new guy that had potential but was a little too cocky for the veteran's liking. When he was brand new to the force, he was very respectful and never gave his opinion unless asked.

His trainee was a young Italian guy who had grown up in the Bronx and had a bit of a smart mouth. "What do you know about hot dispatch lady?" he asked, smiling at his trainer.

Monroy grumbled, "Out of your league, son. Plus, I hear she's off-limits."

"Yeah, maybe," Officer Gallo said, "but a guy can dream. I heard about a case like this once," he said, switching subjects.

"A case like what?" Monroy asked.

"This guy's sister ordered those fancy Omaha steaks as a birthday present, not realizing he was out of town. Her brother's girlfriend found it on the porch and called the police thinking someone had left body parts or something." Gallo chuckled.

"Yeah, I love their steaks. My wife got me some a few years ago. They were delicious." Monroy patted his belly.

When the officers pulled into the driveway, they found a large man and a small woman sitting on the front porch. "Always approach with caution," Monroy warned the new guy.

They both got out of the car and headed toward Mac and Hudson's porch. "Ma'am, did you call the police?" Gallo asked.

"Yes, we got home last night from an overseas trip and found a package on my front porch," Mac explained. "I picked it up and put it in the kitchen, but was so tired that I didn't register anything was wrong with it. The house was dark, and I was more concerned with going to bed."

"Is the package still on your kitchen counter?" Monroy inquired.

"Yes, it is," Hudson said, purposefully staying seated so they wouldn't find him threatening. He'd had that unfortunate experience before. People would assume that he was violent simply because of his size.

"You two stay here, and we'll check it out," Monroy said.

As soon as they opened the door to enter the house, they stopped. The stench was unmistakable. They walked into the kitchen to find a box with dark, reddish-brown gunk seeping from the bottom. Gallo walked over to it, carefully slicing the top of the box open with his pocketknife. Monroy slipped on a latex glove and opened the top of the box.

The dead blue eyes of a woman stared up at them.

Gallo yelped and stepped back. He had never seen a dead body before, let alone a severed head. He thought he might be sick.

The young officer headed for the door, needing fresh air. Monroy followed close behind him. "Dispatch, this is Officer Monroy; please send the cavalry. We have an unidentified severed head."

"Copy," dispatch responded like it was an everyday conversation. "Is there any threat?"

"No, the homeowners found it on their front porch when they got here," he explained.

Monroy stepped out of the house thinking, *Six more months until retirement and then no more dead bodies* as he watched his young trainee lose his breakfast in the sideyard.

CHAPTER
SIXTY-ONE

"YES SIR, YOU HEARD ME RIGHT," Mac explained to Captain Stanton. "A severed head in my kitchen."

"Are you safe?" her boss asked with concern.

"Yes, the police are here now, and they're going to bring everyone else in. I have reason to believe this may be linked to the case at JBLM."

"Why do you think that?" Stanton asked.

"Just my gut," Mac said.

"I know your gut has magical properties," he said, trying to lighten the mood, "but is there any other reason you might think so?"

"Nothing that I can put my finger on at the moment, but it just feels the same. Someone has been trying to get me off this case since the beginning. It only makes sense. Plus, we found some good information in Amsterdam."

"Amsterdam? Why in hell were you there?" Stanton asked, letting out an exasperated sigh. "I thought you two were getting away from it all. I specifically recall you saying you felt stressed and needed an actual vacation."

"We did vacation, kind of…" she said, trailing off. "It was the best lead we had on the case, and we actually found some compelling evidence."

"And what was that?"

"We found out that she's connected to the military in some way, and may have or have had the last name Davis."

"Fair enough. Since this isn't my case, let me get ahold of Kibble and bring him up to speed. I would expect a lot of phone calls in the next few hours, and probably a few visitors as well. Please tread lightly since you were officially removed from the case for your own safety."

"Yes sir, I understand that I was sent home, but no one in my chain of command gave me a direct order to stay off the case."

"Circumstantial evidence shows you were removed, and that's what leadership could hang their hat on if they chose to. I have to go before the word gets out." Stanton hung up the phone.

Hudson finished up his conversation. "So, how did that go?" he asked.

"About as good as yours did, I assume," she said as they watched technicians walk out of her house with the box wrapped in plastic. As they were loading the head into the back of a Spokane Police vehicle, several dark SUVs pulled into her driveway. A large white box truck pulled behind them, blocking anyone from leaving. On the side of the truck, it read in large blue letters, *FBI, WASHINGTON FIELD OFFICE EVIDENCE RESPONSE TEAM.*

"Well, that didn't take long," Mac commented. "Here comes the pissing contest."

Hudson grinned, knowing how right she was.

A man with a weathered face was the first one out of the vehicle. He had tired eyes and an unfriendly scowl. He wore an FBI windbreaker and was clearly the one in charge of his team. The local police bristled at the arrival. Officer Monroy looked equally exhausted as the man approached.

Mac and Hudson watched from the porch. It appeared the two men knew each other from previous cases. Agent Clawson shook hands with Officer Monroy, and they exchanged pleasantries. "Sorry," Clawson said, "we have jurisdiction on this one. Our Seattle office is investigating multiple murders that seem to have one thing in common."

"What's that?" Monroy asked.

"Her," he said, pointing at Mac.

"Shit," Hudson said under his breath, "that can't be good."

"I'm going to need that head and any other evidence your boys have collected," Clawson said to Monroy, leaving little room for discussion.

"You're welcome to this one," Monroy responded. "I'll send our reports over this afternoon. Your tech can take the head now." He said it almost like he had a choice in the matter, knowing very well that it was just a formality.

"Thanks," Clawson said. "I'll be taking her with me as well."

"Suit yourself," Monroy said, walking away to inform his guys that they were off the case. He was slightly pissed at the FBI for swooping in and taking his last case, but really, he had to ask himself if he cared. After all, this would make sliding into retirement so much easier. The problem was that retirement was terrifying. He felt much more comfortable hunting bad guys than he did spending time with the family. He was actually a little worried that his wife wouldn't want him around as much.

Monroy watched as Clawson walked over to Mac, wondering how the case was going to pan out. "Ms. McGregor, I'm Special Agent Clawson with the Spokane FBI office."

"Can you tell me what's going on, Agent Clawson?" Mac asked.

"Not at this time, ma'am. I need you to come with me and answer some questions," Clawson said.

"Are you arresting me?" Mac asked.

"Not at this time," Clawson responded. "It's my understanding that you've been working with Agent Bardot from the Seattle office. She knows about your little trip and wants to know what you found out."

"Fine," she said, turning to Hudson. "I'll be back soon. You may want to head back to your place for a bit."

"Keep me posted," he said with a worried expression.

CHAPTER
SIXTY-TWO

MAC FOLLOWED Clawson back to his vehicle. Once she was settled in the passenger seat, she texted Captain Stanton to let him know she was with the FBI and would keep him posted.

Her phone pinged a few minutes later.

Did they take you into custody? Stanton texted back.

No, just questioning. I'll keep you posted, she responded.

Mac stared out the window as they drove away from her house and down Monroe Street. She knew the area well. Normally she loved crossing the beautiful Spokane River. If she had her way, she would live next to a body of water. She found it calming, but today she just stared past it like it wasn't there. They turned onto Riverside Avenue, pulled up in front of a huge light-gray stone building, and parked.

He led her inside, where her purse had to be searched, and she had to walk through a metal detector. Clawson was pre-vetted and only had to have the guard verify his credentials. They took the stairs up to the second floor. Clawson maintained a position behind her like she might flee at any second. He pointed left at the top of the stairs, and then they took a right into a conference room.

On the screen, Agent Bardot sat waiting impatiently.

"Good morning, Mac. It's good to see you again," Bardot said in her most pleasant bird voice.

"Is it?" Mac asked pointedly.

"Yes, actually it is. After your incident here, I thought you might be in danger. I was pretty convinced of it when I heard you had run off to Amsterdam," Bardot explained.

"Convinced of what?" Mac asked with a bit of venom in her voice. "Were you convinced that I was in danger, or that I was the one causing the danger?"

The little bird woman looked down at her from the screen. She looked odd with her small, sharp features blown up on a big screen. She figured it was meant to intimidate, but Mac didn't intimidate that easily.

Bardot cleared her throat. "Okay, I'll admit that we looked into you and your past. Once we found out about your family, we were very interested in you as a suspect. But then we found out that you had an alibi for the recent murders of Lady Carina and Andre."

"What?" Mac stood there staring at Bardot like she heard her wrong. "What happened?"

"They were found in Lady Carina's apartment in downtown Seattle. Her body had signs of overkill, and it appeared that Andre had just gotten in the way. We now believe that there are two killers, likely a woman and a man. Our theory is that the female killer is a sexual sadist, which is quite rare but lends to her background in BDSM. There are signs of sexual sadism and dismemberment. On some of the earlier bodies, there were signs of necrophilia. Due to the strength it takes to actually strangle a person, we believe the woman tortures the victim by mutilating their body in various ways, and when she's done, her partner kills them. We believe dumping the bodies in water is a forensic countermeasure. They're looking to get rid of the evidence. We were lucky and found seminal fluid inside Alice's body, but we haven't found a match so far."

Now Mac was intrigued. She had also suspected this to be the work of at least two people. "What about Lady Carina and Andre? They weren't submerged. Was there any forensic evidence left behind?"

"Unfortunately, no, the bodies were washed with bleach water, and they either wore gloves or wiped the place down."

"What do you make of the change in victimology and signature?"

Mac asked. "As far as we know, they've never taken on a couple before, and certainly no one as formidable as Lady Carina and Andre."

"It looks like this one may have been an impulse kill. We think they might take turns. Sometimes the male partner gets to choose, and sometimes the female does. It appears that the woman prefers strong young men, and the man prefers small, petite women. The problem is we're just speculating. We have no idea if they're always killing together or if they sometimes go out separately. Hell, we aren't even sure if all the cases are connected." Bardot let out a frustrated breath.

"That's fair, but if you'll allow me to come back into the investigation, maybe we can put our heads together and figure this thing out. Maybe if I come back, they'll come out of hiding."

"Are you suggesting we use you as bait?" Bardot looked intrigued. "Actually, I get the feeling that the present you just received is to taunt you. One of them has a sick little fascination with you."

"If that's the case, then dangling me out there could be too tempting for them to stay away."

"Are you sure, Mac? It could be very dangerous for you."

Mac didn't hesitate. "I'm in."

CHAPTER
SIXTY-THREE

"YOU DID WHAT?" Hudson looked at her like she had lost her mind.

"Yes, they put me back on the case. You know I can't walk away, not with Uncle Don calling me every other day for updates about Alice's killer. The man needs closure, and I can't just run away. He practically raised her, and he's grieving."

"Why can't it be someone else?" Hudson asked, pacing around his small office on base. Hudson had been gone for too long, and there was work piling up on his desk. He ran his hand through his hair, making it stand up on his head.

"I don't know. Maybe because I'm actually good at this," she pointed out.

"Maybe you're just a freak magnet!" he said, raising his voice. "You do realize your house is once again an active crime scene, and you want to taunt this maniac into making further contact with you? We aren't even sure what we're dealing with. For all we know, the woman is innocent and her husband is the killer. She's just in the wrong place at the wrong time. You know how rare it is for a woman to be a stone-cold killer?"

At first she was a little taken aback by the fierceness in his eyes, but then she realized he was upset because he was frightened. She couldn't blame him for that; she was a little more than scared. Finding a severed head in her house when they'd gotten home had been a bit unsettling, to say the least. The technician brought in by the FBI to examine the head had found a note inside the mouth that said, MISSING YOU in red block letters. Now she was going back to the Seattle/Tacoma area and the killer's playground. She just hoped they could catch a break and stop the killings without anything happening to her.

She tried to put her emotions aside and convince Hudson to help her. If he was involved, then he would feel like he had some sense of control and could protect her. Plus, he had some really good instincts. "I know how rare it is for the woman to be the killer, but it's still possible. There are cases out there that substantiate the possibility. From way back in history, there are cases of female sadistic killers like Madame LaLaurie, who killed countless in her torture chamber that she kept in her attic. What about Elizabeth Báthory, the Blood Countess who was thought to be a vampire and killed and tortured servant girls in a torture chamber that her husband had built her? More recently, Aileen Wuornos was a serial killer who took out seven men."

"I get your point, but Aileen killed because she had been sexually abused throughout most of her life and was taking some sort of twisted revenge against her clients while working as a prostitute, if memory serves me correctly. If you're right about this woman being a sexual sadist, then she is indeed a rare breed," Hudson said.

"Yeah, but not impossible," Mac responded. "So, how about you come with me? You could be my bodyguard, and we could unravel this mystery together."

"Well, as much as I would love to guard that beautiful body, I also have a job to do. I'm not sure how much time my commander will allow me to take off, plus we've been having some serious morale issues in security forces after the suicide." Hudson's face showed worry lines.

"Fair enough. Let me see if I can pull some strings and get a fill-in first sergeant to cover for you. If Bardot wants me, maybe I can negotiate a package deal. She seems to have some serious pull with the OSI. They're both federal investigating agencies, so they should cooperate specifically to get this case resolved. If they're connected to the military, then it puts a big ugly mark all over public relations."

"That seems fair, but I still feel obligated to help my squadron. I'll talk to my commander and see if there's a possibility that one of the other master sergeants can take the lead, and I can stay on call while at JBLM with you. Hopefully he can put me on orders. This little adventure is costing me a fortune." He stopped talking and pulled her into a warm embrace. At first she was very still, but then he felt her chest shudder against his and realized she was crying. "It'll be okay," he said.

"I know, I'm just a little worried and exhausted. Sorry for getting all emotional on you, it's just with that thing in my kitchen..."

She pressed closer to his chest and wrapped her arms around his body, trying desperately to feel some sense of safety. "I need to be near you right now. Can you make time?" she said in a soft voice.

"I'll always make time for you," Hudson said, looking down at her with kindness and understanding in his eyes.

He reached over and slid his door shut and clicked the lock. He ran his fingers up and down her back. The sensation of simply holding her and never wanting to let go made the world seem like a better place.

CHAPTER
SIXTY-FOUR

"WHO WAS ASKING QUESTIONS ABOUT ME?" Panic rose in the pit of Mistress Gennavie's stomach.

"A large man slightly smaller than me and a hot little Latina were here to see Goddess Z, and they were asking about you," Mountain said. "I just thought you might want to know."

"How long ago was this?" she practically yelled into the phone.

"About four or five days ago, I think," he said, sounding unsure.

"And why did you wait to call me?" Gennavie seethed.

"Because Goddess Z said you left her, and she was hurt. She said not to contact you, but I was afraid that you were in trouble, so I decided to call," he said, sounding offended.

"Very well, thank you for letting me know. Do you know what Goddess Z told them about me?" Mistress Gennavie asked, trying to keep her voice as calm as possible.

"Just that you sometimes go as Davis and that you carry an ugly military bag with you on some of your visits."

"Is that it?" she said, straining to stay calm.

"She said she missed you and wants you to come back to her," Mountain said softly. "I miss you, too," he added.

"I miss you too. Thank you for calling me. I know that couldn't have been easy for you," she cooed.

"I'll do anything for you. Will you come back?" he asked, but was startled to hear the phone disconnect.

She would never go back there. Goddess Z was cruel to her and treated her like she had been an item she owned rather than a companion. There were so many different techniques that she had learned, but just as many ways to be cruel and self-centered. Goddess Z simply wanted her pet back.

Her mind was reeling. She forced herself to calm down, especially since she was at work. It was beneficial that her husband was out in the field. He would be gone all week getting ready for the big inspection. There was a good possibility that he wouldn't even get the opportunity to call her over the next few days. They were supposed to be roughing it with their new troops, teaching them how to survive in the wilderness. This suited her just fine. She needed time to think and decide how to proceed.

The thoughts that kept popping into her twisted mind were at first jumbled, but then became more calculated. She hated to leave her husband behind. He was the first person she had ever known that understood who she truly was and liked it. Most men enjoyed her sadistic side, to a point. As a sexual sadist, she had become a very good dominatrix. She wanted nothing more than to control her clients, but she could never truly let loose with them.

The first time she had truly let loose ended with a dead body in Amsterdam right before the military PCS'd her back to the States where she had met him. He had been so open and willing to understand her true dark side.

The enticing and thrilling feeling she got when she killed with him was hard to give up. It was like an addiction that she was trying to walk away from. There was nothing she couldn't do in front of him. They had done it all. Most of it involved bondage, mutilation, strangulation, and then the most orgasmic sex she had ever experienced with a consensual partner afterward.

She wasn't sure if she would find anyone like him again, but she couldn't see any other way. If they remained together, then they would always be hunted. Living on the run didn't seem like a great idea. She was a lady who enjoyed the finer things in life, after all, and she wanted to be free to continue killing. *Is he important enough to go on the run?* she wondered to herself.

The day seemed to drag as she saw patients and attended to her duties. The mundane tasks gave her the opportunity to think and come up with a solid plan. By the end of the day, she knew what she had to do.

CHAPTER
SIXTY-FIVE

MAC RELUCTANTLY KISSED HUDSON GOODBYE. They'd decided to stay at his place after the whole severed head thing. She wasn't sure if she would be able to sleep at her place again for a while. It was a good thing she was headed back to JBLM. She felt apprehensive because Hudson hadn't been released to join her in the investigation. She downloaded the Life360 app on both of their phones so he could track her whereabouts. Somehow, it didn't make either one of them feel better about the situation.

She had been in contact with Bardot and Kibble. Both seemed happy for her to return and further assist with the case. She had reservations, especially without Hudson by her side. She desperately wanted to catch the killer, but her anxiety kept her on edge. Something about the case was eluding her, and she just couldn't put her finger on it.

So many unanswered questions were running through her head and were messing with her sleep, which made her brain feel sluggish and unfocused. Her stomach was upset, and she felt off-balance about other things as well. There was only one thing she could do: figure out a way to sleep. Sleep meds weren't an option because they left her feeling foggy and hungover the following day.

It wasn't just the case that was making her feel off. She felt horrible every time she talked to Alice's uncle. She had a nagging feeling that she was somehow responsible or could have prevented Alice's death. She kept replaying the events in her mind but couldn't quite come up with a resolution. The only way to make peace with the beautiful young lady's death was to catch her killer and give Uncle Don some closure.

Her mind skipped to Lola. *What the hell was she thinking?* she wondered as she drove the now-familiar route back to Joint Base Lewis-McChord. This new employer didn't feel right, and she couldn't get over the fact that Lola had a little girl. She was the most precious little person Mac thought she had ever seen. She felt instantly connected to little Olive and wanted to make sure she and her mother stayed safe. Her feelings were still hurt that the only reason she'd found out about her existence was that Olive had been hungry.

They had been there with Lola, and still, her sister was going to keep Olive a secret. She felt hurt and a little betrayed, but also very concerned. If Lola was that fearful, then there had to be more going on than the threat to their family. They had been dealing with that threat their entire lives. It was nothing new to either of them. This had to be something more.

And then there was the issue of Hudson. Dammit, she was falling for him hard. Who was she kidding? She had fallen for him in the beginning but was doing her best to bury those feelings deep, but was being entirely unsuccessful. She even liked his mom and could see why he was such a kind and gentle giant. If she had it her way, she would marry him tomorrow and start a family, but he would have to spend his life looking over his shoulder just like she did. He wouldn't understand, but she would just have to make him. It would be time to leave him soon, and it would break her heart.

Her phone rang next to her, cutting into her destructive thought process. She was relieved for the distraction from her own mental torture. It was one of the things she wished she could change about her personality—she would fixate on a problem and keep mulling it over. It made it almost impossible for her to shut down her brain or focus on other things. Now she was fixated on three different issues that she couldn't seem to solve.

"Mac, when will you get here?" Bardot's voice came over her hands-free speaker.

"I'm on the road now and should be there in about five hours."

"Fair enough. Initial thoughts?" Bardot asked bluntly.

That was something Mac really liked about Bardot. Mac always knew where she stood with her, and there weren't any games except for when Bardot had been investigating her. That was one thing Mac couldn't handle from anyone. She hated deception and playing games with people and enjoyed people who would shoot straight with her. "I think you're spot-on, and there are at least two people involved. I'm a little hung up on the severed head. Don't get me wrong, it had the desired effect and freaked me out a bit, but it doesn't fit their normal modus operandi or signature considering none of the victims have had severed body parts. I'm not saying it isn't possible; it just doesn't quite fit."

"You're very observant. I like that about you," Bardot said.

"Thank you, ma'am. What do you think?"

"I think I agree with you. As you probably already know, the MO is the method they use to kill, which often stays the same but can grow, and the killer can get better at their mode of killing the more skillful they become. With our guys, they've been known to use a distinct rope that has yet to be identified and isn't necessarily a cause of death, but the whip marks and genital mutilation are unique. They never leave fingerprints behind or any other forensic evidence except for the seminal fluid left in Alice's body and a synthetic red hair found on the Collymore body and in the truck that was traced back to a high-end wig. The signature is what's eluding me."

Mac was silent for a moment. "I think we're having a hard time nailing down the signature because it's emotional. We think sometimes they kill together and sometimes separately because there are variations depending on the victim, which is highly probable. They could agree on how to kill when they're together, but sometimes it can be hard to separate when you have two separate sets of emotions. Right now, I feel like we have more questions than answers."

"I agree. Additionally, there seems to be the possibility of a third accomplice," Bardot reminded her.

"Carter just doesn't feel right, but I can't put my finger on why," she said as she passed into the mountains and the call cut off.

CHAPTER
SIXTY-SIX

MISTRESS GENNAVIE'S PHONE RANG.

"She's coming back," Tank told her. "And she knows entirely too much. I'm worried about your safety. Are you sure they have nothing on you?"

"Oh Tank," she said in her sweetest voice. "Of course they have nothing on me, because I've done nothing wrong. Though I do need you to keep her distracted for a bit. Tell me everything she knows."

"She said there was a dead body in Amsterdam right before you came here. Do you know anything about that?" he asked pointedly. He was crazy about this woman, but he knew she was dangerous, which was part of the turn-on. If anyone found out about their little affair, it would ruin everything for him, but he simply couldn't give her up.

"I had absolutely nothing to do with that," she crooned. "I heard rumors about it after the fact. Apparently the man committed suicide in his hotel room."

"Yes, but he was covered in whip marks. Now who does that sound like?"

"Dammit, I said I had nothing to do with it, and that's final," she snapped.

"Okay, okay." His voice softened. "I just have a lot on the line here, and I want to be sure you're going to stay with me. I'm not sure if I can continue without you," he admitted pitifully.

"You know I'm not going anywhere. I'm just as crazy about you," she lied. "Now, keep your ear to the ground and keep me posted on the developments."

"When can I see you?" he practically begged.

It was just where she liked him—wanting and addicted to her kind of crazy. She could make a man do anything she wanted him to do. She lived for the power it gave her. In many ways, it was just like being an alcoholic. She simply couldn't get enough. "Soon, darling. Be patient. You're too close to the investigation, and I don't want to bring any attention your way."

"You're right, we should lay low, but with your husband in the field this week, I just thought we could, um, you know…" he said, sounding like a bashful schoolboy.

"I'll work something out. Since my name is no longer Davis, it should take her a little time to figure things out. In the meantime, find out everything you can about what the FBI, OSI, and local law enforcement know about the case and, more importantly, about me. I need you to distract Mac and keep her away from me. I have some business to attend to. Can you keep her away?" she asked in her best phone-sex voice.

"Yes, my love. I can't wait to see you," he said, but only received a dial tone in his ear.

CHAPTER
SIXTY-SEVEN

MAC CHECKED in with Kibble to review the case one more time before meeting with the FBI the following day. There was very little that Bardot had not already told her, but the news about another potentially related body found near Snoqualmie Falls was a new one.

She felt terrible for the lovebirds who had discovered the cougar snacking on the remains. *That had to put a damper on any romance they had planned*, she thought. The evidence surrounding the bodies of Lady Carina and Andre was particularly compelling. There was little physical evidence left at the scene, but the mutilation of Lady Carina's body was interesting. Clearly the killers were silencing them, but the rage taken out on Lady Carina spoke volumes about how the killer or killers felt about her in particular.

Carter walked into the office. "Hi Mac, nice to have you back. How are things going?"

"Good, just trying to figure this thing out," she said, purposefully vague. She had kept all of her evidence in a folder and encouraged Kibble to keep his folder with him, just in case.

"I'm headed out to do some interviews on a separate case. Do you guys need anything before I go?" Carter asked, not seeming to catch on to the tension in the room.

"No," Mac responded, trying to sound dismissive. "I think we're good."

Kibble and Mac watched him leave.

"So," Kibble said, approaching the subject cautiously. "If he left you that note, what do you think he's getting out of it?"

"I'm not sure, but the puzzle pieces don't quite fit. What could he possibly gain from getting me off the case in the first place? As far as I know, he's a happily married man with a wife expecting their third baby. That doesn't sound like the type of man who would be wrapped up in something like this."

"Yeah, well, I've seen men do some crazy things before. I've had more surprises during my time as defense counsel than I care to think about."

"I can agree with that. Either way, we need to keep this information close to our chests."

Kibble's desk phone rang. "You've reached the Area Defense Counsel's office. Can I help you?"

"Hey, just the guy I've been looking for. This is Agent Whitlock. I've been on the phone all morning with the FBI. It appears we have a match to the DNA found in Alice. Our perp isn't at all what I expected."

"I'm putting you on speaker. Mac is here in the office with me," Kibble said. "So, spill it."

"He's part of the Twenty-Second Special Tactics Squadron and highly trained in special ops, rescue, and personnel recovery, and you're going to love this: the team is all parachute qualified."

"Is that significant?" Kibble asked.

"Yeah, the paracord matches the ligature marks on most of the victims," Whitlock said. "The team lead confirmed that the rope was regularly braided into multiple patterns, which explains why the ligature marks were often the same width but had different markings."

"Why didn't I think of that?" Mac muttered. That made complete sense. "When can we interview him?"

Whitlock was quiet for a few minutes. "That's the complicated part. If we get a confession, then there'll be a jurisdictional mess to deal with. Of course, you want a piece of him for the Collymore murder, but then the FBI wants to charge him in a civilian federal case. He's also wanted in multiple jurisdictions in Washington. I guess what I'm saying is you might have to get in line."

"What about his partner?" Mac asked.

"What partner?"

"There's evidence that he's been working with a woman that at some point went by the last name Davis and Mistress Gennavie," Mac explained.

"I don't know the status of that, but I'll look into it," Whitlock said. "I'm meeting with Bardot in an hour. I assume you guys want in on this?"

"Damn straight," Kibble responded. "We'll meet you there."

CHAPTER
SIXTY-EIGHT

THE LITTLE ROOM was getting very crowded. Mac felt a little claustrophobic with all the law enforcement representatives pressed together. They were watching the interview through a one-way mirror. The young man cuffed to the table was not at all what she'd thought he would look like. It was interesting how the brain formulated an image of a person simply based on their actions.

The young man sitting in the interrogation room looked... Mac couldn't quite put her finger on it, just not what she had expected. He was a muscular young man with a broad smile, blond hair, and fair Norwegian features. Not that he was smiling now, but she had seen a picture of him before arriving; in it he was smiling, standing next to his team in uniform. He couldn't have stood more than five foot eight inches.

Bardot leaned toward the suspect. "Please state your name for the record."

"My name is Staff Sergeant Auston Pierce" he said in a shaky voice. "Why am I here? I haven't done anything wrong."

"Why did you kill Alice Bosold?" she said, staring him directly in the eyes, watching for a reaction.

"What are you talking about? I didn't kill her. I never laid a hand on her," he said, looking frightened.

"Where were you last Monday night?" Bardot asked.

"At home, I think. I usually don't go out during the week because we have to be at work so early," he explained.

Bardot switched tactics. "Who's the redhead that picked up Collymore?"

"I don't know any redhead." His hands were shaking, and he looked like he was going into a full-blown panic.

"We know you've been working with a woman who wears a red wig. Is she also in the military?" Bardot asked.

"I don't know who you're talking about," Auston shot back.

"How many other people have you killed?"

"None, zero. I've never killed anyone."

Bardot changed direction again. "What about the rope we found in your room?"

"What about it?" Auston looked confused.

"That's the exact type of rope used to strangle your victims."

"I don't have any victims, and we all use that rope. It's part of our parachute gear. The whole team has it. You can check," he said hopefully.

"We sent it to our lab for testing. You might as well tell me what happened. We're going to find out anyway. Once Alice's DNA comes back on your rope, you won't have any room to negotiate. I can work with the multiple agencies looking to prosecute you if you cooperate. I'll let them know you cooperated and want to give the families of your victim's peace," she said, softening a little, trying to give him an opening to confess.

He just looked at her, so she took a picture of Alice's white corpse out of her folder and placed it in front of Auston. "What did she do to deserve this?"

His face turned ghostly white, and he looked away from the gruesome picture. "Ma'am, with all due respect, I have no idea what the hell you're talking about, and I want my lawyer," Auston said, sitting back in his uncomfortable metal chair.

"Very well," Bardot said, gathering her file and leaving the room.

Inside the small observation room, there was an audible grumble from the task force. A lawyer would slow things down and ultimately stop any questioning. It would be hours before his attorney could be appointed, let alone have time to meet with his client. The only upside was that they could hold him, and he wouldn't be able to hurt anyone else. They were stuck, and everyone was feeling frustrated.

Mac hoped the lab would find some usable evidence. They were combing through Auston's apartment during the interrogation. Now all they could do was wait. She thought about what they might find. The fact that Auston's DNA was found inside the victim was damning and could quickly get him convicted, but Mac knew a good defense attorney could poke holes in it if there was no other evidence to corroborate his involvement.

CHAPTER
SIXTY-NINE

GENNAVIE PACED AROUND the clinic where she worked, trying to figure out the best next move when her phone rang. "Hey, I heard I was arrested today," Vincent said sarcastically.

"Are you still in the field?" Gennavie asked.

"Nah, when OSI came out to the field I nearly shit myself, but they took Auston. Did you have something to do with that?"

"Why do you always have to be so vulgar? Of course, I did. If I left things up to you, then we would likely be in prison right now, and this lady wouldn't do well in a cage," she said, referring to herself.

"Well, well, aren't you the clever one. How did you set him up?"

"It's none of your concern. Just know that it's taken care of. Now grab your go-bag and meet me at the place we discussed."

He sensed concern in her voice. "Don't worry, we planned for this. I know you don't want to go on the run, but there's no other way," he assured her.

"I know, I just hate to have to start from scratch once again, and even more so, I hate to be on the run," she admitted. "But it beats the alternative."

"Agreed, my love. Don't forget your passport. I'll meet you there. Be safe," he said, and hung up.

She found her supervisor in the back storeroom taking inventory.

"Hey, I hate to ask, but I have an emergency. My mom is really sick, and I need to fly home to Ohio. Can you approve me for twenty-five days of leave?" she asked sweetly.

"Um, don't you want to go through the Red Cross and get on emergency leave, so we can possibly get a grant from the Air Force Aid to help pay for the trip?" Master Sergeant Ellis asked.

"No, I have the money. I just want to get to her as quickly as possible," she lied. Her ability to deceive was one of her best assets. It was one of the reasons she went to such great lengths to be a star airman. People wanted to trust and help her, which went a long way when she had to flee.

Master Sergeant Ellis hesitated for what seemed like a long time.

"Look, boss, I rarely ask for leave, and I've done a good job for you. If you can sign the leave for twenty-five days, it doesn't even have to go through the commander. I should be able to get everything taken care of for her that quickly. We would have to get him involved if it was over thirty days. This will just be quick and easy. No hassle, and I'll be back before the inspection." She gave him a pleading look.

He couldn't say no to her. Being her boss was one of the most challenging things he'd had to endure. He had feelings for her that he could never reveal to anyone, especially not his wife. Even if he wanted to pursue her, it was against the Uniform Code of Military Justice, and he wasn't going to slip up right before the end of his career. She mesmerized him, but he wasn't that stupid.

"Sure, log in to leave web and put in the request. Let me know when it's done so I can approve it," he said.

"Thanks, boss, I'm on it. I'll turn my stuff over to the rest of the team and have it to you shortly. I really appreciate your understanding and flexibility," she said over her shoulder.

I really love her smile, he thought as he watched her walk away.

CHAPTER
SEVENTY

AUSTON'S REACTION to the picture of Alice's corpse didn't seem right to Mac. He wouldn't have turned pale like that if he had killed her. The physical reaction to the photo was something that Auston had no control over. His eyes had dilated, showing a spike in adrenaline when he realized Bardot was accusing him of murder, and he looked up and to the left when answering her questions. If he had looked up and to the right, it would generally mean that he was lying. This usually indicated that the suspect was trying to remember and telling the truth.

Mac wasn't sure what to think. These troops were trained in evasion and interrogation techniques, so he may have been able to fake his eye movements, but she didn't think he could fake the blood draining from his face. Something just wasn't right.

Kibble walked into the conference room at the FBI office. She was still sitting there going over information. He handed her a cup of coffee and sat down.

"Thank you," she said.

"So, what do you think?" Kibble asked.

'Not sure, just working through what we know. Have they come back with anything yet?"

"Not that I know of, but hopefully there will be more at his place," Kibble said.

"Any indication of a woman in his life?" Mac asked.

"Nothing that we've been able to find. He has a roommate that said he dates a lot, but no one is serious. I would think a partner like her would be somewhat serious."

"You would think so. Are the IT guys running his phone, social media, and computer?" Mac asked.

"Yeah, they have it all covered. Why don't we head back to base?" Kibble suggested. "They'll let us know if they find anything. Plus, I have some things I need to take care of."

"That's a great idea. I can't tell you the last time I got a good night's sleep." She yawned and stretched, then collected her files.

CHAPTER
SEVENTY-ONE

MAC SETTLED into the bed in her hotel room, finally ready to sleep. She was wearing one of Hudson's old t-shirts that still carried his scent. It made her feel safe. Just as she was about to drift off to sleep, the phone rang.

She picked it up. "What?"

"Ma'am, I'm sorry to bother you at this hour," came the voice of Bardot's right-hand man.

"Sorry, Weidman, what can I do for you?" She tried to stifle a yawn.

"Bardot needs to see you as soon as possible—without Kibble."

"What's this about?" Mac asked, now feeling alert.

"There have been new developments, but that's all I can tell you right now. Can you come back in?" Weidman asked.

"Of course, I'll be there as soon as I can." She hung up, pulling Hudson's comfy t-shirt off and putting the same clothes she had worn all day back on. She went into the bathroom and splashed water on her face to wake up a bit. She couldn't remember the last time she was this tired. Her entire body ached, and she looked like shit. She contemplated putting on some makeup but then abandoned the idea and grabbed her bag.

She arrived back at the FBI building, but it was completely deserted at this hour. There were few cars on the streets, and the building had a spooky quality. Mac already felt on edge but being out on the street by herself at night with an actual boogeyman on the loose didn't sit well.

Her heart was pounding in her chest. She quickened her pace and was relieved to see Weidman waiting for her just inside the building. "Thank you for coming back so quickly," he said, holding the door open for her.

"No problem. What's going on?"

"I think Bardot should walk you through everything," he said, leading the way back to the elevator.

They entered the FBI offices to find the place deserted, minus Bardot and a woman in a lab coat. "Mac, thank you for coming back. This is Dr. Vandenberg, our lead forensic scientist. She has some interesting news." Bardot stepped back from a large screen, indicating for the doctor to explain.

"As you know, we found seminal fluid inside the victim after her body was discovered in the water. Surprisingly, it was a good sample since the body had not been submerged for any period of time. What surprised me was there are three distinct DNA indications present," Dr. Vandenberg explained.

"Three? How is that even possible?" Mac asked.

"That's precisely the question we're trying to answer. There are a few explanations that make sense, like a threesome. You knew the victim. Do you feel that's something she would participate in?" the doctor asked.

"Not at all," Mac said. "The woman I met with was devastated to lose Collymore. She was grieving and mourning the loss of not only her future husband but the plans they had for a life together. All she could talk about was getting married and having children. She was concerned about some of the things he was researching, but she seemed more appalled and concerned and not at all wanting to participate in that lifestyle."

"That was my understanding as well," Bardot said. "We looked into her background, and she's a religious woman, which doesn't suggest an interest in group sex."

"Okay, so what's the other explanation?" Mac asked.

"That's why I brought you in. Auston's attorney has spoken with his client and agrees that Auston has some information that might clear him, and has agreed that Auston can be interviewed again as long as he's present," Bardot said.

"Why did you instruct me to leave Kibble out of this?" Mac asked.

"Just a hunch," Bardot said. "And having two lawyers go at it won't help Auston feel at ease. I've already questioned him and feel you would be well equipped to get the information needed from him. There are pieces here that just don't fit. You need to get him to open up, especially if he has information that could clear his name. Are you up to this?"

"Yes, ma'am, I'll do my best."

CHAPTER
SEVENTY-TWO

MAC SIPPED a cup of coffee as she waited for Auston and his attorney. The evidence response team had returned with everything from Auston's apartment and was busy testing and processing the evidence. She wondered if they would work through the night or if it would wait until morning. She knew there were strict rules surrounding the process.

Years ago, there was a case she was involved in where the defense counsel had poked holes in the chain of evidence and processing because the person in charge of the process had not slept in almost twenty-four hours. The defense brought in a sleep expert to testify about the diminished cognitive abilities associated with sleep deprivation. Ultimately, the case was thrown out on a technicality due to the piss-poor way the evidence had been processed. In that case, Mac had strong beliefs that the accused had, in fact, been guilty of rape and should have gone to prison. She knew the defense's job was to always do what was in the accused's best interest regardless of their thoughts about them as a human.

Overall, Mac enjoyed defense more than prosecution because she liked helping people, but there were some cases where justice simply wasn't done, and a rapist was set free. She truly believed in the military justice system. She thought at times it was entirely too strict, like when she had a client who was eighteen years old and did a line of coke to impress someone but was now being put out of the military with a federal conviction. It left the young man with few options except to possibly become a drug dealer or some other unsavory career field.

Auston and his attorney were brought into the interrogation room. Mac stood up and shook their hands. "Good evening, I'm Technical Sergeant Evelyn McGregor, but you can call me Mac if you'd like."

"I've heard of you," Auston said. "Aren't you that lady who solved the serial-killer case at Fairchild?"

"Yes, one and the same, but that's not why we're here. I understand you may have some information that could be useful to exonerate you and shed some light on this case," Mac said.

The attorney sitting next to Auston cleared his throat. "I'm Joseph Admier. I've verified that Auston has been read his Miranda Rights and Article 32 rights and understands them. I'm here to protect the interests of my clients and will terminate the interview if I believe it's in his best interest."

"I would expect nothing less," Mac said, smiling to put them both at ease. It was crucial that she came across as an ally versus an adversary. "I'm here to help us get to the bottom of this and have no interest in getting the wrong person prosecuted. Now, why don't we start at the beginning and go from there."

Auston looked at his attorney for confirmation. The attorney gave him a slight nod. "So, I first want to say that I'm not a bad guy."

"No one said you were," Mac assured him, keeping eye contact.

"Okay, so I've never met Alice, the victim. I didn't have sex with her, but I may know what happened. But it may sound really far-fetched."

"Try me. I'm pretty open-minded," Mac encouraged.

"She's good at this," Bardot commented to Dr. Vandenberg, who watched from the other side of the one-way mirror.

"So," Auston continued, dropping his eyes to his hands for a moment, "I had sex with my buddy's wife." He paused, trying to collect himself. "I'm not at all proud of what I did, but this woman is, um, irresistible. She has a way of getting what she wants from people."

"Who is this woman?" Mac asked.

"She went by Ares, but I don't know if that's her actual name. The way she said it almost sounded like she wasn't used to it or something. I know that sounds crazy, but I know she's on active duty, and her name isn't that, or at least I don't think it is."

"What do you think her name is?" Mac asked.

"Well, my buddy's last name is Wulf—Vincent Wulf—and he always referred to his wife as Gennavie, not Ares. I should have never slept with her."

"Why do you think this has anything to do with Alice's murder?" Mac asked, trying to keep him focused.

"Well, um." Auston looked down at his hands again and then back at Mac, "When I, well, she kept the condom after I—well, you know. I don't think she thought I saw her, but she twisted the top. My eyes were slightly closed, but I looked down right when she did it. At first, I thought she was just taking it off to throw it away, but then she put a clip on it. I thought it was just a bizarre thing to do."

"That is weird," Mac said. "Did you ask her about it?"

"No, I didn't know what to think," Auston said.

"Did anything else happen?"

"She got up and went to the bathroom. All her stuff was in there, so I assumed it went into her purse because it wasn't in the trash. I thought it was some kind of weird fetish of hers, so I just let it go."

"When did this happen?" Mac asked.

"It was the Saturday before they said I killed Alice. I'm not sure if that helps my case, but under the circumstances... I know I never had sex with this Alice woman. I don't even know who she was. The only person who had access to my DNA was Ares, or whatever the hell she goes by."

"What else do you know about her?" Mac asked. "Do you know where she works or where she lives?"

"I've been to her place once while her husband was in a training session. I had already been through the training, so I didn't have to attend."

"Do you recall where the house is?" Mac asked.

"Oh yeah, it was stunning. It sits right on the water and has multiple levels. It's not far off of I-5 but is tucked down a back road. It's the last house before the road ends. I'm not sure how they afford it, but I can tell you it's fun to play there."

"Do you think you could show us where it is on a map?" Mac asked.

"Sure, no problem."

"Is there anything else you can tell me about her?" Mac asked.

"Nah, just that she's a bit of a control freak. I'm honestly not sure what she was doing with me. I mean, she really didn't seem to care if she got caught by her husband, and I got the feeling that I wasn't the only guy she was messing around with."

"What gave you that feeling?" Mac asked, thinking this was a goldmine of information. If any of it panned out, they might solve this thing after all. She could feel her Spidey senses tingling—that feeling all investigators get when they're close to solving a case.

"Well, this attorney guy stopped by my apartment the next day and just wanted to chat. He said he had some questions about some guy named Collymore and wanted to know if I had any information about his death. I thought it was weird because it was a Sunday. When he started asking questions, it wasn't about the Collymore guy at all. He wanted to know if I had been sleeping with Gennavie, and he seemed a little jealous. He wanted to know details about how long we had been sleeping together. I mean, she told me not to tell anyone, but I wasn't about to lie to an officer. I could get into real trouble for falsifying information."

Mac hadn't been expecting that. "Can you describe this man?"

"Yeah, he kinda resembled a bear. He was wide and not very tall. He said his name, but I can't remember what it was. I just know he's a captain," Auston said.

"Could it be Captain Kibble?" Mac asked, caught off guard.

"Yeah, that's the guy," Auston said, smiling for the first time.

CHAPTER
SEVENTY-THREE

BARDOT BROUGHT in a map for Auston to point out the property. Most of what Auston had said backed up the current evidence they had in their possession. It was after 2300 hours by the time they called it a night. It would be morning before Bardot could get a search warrant for the property.

Mac woke the following day feeling like she had been hit by a Mac truck. She hauled her carcass out of bed and took a quick shower. She was due back at the FBI office by 0800 hours. She lied to Kibble, telling him that she had other business to attend and wouldn't be in until later that afternoon. She hated lying, and it went against what she believed in, but she wasn't willing to jeopardize the investigation without knowing Kibble's full involvement.

When she arrived at the FBI building, Dr. Vandenberg told her they'd discovered that a rope found at Auston's apartment had Alice's DNA on it and had a hair on one end left by none other than Captain Kibble. None of Auston's DNA was found on the rope, even though it was discovered under his bed.

Mac really couldn't understand what was going on with Captain Kibble. He seemed like such a good man. How could he possibly throw his life away to cover up murder unless he was involved in the murders himself? Mac let that thought roll around in her brain for a little bit. It didn't feel right, but then she thought back to her previous case. She would have never thought that her mentor and confidant could be capable of murdering multiple women.

Even so, Chief Master Sergeant Deleon had once been a good man but had changed due to a traumatic brain injury. Nothing like that had happened to Kibble, as far as she knew. There had to be something she was missing about the man. Her thoughts went to his wife and four kids. *How could he do that to them?* she wondered.

Bardot walked into the office. "Ready?"

"I was born ready," Mac said, smiling.

"My team is sitting on the property now. They've been there overnight, and no one has come or gone. We're fairly certain that no one is home," Bardot said, heading to the elevator.

"What about the husband and wife? Have they tracked them down yet?" Mac said, feeling encouraged. "Maybe we can find some evidence to lead to this couple and answer some of the questions."

"No, unfortunately it looks like someone tipped them off," Bardot said. "The woman in question is Ares Wulf. She's a medical technician at JBLM. She is a model airman and has won several awards. Her leadership loves her and is convinced we have the wrong person. I spoke with her supervisor, Master Sergeant Ellis. He said that she came to him late last week and asked to be put on leave. She said her mother was sick and had to fly home to Ohio."

"Well, at least we know where she's headed. What about Vincent?" Mac asked.

"We have all airlines keeping an eye out for anyone matching their description. Vincent Wulf's leadership says he called in sick this morning and hasn't been seen."

Bardot and Mac drove up to the property, finding a traffic jam full of cop cars, FBI, and civilian vehicles. It was a narrow entrance to the property to begin with. The drive opened up a bit closer to the garage, but the entrance was small. There was very little room to maneuver and didn't leave much of an exit option. Mac wondered if maybe they'd gone by boat at some point, but she could see armed men out on the dock, patrolling the area. No one had been permitted to enter the property until Bardot arrived.

"Follow me," she said, looking at Mac. They walked up to a giant man covered head to toe in tactical gear.

"Ma'am," was all he said, and handed them both bulletproof vests. "We ran thermal imaging and found no signs of life."

"Is your team ready?" Bardot asked.

"Yes, ma'am," he responded.

"Go in and clear the house. Make sure you check any hiding places. There's been no sign of either suspect, so we can't assume they're not inside," Bardot instructed.

He spoke into his headset: "In five."

Mac watched as four men approached the property—two in the back near the dock, and two in the front. The rest stayed back from the perimeter until it was cleared. The team cleared each area methodically, shouting "clear" after each room. They worked from the bottom floor up and found nothing. It was standard protocol to have a property cleared in the event that explosives or booby traps were present.

The team came back out of the house. The lead man said, "It's all clear, ma'am."

The evidence collection team handed boot covers and gloves to everyone who'd received authorization to enter. Bardot took control of the scene, handing a clipboard to one of the officers standing by. Everyone signed in before entering, per protocol.

It was a stunning place. The thick mahogany door swung wide to reveal marble floors and chic leather furniture. Mac found herself looking around, astonished that this might be where her killers lived. People never cease to amaze her.

She followed Bardot through the house. The main entrance led to the second floor, so they started meticulously walking from one space to the next, taking care not to disturb any evidence. "Do you see anything that stands out?" Bardot asked.

"Not at the moment, other than the house feels a bit staged, almost like no one really lives here," Mac observed.

"I agree. What else do you see?"

Mac walked from one place to the next. "Obsessive cleanliness. There isn't even dust, which is hard to avoid when living next to the water."

They headed to the next level up.

On the house's third floor was a spotless kitchen with modern stainless-steel appliances and a large table that could fit at least twelve people. It was small and orderly like the previous floor had been. They went through the cabinets and found unpriceable food, neatly put away, almost like they each thing had a designated spot. The refrigerator was the same: everything was neatly lined up in rows with the labels facing out so that when the door was opened, you could see everything. "It looks like only one, maybe two people live here by the amount of food stored in the house," Bardot said.

"Let's go look at the top level," Mac suggested. The stairs were narrow up to the top floor. There was a small full bathroom off to the right as they walked in. It was just as orderly as the rest of the house. The towels were plush and neatly put in place. Mac started to wonder if there was a cleaning lady. Most people didn't take the time to be this meticulous in their own homes.

There was a prominent California king bed in the middle of the room with a nice sitting area off to one side. Large windows looked out over the water like the rest of the house. It was truly stunning and had to cost well over a million dollars, especially in the Seattle area. The room was neat and orderly. Along one wall there was a walk-in closet to the left, and to the right was a corner fireplace.

Inside the closet hung two sets of uniforms, neatly pressed. One was small and clearly made for a woman, and the other was a bit larger. The boots and dress shoes were lined up in an orderly fashion. There wasn't any dust in sight, and the shoes all looked like they had been wiped down recently. Mac wondered if it might be to eliminate any evidence. There was a row of high-end women's clothes on the other side of the closet with all the trimmings. "Look at this." Mac pointed to a green dress. She moved a few things aside and found a box. She removed the top to reveal a long red wig. She made sure not to disturb the evidence as she set it back on the floor.

"Ma'am, you should come to see this," came a male voice from one of the lower levels.

They headed down the stairs to find Agent Weidman on the third level, waiting. "What did you find?" Bardot asked.

"Follow me." He led them back down to the second level and then down the narrow stairs to the first floor. As they hit the bottom floor, they found a room with a glass wall with a view out to the water. It didn't lend much privacy, but no one could see unless they had a high-powered telescope or were out on the water. It was just as clean and stunning as the rest of the house.

There was a large bathroom off to the left with a nice clawfoot bathtub along one side. Weidman continued past another bedroom that sat off to the right. "In here." He pointed to the end of the hall. This room was different from the rest. Blackout shades had been draped across the large window, eliminating all-natural light. There was a leather board against the left wall with large rings attached to it. Off to the right, the wall was lined with whips, flogs, dog collars, and an assortment of leather clothes. In the center of the room, a sex swing hung from large hooks in the ceiling.

"Interesting," Bardot commented. "Has the evidence team processed this room?"

"No, ma'am. This one is next," Weidman said.

CHAPTER
SEVENTY-FOUR

GENNAVIE WANTED to scream as she watched the commotion from her boat. She did not like people in her space and going through her things. It had taken her a long time to get everything exactly the way she wanted it, and they were ruining everything. Her temper was getting out of control.

She knew there was nothing she could do about her situation or her husband. When she'd shown up to get her go-bag, she saw two men approach the house and take a position on the other side of a rock wall. She hadn't seen them at first but caught movement out of the corner of her eye. She'd left everything and headed out the back to her boat. She just hoped Vincent had gotten out in time. She had heard movement on the third floor but hadn't taken the time to see if it was him or the cops. All she could do was sit on her boat and watch the drama unfold.

The beauty of the house was that she could sit on the water tucked back in a little cove and see everything happening inside except for when they went into her dungeon. *Damn those curtains,* she thought. Whatever they were looking at couldn't be good. All she could do was sit back and helplessly watch her latest pretend life get picked apart little by little.

She saw Mac walk near a window and seriously thought about picking up her rifle and taking a shot. Ever since making expert marksman in basic training, she had honed her skills for just such an occasion. She was considered one of the best on base. The shot would give away her position, but it would be worth it, probably. She fixated on Mac on the other side of the window. They wouldn't have been caught if it hadn't been for her. Why the hell hadn't Mac been able to just walk away? She looked through the scope, getting a close-up of Mac and badly wanting to take the shot. She rested her finger on the trigger, contemplating. *Could they get to her fast enough?* she wondered.

If she'd made the shot and then taken off in the boat, they might not even have had time to react, but there were other boats on the water. She couldn't be sure that one of them wouldn't come after her. The boat rocked slightly, causing Gennavie to press her weight against the railing. It would be a tough shot from this distance and on the water, but she thought she could do it. The waters would have to be calm, but she thought she could still hit Mac and maybe that bird woman from the FBI. What the hell was wrong with those two?

After five intense seconds, she lowered the rifle and waited. They would have to leave eventually, and then she could go back in to get her supplies and, most importantly, her passport. Everything was hidden inside a small box underneath the floorboard on the first floor. There was no way the investigators would find it.

CHAPTER
SEVENTY-FIVE

MAC WALKED UP TO BARDOT. "They'll be processing for a while. I'm just going to step out and make a few phone calls to update my leadership and Hudson."

"Only give them essential information and make sure Stanton knows to keep Kibble out of it until we know his involvement," Bardot instructed. "I know those two are friends, and I don't want that to cloud his judgment."

Mac nodded and walked out of the house. Gennavie watched from the safety of the water as Mac made her way to the side yard. It was a nice area behind the separate garage. Paddleboards and kayaks hung on the back of the garage, and beyond the garage was a nice grassy area with lounge chairs. Mac thought she and Hudson should get away when this was all done. She sat in one of the chairs, pulled her phone out of her back pocket, and dialed Hudson.

"Hi hon, how are you doing?"

"Worried sick about you," he said, sounding agitated. "I thought you were going to keep me up to date. What happened when you got called in by the FBI?"

"I'm sorry, hon, it has been a whirlwind. We're actually at—" The words got caught in Mac's throat as she felt the barrel of a gun press against her right temple.

"Mac, are you there?" she could hear Hudson say as she lowered the phone.

"She won't be for long," Vincent said into the phone.

Hudson felt the blood drain from his face.

Gennavie watched the scene unfold from her perch, knowing it was extremely unlikely that her husband would walk away from this unscathed. At least now she knew what had happened to him. He must have been the noise she had heard from the third floor before she ran. He must not have seen the cops approach the house until it was too late. Maybe there would be a positive that came from it, and he would kill Mac once and for all, clearing the path for Gennavie to get away. She watched, not realizing she was holding her breath.

Vincent pressed his body against her back, snaking his dirty arm around her neck and pressing the gun hard against Mac's head. "Don't scream, or I'll shoot you."

"What do you want, Vincent? I can help you." Mac dropped her voice to keep the situation calm. She had done some training in hostage negotiations, and she was trying to remember what the instructor had said. The only thing that popped into her mind was, *Keep my voice low and offer to help.*

"Damn straight you're going to help me. You're my ticket out of here," he growled.

"Okay, what's your plan?" Mac asked him, softening her voice further. She found that it actually helped her stay calmer as well. Nice side effect.

"You'll walk out of here with me and make sure no one follows us."

"Okay, I can do that. How do you want to leave, and where do you want to go?" Mac asked calmly, trying not to breathe in his scent. He smelled of sweaty body odor, dirt, and fear. He must have been hiding all night while the house was being watched.

Hudson was frantically texting Bardot. *Mac held by gunpoint!* Thankfully Mac had left Bardot's number with him in the event of an emergency. He didn't want to break the line with Mac in case there was pertinent information to pass along. He was pissed at himself for not going with her. Screw his commander and all the problems. None of it would matter if the love of his life was murdered.

He waited, holding his breath until the text came back.

K, I have them, was all she responded with.

He heard the man on the other end of Mac's phone say, "You're going to be my human shield and get me out of here in one of those bulletproof SUVs."

"I can do that," she said calmly. "I'll need to get some keys."

"Fine," he said, pushing her back toward the garage. They came around the side to find every armed FBI and local police officer pointing their weapons at them. "Shit," he breathed into her neck.

Mac had kept her phone in her hand the entire time and knew Hudson was listening. "It's okay. We can work this out," she said softly back to him. She also meant the message for Hudson. She knew he had to be frantic.

"What are you talking about? They're going to shoot me," Vincent seethed. She could feel his fear bubbling to the surface. He was sweating profusely against her back, and her neck felt slimy with his sweat.

"If you turn yourself in, no one will get hurt," she tried.

"Never gonna happen. I'm not made for a cage." It was the one thing he and his wife had agreed on if it ever came to this. He hoped she had gotten away before the shit hit the fan and they came to their house. He was pissed at Auston for turning them in, but it was to be expected since she'd set him up to take the fall.

"Okay, let's stay calm," Mac said.

"Vincent, let her go," Bardot said, stepping forward.

"Ma'am, he wants the keys to your vehicle," Mac explained.

"No one is going anywhere." Bardot steadied her voice.

Mac made eye contact with her. They needed him alive if there was any chance of catching his partner.

CHAPTER
SEVENTY-SIX

MAC FELT Vincent loosen his grip slightly on her neck. She seized the opportunity and dropped her entire body weight onto the ground. She heard two gunshots ring out, but they sounded far away. She whipped her head around just as one of the bullets sliced across her neck and another exploded in her chest. The bullet in her vest knocked her back but Vincent reacted quickly, grabbing her hair and pulling her back into place as his human shield.

"Get down," someone shouted as the entire cavalry hit the ground. Mac stayed in place, Vincent holding her close to his body. He looked down the front of her to see a bullet lodged into her vest.

Bardot looked up to see the two were standing in place. "Are you hurt? Mac, talk to me." Bardot pushed herself closer. There was blood streaming down Mac's neck.

"Stay back or she dies," Vincent yelled.

"It hurts like hell, but I'll be okay," Mac said, trying to project her voice toward her phone so Hudson would know but keep it low enough not to excite her captor.

"Who the hell took a shot?" Bardot asked.

"Ma'am, it came from out on the water. We just radioed for the Port Police to send boats to investigate," one of the uniformed policemen said.

"Good. My guess is it's his partner," Bardot said. "Now Vincent, let her go so we can work this out. No one else needs to get hurt."

"I still want out of here. Now be a nice lady and give Mac the keys before she has to die," Vincent said.

Bardot could see the wildness in his eyes and knew she needed to figure out a way to defuse the situation. Her vehicle was LoJacked with GPS, so even if he got in the SUV, they could track them.

"Okay," she said, holstering her gun. "I'm going to approach Mac with the keys so you two can leave," Bardot said, moving slowly and keeping an eye on the gun pressed against Mac's temple.

Hudson was screaming into the phone, but no one could hear him. He desperately texted Bardot, asking what she was thinking, but unsurprisingly it went unanswered.

Bardot placed the keys into Mac's hand and stepped back, not wanting to give Vincent any reason to pull the trigger. "Okay, you're free to leave."

"Tell your people to lower their weapons," Vincent barked.

"Drop your weapons," Bardot said without taking her eyes off of Mac and Vincent. Everyone stepped back, giving the two a wide berth and watched while Vincent backed away from the group of law enforcement so they wouldn't shoot him in the back of the head.

They got to the vehicle and Vincent pulled her to the driver's side. "Get behind the wheel," he said. She did as she was told. "Take off your vest."

"Why?" Mac asked.

"Just do what I tell you."

She stripped the Velcro off and awkwardly removed the bulky vest while staying in the seat. The vest had been pressing against the place where she had been shot, but when she took it off the pain seared through her chest, making her inhale sharply.

She hoped he was going to the passenger side, which would give her enough time to lock herself in the truck, but he slid behind her, keeping the gun trained on her head.

CHAPTER
SEVENTY-SEVEN

MAC TOOK A DEEP BREATH, pulling on her seatbelt and willing herself to stay calm. "Where do you want me to go?"

"Take us out of the neighborhood and hang a left," Vincent said.

Mac did as instructed, navigating the SUV out of the driveway and down the street. "Where do you want to go from there?" If she could figure out his endgame, then maybe she could get out of this in one piece. She could see several government vehicles and a few cop cars following at a safe distance behind. She was sure Vincent saw them as well, but he didn't seem to care.

"Just drive and I'll tell you which way to go," he said, pushing the gun into the back of her head.

"How long have you two been married?" she asked, trying to distract him.

"Don't try building a rapport with me. Just do what you're told and you won't have to die."

"But I thought you liked killing people," Mac said softly.

"It's the biggest rush you'll ever experience, but right now I need you alive so you can get me out of here. Prison is not an option for me. Either you get me out of here, or we'll both have to die."

"Okay, what makes taking another person's life so exciting for you?" she asked, doing her best to keep her voice steady. She looked in the rearview mirror to make eye contact with him and check to make sure she still had people following her.

They took an onramp onto the highway and drove for just a few moments before Vincent said, "Take this exit." He hadn't answered her previous question. They were getting close to the water.

"Is this where your wife is picking you up?" Mac guessed.

"You're a very smart girl, and you get the pleasure of coming with us. We might even play with you for a while."

Mac pulled up to a beautiful area with a small pier where several boats were parked. She slowed and pulled the vehicle into the parking lot near the dock. "Now what?"

The little pier was deserted. She looked in the rearview mirror to see the panic in his eyes. She might have had a chance if they got out of the bulletproof SUV on the way to the boat that was supposed to be waiting, but no one was there. Mac wasn't entirely sure what he was capable of, but she worried that his alternative plan would get them both killed.

"Where the hell is she?" he screamed. He had watched her speed away on the boat and they had worked out this plan way in advance. If the authorities showed up at the house, she would take the boat and meet him here. She had promised.

Mac sat silently, not sure what to say, and then she had an idea. At this point, she was willing to do anything to survive. If she did nothing, she would surely die but she couldn't let that happen. She needed to get home to Hudson and be there for her sister Lola and her little niece. It was amazing how quickly she had built a little family unit that meant so much and she wasn't about to let this asshole take that away from her.

Visions of that terrible night when she and Hudson had been pushed into the Tacoma Pier ran through her mind. Her heart raced as she thought about hitting the unforgiving ice-cold black water and quickly sinking. But then Hudson had shown her what to do to survive. Could she do it again without his help? She was about to find out.

She dropped the SUV into gear and hit the gas hard, launching both of them off the pier. She quickly lowered the windows like

Hudson had told her to do. Her heart felt like it would pound out of her chest. She tried to focus on relaxing her body and not lock her arms on the steering wheel.

She took several breaths in and out as the vehicle went airborne. She could hear Vincent screaming in the back and fumbling to get his seatbelt on, but it was too late. They hit the water hard, lurching Mac forward. She took comfort in her seatbelt locking around her body and keeping her in place as she heard Vincent's head smack against the back of her seat, and then nothing. She looked back to see blood running down the side of his head.

She followed the same instructions Hudson had given her the last time they were sinking in a car. Funny how that type of knowledge could help in a pinch. She watched the water rush into the open windows, trying to remain calm as it started rising up her chest. Vincent had actually helped her out by making her take off the vest. It would have made getting up to the top of the water much harder.

The heavy SUV with its bulletproof reinforcements sank much quicker than her compact SUV had. She kept her wits about her, feeling panic at her inability to swim. As it sank, she released her seatbelt at just the right time in order to let the water lift her up and slide into the back seat. She hooked her arms around Vincent's unconscious body, relieved to feel he was still breathing and pushed off the seat and out the window as the vehicle fell below.

There was a moment in the dark water when she thought she was going to lose her grip on Vincent but then felt strong hands wrap around her waist and another taking Vincent from her. Relief swept over her as they crested the water and were led back to shore. She had banked on them coming in after her, knowing full well that she wasn't strong enough or a good enough swimmer to bring Vincent up to the surface.

They laid her down on the soft grass and Bardot came running over and checked her pulse to find it beating strong, and she sighed in relief.

Mac slowly opened her eyes, worried to see Bardot's reaction.

"You could have gotten yourself killed," Bardot said.

"Did Vincent survive?" was all Mac wanted to know.

Bardot looked at the officer who had helped pull Vincent out of the water, and he gave her a thumbs-up. "It looks like he'll live."

"What about Gennavie?"

"She was out on the water taking shots at you, but she's gone now. The Port Police sent boats after her, but so far nothing. They should have her in custody before long."

An emergency medical team with four medical professionals rushed over. "Ma'am, I need you to move aside," one of the EMTs said to Bardot.

She stood up, dusting herself off, and moved out of the way so they could work.

"Let Hudson know I'm okay," Mac said as Bardot moved aside. She listened as Bardot called Hudson, letting him know she was okay. Mac had no idea where her phone had ended up.

Two of the EMTs were working on Vincent while the other two looked over Mac's injuries. She could smell burnt flesh from her neck wound, which scared her, but at least she was still breathing. "Ma'am," she heard one of them say soothingly, "I see no major injuries. How do you feel?"

A female EMT was checking her legs and lower extremities for injury. She looked up into the weathered face of an older man. "What's your name?" the man asked.

"I'm Mac, and I think I'm fine. Just a couple of scrapes, I think."

"If you call a couple of scrapes being shot twice and then driving your vehicle into deep waters, then yeah, you have a couple," he said, smiling down at her. "Are you okay if I poke around a bit?"

"Sure."

"Okay, I need you to keep this pressed against your neck while I check to see if the bullet made contact." He was relieved not to see any blood. He pressed a clean gauze against her neck, placed her hand over it, and moved down to her chest. He asked the female paramedic to assist. "Is it okay if we lift your shirt and check to see if anything is broken?"

Mac nodded and then winced. Now that her endorphins were starting to wear off, she could feel the pain coming from her neck. She felt him lift her shirt and press lightly on her ribs. "Okay, so I think we should get you X-rayed, but overall, it looks like you'll have some bruised ribs. Nothing is broken. Do you think you can stand?" He was relieved that the vest had done its job.

"Yes," she said, and the two EMTs flanked her sides and hoisted her gently by the arms. She looked back at her captor to see him sitting up with his head dropped down to his chest.

CHAPTER
SEVENTY-EIGHT

MAC WAS nursing her third cup of coffee after being given the opportunity to take a shower and change her clothes. Now she was waiting at the FBI building. She didn't understand how people operated without large amounts of caffeine during these times, but she was going for a bubble bath and her favorite wine when this was all over. Her whole body ached from being shot, but she felt very blessed to still be breathing.

She was waiting while OSI and the FBI argued about jurisdictional issues. Their suspect was being held. Thanks to his earlier stunt, they were able to charge him with assault with a deadly weapon. This meant he could be accused of that until they had enough evidence to charge him with the murders.

Her phone rang, and she welcomed the distraction. She'd dropped it on the ground when Vincent shoved her into the driver's seat. Now, all she wanted was a little sleep.

"Hi hon, how's everything going?" came Hudson's voice on the other end of the line.

"Good, I'm just bone-tired and want to come home," she said. "I'm in a holding pattern while they figure this thing out. OSI wants jurisdiction because of my status as a military member and Collymore's murder. The FBI wants jurisdiction because of everything else. I think they might end up prosecuting him in both jurisdictions, but it's hard to tell because they're both federal. Not to mention the state wants a piece of him. It'll be interesting to see how it all works out. How are you doing?"

"Not bad. Much better now that you're safe. Any sign of Gennavie or Davis or whatever her real name is?" Hudson asked.

"Nothing so far. All we know is that she took off in a boat, and as far as I know, they haven't found her yet."

"I'm sure they'll track her down. She can go only so many places, and she certainly can't stay out in the water forever. Are they still watching the house?" he asked.

"Yeah, they found her stash with her passport and money under a creaky floor panel. It was actually a fluke that they found it. One of the evidence technicians walked into the corner of the dungeon and accidentally stumbled across it. It looks like the police showed up right after she arrived to gather her supplies. She ran for the boat and wasn't able to get her go-bag or her husband, which was definitely in our favor."

"Did she have a full-on dungeon in her house?" Hudson asked, amazed at how twisted the case was. He was intrigued by her way of life, though a little put off. Their fascination with why people do what they do was one of the things they had in common.

"Yeah, it had everything, even a sex swing," Mac said.

"Interesting, so what now?"

"Not sure. I'm just waiting to find out what they're going to do with me. They want to put a protective detail on me until Gennavie is caught and in custody since circumstantial evidence shows she was likely the one who shot at me from the water. It's the only conclusion that makes any sense," Mac explained. "Of course, everyone has an opinion on this thing."

"Well, you know the old saying: opinions are like assholes—everyone's got one, and some people's stink. More importantly, what's your opinion? What do you think they should do with you and the suspects?"

She loved that about him. He always cut to the chase and wanted to know what she thought. There had been too many times in the past where her opinion didn't seem to matter, either because she was a lower-level enlisted member at the time or because she was female. She liked that he always wanted to know her take on things. "Well, I think the FBI should take the lead and work with OSI in a concurrent investigation. There will be sticky wickets if there are too many people leading."

"What the hell is a sticky wicket?" He laughed.

"You know, one of those difficult situations where too many people stick their hands into the pot and screw it all up. In this situation, we need one team or person leading and the rest reporting to her, and I think that person should be Bardot. She's proven to be organized, meticulous, and resourceful. I feel she'll do everything in her power to get justice for the victims. What do you think?"

"I don't know much about Bardot, but I trust your judgment. Someone definitely needs to lead the show. Did they release Sergeant Auston Pierce?" Hudson asked.

"For now, the evidence backs up his story. They're trying to obtain Gennavie's DNA from her house to compare to the third DNA indicator found in Alice's body. If they come back with a match, then Auston will likely be off the hook, and Gennavie will have some explaining to do," Mac said. "Hey, I've got to go. They just finished their meeting."

"Okay, call me when you know something."

"Will do." Mac hung up the phone, not at all liking the look on Bardot's face. "So, what's the plan?"

Bardot took a moment to answer. "The FBI gets the first crack at him, which is good. They're also bringing Kibble in." She let the statement hang in the air for a moment. "I know you two worked together, but I'd like you to interview him with me. You're the only person who's spent time with him, and you know how to speak military law, and I don't."

"Okay, I can do that. Will OSI be involved?" Mac asked.

"Yes, they're going to read him his rights and procure military counsel for him if he requests it. If he lawyers up, then our meeting will be very short, plus it'll take time to find an attorney in the JAG Corps who doesn't have a conflict of interest with Kibble. I understand that he's been prosecuting and defending cases for years and knows a lot of people."

CHAPTER
SEVENTY-NINE

WITHIN THE HOUR, Sergeant Vincent Wulf was brought in for interrogation and was read his rights by OSI. He declined counsel in writing and was ready to talk. He had also been cleaned up and had a fresh set of dry clothes on. They let him stew for another hour and finally went in. Bardot and Mac took their seats across the table from the suspect. He looked utterly relaxed, like he was just there to have lunch with friends.

"Good afternoon, Sergeant Wulf," Bardot began.

"Ma'am," was all he said.

"Do you know why you're here today?" Bardot asked.

"I suspect it's because I put a gun to this pretty little lady's head," he said, pointing at Mac.

"Yes, well, that's part of it, but we would also like to discuss your wife and your involvement in a string of murders," Bardot said, trying the direct approach.

"Mmmm, nope. Not going to talk about that. I'm willing to negotiate the whole weapons thing, but nothing to do with my wife," he said forcefully, but immediately smiled. "That little scratch you got has to hurt."

"It stings a little," Mac admitted. "Do you know where your wife went in her boat?"

"You may be smart, but you'll never find her unless she wants to be found, and she doesn't." Vincent focused all his attention on Mac and acted as if Bardot wasn't even in the room.

Bardot stood up. "Does anyone want something to drink?"

"I would love some water," Mac said in a soft voice, catching on to what she was up to.

"Nah, I don't want anything from the likes of you," Vincent spat.

"Very well," Bardot said. She closed the door behind her and left the room.

Mac sat back in her chair, letting silence fill the room. She had always found that people felt they needed to fill quiet space. She opened her folder and started going through the reports she had been given. Mac had received Vincent's security clearance and background report that the military had provided. He was highly intelligent but impulsive and tended to act without thinking things through. This had gotten him in trouble a few times in the military. Mac found it interesting that he hadn't gotten into more trouble, but that was clearly because he had found an outlet.

"So, what do you think they'll do with me?" he finally asked in a calmer voice.

Much better, Mac thought. "It depends if you want to make a deal or go down for assault, not to mention the laundry list of murders the two of you are connected to."

"The only thing you have evidence on is when I lost my cool at the house. Everything else is circumstantial at best," he said confidently.

"Are you sure about that?" Mac asked with the intent of throwing him off guard. "What about your wife? Will she turn on you when we find her? Will she make a deal to save her skin rather than protect you?"

"She would never turn on me, and you'll never find her. She's just that good. It's why I knew I could trust her."

"Trust her with what?" Mac asked.

"Not to turn on me," he said, leaning back in his chair to match Mac's body language.

"So, you already know about the others?" Mac asked dismissively.

"Um, well yeah, sure I do."

Mac waited in silence for him to process the question further. After analyzing his personality and talking to his leadership, she knew he was a narcissist. There was no way he would be okay with sharing his wife unless he was in control of the situation. She hoped he would view it as a betrayal if she had gone behind his back. So, she waited silently, taking pictures out of her folder. She meticulously and slowly lined up photos of Auston, Kibble, Lady Carina, and Goddess Z. She knew Bardot was on the other side of the one-way mirror, reading his facial expressions. She pulled out three different pictures of victims they suspected were killed solely by Gennavie due to the wound patterns and manner of death.

"Do you know this man?" She pointed at Kibble's picture.

"No," he said.

"What about this woman?" She pointed to Goddess Z.

"No," he said again.

"Did you know your wife was involved with all these people?"

"Involved?"

"Yes, as in she was having sexual relationships with all of them. Each one is willing to testify against her. Did she tell you about her extramarital relationships?" Mac asked in a low, even tone.

"She wasn't sleeping around behind my back," he said, getting angry, which was precisely how she wanted him.

"Oh, so she told you about her other relationships?" she asked. "What's it like having an open relationship like that? I've always wondered if it would be exciting."

He smiled mischievously. "I could show you if you want."

"Not interested. You're fixing to be someone else's bitch in prison. A nice young man like you—they're going to enjoy you on the inside."

That shut him up. The thing he feared the most was being locked in a cage. He was able to kill because he was more intelligent than most and used the element of surprise, not because he was a massive man that could overpower others. He knew he would have a hard time without weapons to give him an advantage in prison.

"Do you really think Gennavie will come back to rescue you?" she asked.

His mouth fell open slightly at the mention of her name, and he looked at his hands.

"She's going to leave you here to rot. Do you really think those shots were only meant for me? If she took you out, then she wouldn't have to worry about you turning on her. She's only worried about saving her own skin and is willing to do anything to remain free. She'll replace you within a matter of weeks. She won't even shed a tear for you. She already has several lovers lined up. She seems very fond of this one." Mac pointed to Kibble's picture again.

There was some truth to what Mac was saying. Vincent knew they had agreed to either flee the country or die together in a hail of bullets with suicide-by-cop ending. They had never talked about only one of them getting away. He thought they would always stick together, and now he was in here, and she was out there enjoying her freedom. He almost hoped she would get caught so he could be near her. Maybe if he made a deal and told Mac what he knew, she could be close to him again.

He felt his anger rise at the thought of her playing on a tropical island with a new man while he rotted in prison. He knew the guy Mac was referring to was her informant on base, but he hadn't known she was having sex with him. How could she do that to him? It had always been about her and what she wanted. How could he have been such an ass?

He looked at Mac sitting across from him. *Why couldn't I get a woman like her?* he wondered to himself. "She would never betray me."

"Are you sure? Did you ever ask yourself why she chose to frame Auston, knowing he would lead back to you? She could have picked up any random guy. How did she even know about Alice? Did she follow you, waiting for you to make a move like that so she could plant evidence? She knew you were too smart to leave any evidence behind, so she went for your buddy to buy herself a little time rather than directly implicate you. She knew we would bring Auston in, which would delay the investigation, giving her the time she needed to get away before you were caught."

He stared at her silently, and she waited patiently. "What kind of a deal?"

Mac sat in silence for a few moments. Bardot watched along with a team of investigators, hoping they would get a confession. In actuality, they didn't have much solid evidence. Without a full confession, it was mainly circumstantial at best. Once they knew the whole story, they could start piecing the evidence together, but without a confession they would likely have to charge him with assaulting Mac and hope the judge threw the book at him. The murders would all remain unsolved.

"What do you want?" Mac was surprised that he was even entertaining an offer. She thought he would be harder to crack and was careful to keep a straight face.

"I want immunity and to stay out of prison," he tried.

"That's not going to happen, but depending on what you tell us, it's possible to spend less time on the inside," she counteroffered.

"I want you to go talk to all those stiffs on the other side of the mirror and work out a deal for me, and then we'll talk."

"No problem. Can I get you anything to eat or drink?"

CHAPTER
EIGHTY

AFTER HOURS OF WAITING, negotiating, and bringing in a lawyer for Vincent to discuss a deal, everyone finally agreed on taking the death penalty off the table in exchange for a full confession. At the end of the day, Vincent decided he really didn't want to die, and he certainly didn't want to sit on death row for years. Vincent wanted to confess only to Mac and no one else. The entire team that had worked on the case was in a mood to celebrate until the confessions began.

Mac sat across from Vincent as he detailed everything he knew, starting with his honeymoon and the murders they'd committed together in Hawaii. The task force had already started tracing their whereabouts and looking at different murders in places the couple had been together and separately, but now Vincent was making it all a lot easier. He went into such detail that Mac had difficulty keeping a straight face. She had to listen to the gruesome details about how they tied their victims up and his wife mutilated the victim's genitals and whipped them so severely that they would pass out from the pain only to be revived and further tortured.

He talked about the thrill he would get when preparing his ropes for the kills. Each one was unique and matched the outfit Gennavie planned to wear during the act. She would dress up in her favorite dominatrix outfit, and he was into voyeurism. At first, it was all about seduction and control, getting the victim to comply and do what she asked. With a body like hers, it wasn't all that difficult. Once the victim was all nice and tied up, she would bring her bullwhip out and destroy their bodies.

The end was his turn. He became excited watching her torture people, and when she was almost done, he would strangle the victim while she had sex with them. She got off on watching the life leave their bodies. "It was so hot. It was nothing I had ever seen before. She would get so excited at that moment when their eyes started to bulge from their head. It was a magical thing, and the sex afterward was mind-blowing. She would be insatiable. We would have sex for hours with the dead body lying next to us. Sometimes she would touch the dead guy right before she orgasmed. It was something else."

Mac was doing her best not to visualize or lose her lunch. She had never heard anything quite so disgusting and was relieved when there was a knock at the door.

Bardot stuck her head in. "Hey Mac, can I speak with you for a moment?"

Mac stood up from the table. "I'll be right back, Vincent," she said like they were friends. She knew she needed to keep him talking. She still needed locations and information about how they disposed of the bodies. He had given general details, but not the specifics. They had to have solid evidence to ensure a conviction, and they simply didn't have enough yet.

"We have news," Bardot said. "Gennavie's boat was found floating near Bainbridge Island. It was set on fire and was drifting toward the island. There is no sign of Gennavie. We're sending out a dive team, but it would be nearly impossible to find her if she did go into the water. The current in the Puget Sound would likely take her out to the Pacific Ocean, not to mention the different species of shark that would enjoy a snack."

"Okay, so is there any way she could have gotten to shore?" Mac asked.

"Not without help. My guys are canvassing the area, asking

everyone if they saw anything. It's going to be a while before we know."

"Fair enough. I'll keep working on Vincent. Please let me know if there are any developments. I'm going to take a break before I go back in. It's hard to stomach. How can he talk to me like he's telling me about a nice date he had with his wife? I just don't understand," Mac said, shaking her head.

"If he's a true psychopath, he likely has no connection with people and views them as objects rather than human beings."

"How is his wife any different? He seems to truly care about her," Mac asked.

"He might in his own way. Many psychopaths feel isolated and alone. They have a connection when they find someone who will play in their sick and twisted world, but I'm not sure if you could call it love like normal people know it."

"Okay, I may be able to use that." Mac took a deep breath.

"You're doing a great job, Mac. Don't give up. He's opening up to you, and if you can get the information we need, there are a lot of families that will receive closure and justice for their loved ones."

"I know. Uncle Don calls me every other day wanting to know if we caught the sick bastard that destroyed his niece. I would love to tell him we nailed the guy." Mac took another deep breath and took a long swig of water. "K, wish me luck."

She walked back into the room to find Vincent calmly waiting. "Can I get you anything?" she asked.

"Some hookers and blow," he said, smiling.

Mac didn't even acknowledge his comment. "Okay, let's start from the beginning." She took her pen and notebook back out of her file and recorded the date when the couple had first met.

By the end of the day, Mac had recorded the murder and mutilation of seventeen victims, the locations of their bodies, and where they had been killed prior to being discarded. She was amazed that he had given up so much. He'd even told her where he kept his trophies. She had lied, telling him she would see about getting them returned to him in jail.

He had taken an assortment of rings, necklaces, bracelets, hair, and other items from the people they had killed. The FBI and local authorities rushed around to recover the evidence and run tests on everything to link them to the victims.

CHAPTER
EIGHTY-ONE

MAC FELT ABSOLUTELY WRECKED after finishing her interrogation of Vincent, but she was pleased with her progress and his guaranteed conviction. The mountain of evidence was pretty damning. There was little to no way the prosecution couldn't get a conviction at this point, or at least she hoped nothing would be thrown out on a technicality.

She needed to do one more thing prior to slipping into a nice hot bath and drinking a glass of wine. She called him and made the arrangements.

Uncle Don was waiting for her when she arrived. His tiny house sat upon a hill at the end of an old street. The lawn had been meticulously kept with tulips growing along the front of the house. The tulips looked like they were beginning to wilt, just like Uncle Don, who appeared to have aged ten years since the last time she saw him. She couldn't believe that was only a short few weeks ago.

"Mac, it's so good to see you." Uncle Don wrapped her into a warm hug.

"It's good to see you too. How are you holding up?"

"I miss Alice every day, but I'm slowly making peace with it. She was like my own daughter. This one is just going to take some time." Deep sadness was present all over his face. He simply looked deflated.

"I understand, and I'm so sorry for your loss. I feel responsible for what happened to her," Mac admitted.

"You had nothing to do with it. My Alice was just at the wrong place at the wrong time and ended up in the crosshairs of that monster."

"I suppose so, but I wish I had provided her some protection. I don't know." She looked down at her feet. *Even though they caught Vincent*, she thought, *it was at such a high cost.*

"Tell me"—Uncle Don brightened for the first time—"did you catch the guy?"

"Yes, we did, and he gave a full confession. The man embodies pure evil."

"How soon is the court, and when will Alice's body be released for her funeral?"

"Um, I'm not entirely sure. They're still fighting over jurisdiction. The military has a right to prosecute, and so does the FBI. It's a complex case, and everyone wants a piece of this guy," she explained. "As for Alice, I'll find out for you. It shouldn't be long now since we have a confession."

"Thank you for bringing my Alice's killer to justice. I know you had to put yourself in harm's way to do it, and I appreciate your sacrifice."

"It was the least I could do." She stood up, ready to leave. She would surely drive off the road if she tried to head back in her current state. She needed a good night's sleep prior to her return trip home.

"You go get some rest and make sure you keep in touch," he said. "I'll let you know when Alice's funeral is. I know she would want you to be there."

"It would be my honor. Thank you for inviting me," she said, giving him another hug and heading to her SUV.

CHAPTER
EIGHTY-TWO

THE FOLLOWING day was much more difficult than she had anticipated. She walked into the room and looked at Captain Kibble. He wouldn't make eye contact with her as she sat down on the opposite side of the table. The interrogation room seemed like the wrong place for someone who seemed so kind.

"Good morning," she started out. "I brought you a cup of coffee." She slowly slid the warm cup across the table.

"I don't deserve your kindness," he said, still not looking at her.

"Why don't you tell me what happened? Just start from the beginning."

"I don't know what to say except that I'm an idiot and fell for her manipulation and games."

"I understand how that could happen," Mac assured him. "From what I understand, she's very good at what she does."

With sadness in his eye, he finally looked at her. "I'm really sorry for leaving that note in the Collymore file. You have to understand, I was just trying to protect you and get you off the case before something bad happened."

"I appreciate you thinking of me. If you get it off your chest, you'll feel much better."

"I may be an idiot when it comes to that woman, Mac, but I'm no dummy when it comes to the law. I have a right to remain silent just like anyone else, and I plan to remain silent."

"That's absolutely fair and probably in your best interest at the moment, but I may be able to work a deal for you," she said, looking at Bardot for confirmation.

Bardot sat beside Mac silently for a few moments. "The FBI is willing to offer you immunity for your testimony."

"What about the military?" he asked with hope in his eyes for the first time.

"We're still working on that issue," Bardot said. "Apparently you've worked with many attorneys in the JAG Corps, and we're having a hard time finding a military lawyer that doesn't have a conflict."

"In that case, I'll tell you everything I know, provided I have full immunity for my involvement through the FBI, OSI, and all local jurisdictions. I want all possibilities of prosecution taken off the table, and I want my military record clean. My career reinstated as it was before," he said, his eyes brightening.

"I'll see what can be done," Bardot said and left the room.

Mac squeezed Kibble's hand. "I know you're sorry for getting mixed up in this, but I'm rooting for you, just for the record. I hope they can work it all out," she said as she got up from the table.

She had mixed emotions about Kibble. She liked him as a person, but he had crossed the line on several occasions. He had shared confidential case details with a suspect and tried to plant evidence to convict another airman. She hoped he would be okay, but she didn't think he should get off scot-free.

CHAPTER
EIGHTY-THREE

THREE WEEKS LATER, Mac and Hudson were getting all dolled up in their Mess Dress uniforms. He looked debonair in his tuxedo-style uniform. On the other hand, Mac hated the way the female version fit. Her short waistline and large chest made the uniform fit her oddly, to say the least.

Hudson walked over to her. "You look amazing."

She smiled. "Thank you, but it isn't in your best interest to lie to me."

"I would never." He came up behind her and wrapped his arms around her. "You're the most beautiful woman I've ever met." He nuzzled his face into her neck and started kissing her.

"Oh no, you don't. That's going to have to wait. We have to be at rehearsals in thirty minutes."

"Come on, they won't mind if we're a little late," he said, reaching up to cup her left breast.

She swatted his hand away. "Sorry, sugar, you're simply going to have to be patient. It took me way too long to get my hair done and put all this together," she said, smiling as he pouted. "Don't worry—I'll make it worth the wait." She turned and kissed him deeply. "Now, let's go."

"Fine, I guess," he said, swatting her on the backside as they headed for his truck. He watched as she hiked her skirt up to climb into the vehicle. "Damn woman, this is going to be a long night."

The Red Morgan Center on Fairchild Air Force Base was decked out. It was a big event. Mac and Hudson had been last-minute submissions for the award ceremony. The wing commander had received a call from Agent Bardot, singing their praises about their contributions to the case.

They were led through the rehearsal, and a young airman showed them to their assigned seats. Captain Stanton was there, along with some of her and Hudson's coworkers and friends. She actually hated getting up in front of people and disliked public recognition, but she was proud of their work.

The ceremony got underway, and they stood on the side of the stage, waiting to be called up. They walked up on stage and stood at attention as they heard their names. "Master Sergeant Gavin Hudson and Technical Sergeant Evelyn McGregor distinguished themselves by an act of courage at or near Joint Base Lewis-McChord in the investigation of Staff Sergeant Vincent Wulf and Staff Sergeant Ares Wulf…"

In the back of the room, Gennavie watched as they stood up there, being recognized for ruining her life. Her hair was now blond and swept back into a ponytail. She was dressed just like the other wait staff. Her eyes were now chocolate brown, thanks to colored contacts she had bought online. Even her uncle would have a hard time recognizing her.

Uncle Frank had truly been her savior. He had called in yet another favor for her and had a friend of his in the area pick her up, no questions asked. The older man who'd plucked her from the boat didn't bat an eye when she lit her boat on fire. The pull her uncle had made her sometimes wonder what he was really into. He was able to get pretty much anything done at the drop of a hat, and that didn't seem like something that could be a result of his job as a defense attorney. Who was she to question? She certainly wasn't what she appeared.

It had been a bit of a trick to get on base. She liked the thrill of getting away with it, as long as her luck held. If someone had stopped to look more closely at the military ID card, she had lifted from one of her colleagues at the clinic, her ruse would have been up. If they had, they would have seen that she didn't really look like the woman on the card. The hair and eyes were the right color, but that was where the similarities stopped.

She watched, pleased to see both Hudson and Mac focused on the back of the large room. It was common practice when standing at attention. There was no wiggling or looking around allowed, so most military just stared at the back wall or the top of someone's head. She took a deep breath, grabbed one of the large round carrying trays, and lifted it up to cover her face. No need to take unnecessary chances.

She stopped at several tables with her back to the stage to pick up dishes. She slowly and methodically made her way to Mac and Hudson's table. She picked up both wine glasses with her gloved hand, carefully placed them on her tray, and walked away without looking back. Once she returned to the kitchen, she sealed the wineglass in a sterile plastic bag. Now that she had what she wanted, Gennavie slipped out the back.

Her thirst for vengeance ran deep. Mac had ruined everything, and she wanted to see her suffer in unimaginable ways. Her original plan to set up Mac and Hudson to take the fall for murder would pale in comparison. Now she wanted to watch Mac suffer and to take Hudson away just like she'd taken Vincent. This would take a long time to come to fruition, but Gennavie was nothing if not patient.

THANK YOU FOR READING MY BOOK!

I appreciate all your feedback, and I love hearing what you have to say.

I need your input to make the next book and my future books better. Please leave me an honest review, letting me know what you like and didn't like so I can keep the good stuff and get rid of the not-so-good.

RECEIVE A FREE SHORT STORY

Join Julie Bergman's newsletter and get your free short story, updates about future books and get to know the author only at juliebergman-author.com.

ACKNOWLEDGMENTS

I would like to express my deepest gratitude to everyone who has supported me throughout this journey. A special thanks to my editor and mentor Shavonne Clarke who has openly answered all my questions and concerns along the way. Without her help and support, I would not be here. Additionally, a special thanks to the Woman's Business Center and specifically Sam Dascomb for all her help and support in setting up my website, marketing, and helping me launch my veteran-owned business.

ABOUT THE AUTHOR

Julie Bergman is a retired military veteran who served her country for over 20 years. She lives in beautiful Spokane, Washington with her supportive husband, four wonderful children, and a slobbery Olde English Bulldog with attitude. After over 17 years in the JAG Corp and a master's degree in forensic psychology, her fascination with crime and the dark side of humanity has spilled into a military-based serial killer series that you won't be able to put down.

Made in the USA
Middletown, DE
22 September 2023